UNDER STONE

Volume Four of The Ambeth Chronicles

HELEN JONES

For my family

CONTENTS

CHAPTER 1
TRAVELLER

Midsummer's Eve, 1927, North Wales

LLEWELLYN DAVIES DREW HIS BICYCLE TO A HALT AT THE EDGE OF *the meadow, his breath coming hard. Dismounting, he leaned it against the low stone wall and stood, hands on hips, looking up the grassy slope. Unhooking a leather bag from the handlebars, he slung it across his shoulders before climbing over the wall, brushing dust from the dark wool of his trousers as he started up the hill. Four standing stones came into view, lit red-gold by the last of the sun. When he reached them he stopped, breathing deep, enjoying the quiet calm that comes in the Welsh hills, in the old places.*

Where he was now was one of the oldest, he was sure.

The other scientists had scoffed at his theories, laughing him out of the lecture hall at the university when he'd gone to present his findings, but he knew he was right. And now he was going to prove it.

Rummaging through his bag he retrieved a small item, wrapped in soft leather. Carefully, he unwrapped it to reveal a small flat purple stone, patterns shimmering like oil across its surface when it caught the light. Closing his hand around the stone he shut his eyes, focusing on his breath and the stillness he'd learnt in India years before. He'd found the stone in India too, bartering with a street merchant who, though he didn't know what he had, knew it to be special. 'It came from the wrist of a maharajah, a holy ruler,' he'd insisted, and Davies knew he had to possess it. Finally, after a shouted discussion over the noise and heat of the crowded market, the two of them had agreed a price and Davies had left with his prize, elated with his discovery. For this was a travelling stone, he was sure of it. He'd read about them in ancient manuscripts, searched dusty libraries for vague references, examining curling documents with his magnifying glass as he sought the answer to his quest. And it was this that had brought him here, on one of the great Feast Days, to a rapidly darkening meadow in the Welsh hills not far from where he was born.

Sinking to his knees before the two centre stones he held the gem out. It began to glow with a soft golden light, warmth pulsing through the thin leather on his palm, echoing his heartbeat. It was true, it was happening! Getting to his feet, Davies closed his hand around the jewel and stepped between the stones. Air and light warped around him and he was gone, leaving only the sheep to wonder when he would return.

CHAPTER 2
POWER STRUGGLE

Ambeth –Present Day

'YOU WISHED TO SPEAK WITH ME, ARTOS?'

Artos of the Light turned to see Denoris, the Dark Elder, emerging from the shadows of a high hedge. He was armour clad, his expression mild; the former was not unusual, the latter, however, was. Beyond the hedge the Palace loomed, ivory walls gleaming in the pale winter sunshine. Artos, out for his morning walk, did not need the King's warning to know he had to tread carefully. After all, they hadn't actually *seen* Deryck go through a Gate. Still. There were matters that were long overdue for discussion, especially regarding Alma. He smiled, bowing slightly.

'Well met, Denoris. Yes, I wondered if we could have a word about your son.'

The blond eyebrows rose. 'My son? Since when has he been your concern?'

Artos spread his hands wide. 'Only since he started seeing my granddaughter – oh, do not act surprised, Denoris, I know you knew who she was.' Artos stopped, taking a short breath. 'Anyway.

Your son seems to still have feelings for her and, well, he was seen yesterday. At the Garden of Shadows.'

Denoris pursed his lips. Then he smiled. 'Shall we walk together? I have to be somewhere shortly, so perhaps we can discuss this along the way.'

Artos paused before nodding. 'That would be fine.'

He fell into step beside Denoris, gravel crunching beneath their boots as they headed along the Long Walk, attracting more than one curious glance. Artos hid a smile, all at once amused. Well, at least while he was distracting Denoris he knew Alma would be safe. Then Denoris spoke.

'My son is an Opener, you know.' He spoke casually, as though the words were nothing of import and Artos struggled to contain his reaction, his amusement gone.

'Is that so?' There was a slight tremor to his voice and he cursed, inwardly. He cleared his throat. 'You must be pleased that he has inherited your Gift.'

Denoris nodded, a glint in his green eyes. 'I am. And so, I suppose, you would be, should your granddaughter display the power her father held.'

'Oh, well, I don't know about that,' Artos dissembled. 'She is half-human, after all.'

'And yet, she managed to evade the Dark Hunt and Thorion's guards, as well as attract the attention of my son – no, I think her far more than that.'

Artos shrugged, though inside he was cold. 'Well, she is definitely special,' he said. 'So perhaps you can understand my concern.'

'Deryck is entitled to visit the Garden of Shadows whenever he wishes. It is a place of the Dark, after all.'

The words were smooth, and Artos felt a stab of anger. So this was how it was going to be. Fine. He could play this game. The path turned, taking them deeper into the gardens, and he kept pace with Denoris, unwilling to give ground. 'And yet he remains on probation. Opening Gates is probably not in his best interest, especially if he seeks Alma. Not to mention the ban on crossing, of course.'

Denoris looked shocked. 'Do you think he opened a Gate? I would hope not.'

'As would I. The King is also concerned.'

The Elder huffed out a small breath, cloudy in the frosty air. 'I imagine – no, wait,' Denoris put his fingers on his chin, looking up briefly. 'I *know* that he is having the boy watched.'

'And? Would you expect anything less? You're lucky he did not exile him, like Etras.'

Denoris tilted his head to one side. 'Am I?' His handsome mouth curved in a half smile. 'Or perhaps there's more to it.' Artos narrowed his eyes, but said nothing. The grin curved deeper. 'It seems to me that, with things as they are, Thorion perhaps would be happy to see Light partnered with Dark. That it would be in his interests, should such a match be made. We both know,' he leaned in closer to a stunned Artos, 'that nothing of power happens in this realm without his knowledge. *If* the boy did cross to seek her, the King would have known. And yet he did nothing.'

They stopped at a point where the paths branched, one leading towards the apartments, the other further into the gardens. Artos swallowed, pushing down the rage burning in his chest. It had taken him long centuries to master his temper, and he was close to letting go. But he could not, for Alma's sake.

'Are you implying that the King is plotting to marry off my granddaughter behind my back? Because I can assure you–'

'Of course, this is just speculation on my part,' Denoris cut in. 'I didn't mean to suggest any sort of impropriety, you understand.'

'Oh, I understa–'

'It's just, I know our King is always working for the greater good and so, perhaps a match between my son and your grand-daughter might work in his favour.'

'What?' Artos shook his head, wondering if he was hearing right. This was not how he'd expected the conversation to turn. 'And what of Alma's choice in the matter?'

'How do you know that she wouldn't want such a match? Come, we both know how they felt about each other. A lover's tiff is soon resolved.'

Artos stared. 'A lover's tiff? He murdered her friend! In front of her! He—' Artos stopped, taking a deep breath through his nose and blowing it out.

'And yet women are as mysterious and changeable as the tides, are they not?' Denoris winked at him, actually winked. Artos didn't know whether to laugh or hit him. He did neither. Denoris went on. 'After all, what could you say if it was what she wanted? If she came through under her own volition and sought out my son? Surely you wouldn't put your own desires ahead of hers? That is not the way of the Light, as I understand it. Of course, if she did come through I would welcome her into my home. And then let you know that I had her.' The green eyes narrowed, just for a moment. Artos' mouth dropped open, but before he could react further, Denoris clapped him on the arm. 'Just think about it.' Grinning widely, the Dark Lord turned away, taking the path leading to the apartments, his cloak swirling behind him.

Artos felt as though he had been punched in the stomach. *Think about it?* Denoris must be mad to even think he would consider such a thing. And, Denoris would 'let him know when he had her'? Artos needed no Gift to hear the threat implied.

Turning, he took the path leading back to the Palace. He needed to move, and he needed to do it now.

ELLERY SAT AT HER DRESSING TABLE, TUGGING AN IVORY handled brush through her long dark hair. She still couldn't get over her brother's revelation that he'd been in love with Alma, that he still was. She'd suspected as much, of course she had, but to have him confirm it had been a shock. Her reflection stared back from the mirror, pale and serious, her green eyes shadowed. Perhaps she should go and find him, see if he wanted to talk. Darkness knew she needed someone to share her life with.

Putting down her brush she stood, smoothing down the folds of her dress, velvet soft beneath her fingers. She picked up her shawl, pulling it around her shoulders before stepping into the hallway... to find Gwenene standing there, as though waiting for her.

'Ellery,' the Dark Elder said, a slight curl to her lip. She was dressed in blue, as she usually was, jewel-bright in the dimly-lit corridor.

'Good morning, Gwenene,' mumbled Ellery. She tried to go past, but Gwenene stepped into her path, hands on hips, a faint smile on her beautiful face. Ellery stopped, only because she couldn't do anything else.

'You are growing up.' Gwenene tilted her head to one side, blue eyes narrowing. She picked up a lock of Ellery's hair, running it through her fingers and Ellery stiffened, trying to keep her face under control.

'Let me pass, please.'

'You look like your mother.' Her fingers twined more tightly in Ellery's hair.

Ellery swallowed. 'So I'm told.'

'Your father spent too much time with her for my liking.' Gwenene let go of Ellery's hair, a slight frown marring her perfect brow. 'And you are just a nasty little reminder of her, a pitiful human – huh!' She snorted, her hand coming to the curve of Ellery's waist. Ellery flinched. Gwenene laughed.

'Oh, don't worry, I have no desire for women. Your father, on the other hand, has much.' She leaned in so close Ellery could smell her perfume, her hand tightening painfully on Ellery's waist. 'So I would be careful, pretty one. I do not like to share.'

'What the hell?' Ellery went cold. 'What are you saying?'

'Just a friendly conversation, nothing more,' Gwenene released her and stepped back. 'Your father loves you, of course.'

Oh, that was too much. 'Does he?'

'How can you doubt it?' Gwenene looked annoyed. 'He feeds you, houses you – he even gave you a tallus stone!' Her eyes went briefly to Ellery's necklace. 'He didn't have to do any of those things.'

'He would do the same for any creature he had care of, apart from the necklace.' Ellery paused, pain in her heart at the thought of her father's betrayal with the tallus stones. She hadn't let her necklace touch her skin since she'd realised he was using the stones to control them. 'I don't deceive myself that I hold any special place in his heart.'

'Do not speak so of him! You know not what is in his heart!' snapped Gwenene.

'And you do?' Ellery glared at Gwenene. 'He's just using you, like everyone else in his life.'

Gwenene slapped her, the sound echoing in the hallway. 'You little–'

'What is this?'

Ellery turned, her hand to her stinging cheek, to see Deryck approaching. He was dressed in cream and brown, his handsome face tight with anger.

'Ellery, are you all right?'

She nodded, her throat too choked with tears to answer. Deryck turned to Gwenene. 'What's going on? Why did you strike my sister?'

'Your sister needs to mind her tongue,' hissed Gwenene.

Deryck clenched his fists, his broad shoulders curving forward. 'And I'm sure you said nothing to provoke her,' he snapped. Gwenene's blue eyes widened. She tilted her head, her hand coming up to trail across the front of his tunic.

'You are very like your father, you know,' she purred. Ellery's skin crawled. Deryck angrily pushed Gwenene's hand away.

'You are my father's favourite, and that is the only reason I do not ask you to leave. But do *not* touch my sister again.' He put his arm around Ellery and moved her swiftly along the hallway and out the front door, not stopping until they were outside, in the shelter of the trees. He turned her to face him, keeping her in the circle of his arm, his other hand coming up to her cheek. She flinched.

'Are you all right?' he asked again, but she still couldn't answer, sickness in her heart. He put his other arm around her, pulling her into a hug and she broke, sobbing against his shoulder.

After a few minutes she lifted her head, wiping her eyes. 'I'm sorry.' Deryck released her, fishing in his pockets for a handkerchief which he handed to her. 'Thanks,' she said, taking it from him. 'She is just such a—'

'Bitch?' Deryck raised an eyebrow. Ellery huffed out a laugh, despite her upset.

'Yeah, that sounds about right. She was, Deryck, she said something...' She shivered, pulling her shawl tighter around her shoulders. It wasn't just the cold air making her shake — she felt cold to her core, as though the frost lining the branches with silver had crept inside her.

'Hey.' Deryck touched her arm. 'What is it? What did she do? Do I need to speak to Father?'

'No!' Ellery stopped, her gorge rising. 'She said that... ugh!' She shook her head. 'I need to sit down, I think.' She went to a nearby bench and Deryck came to sit next to her, his hands on the edge of the seat as he looked at her enquiringly, worry in his green eyes. 'She said that I looked like my mother. And then she implied that Father, that he would be attracted... ugh!' Clearing her throat, Ellery turned and spat into a nearby bush. Surely Gwenene hadn't meant what she'd said, not in that way.

Deryck had gone pale. 'Are you serious?' His breath puffed

into the air. 'Ellery, I promise you I'll do what I can to protect you.'

Her heart sank. 'So you think he could, that he would do something like that?'

'I told Alma once,' he said, his voice low, his green eyes distant, 'I told her that even I didn't know what he was capable of. I still believe that.' His face twisted. 'But I swear, I won't let him hurt you like that, not if I can stop him.'

Ellery stared at him. 'And what if you can't?' Her voice caught against the sickness in her throat. She took a deep breath, trying to pull herself together. 'M-maybe she was just joking, playing with me? It wouldn't be the first time.'

'Huh.' Deryck leaned forward, hands clasped between his thighs. 'Well, I wouldn't put it past her.' He glanced at her. 'But I think we need to stick together, you and I.'

Ellery nodded. 'Okay,' she said. 'It's good to know I can rely on someone.'

Deryck leaned into her, nudging her with his shoulder. 'You can. C'mon, shall we get something to eat? I think it's near to lunchtime. And it's too cold to stay out here.' He stood up, offering his hand to Ellery and pulling her to her feet. She wasn't sure if she could eat but linked her arm with his, wanting the contact. The two of them set off through the gardens together.

CHAPTER 3
OF JEALOUSY AND RAGE

'Your children are annoying.'

Denoris entered his study to find Gwenene seated on the sofa, a frown on her lovely face.

'What?' He was in no mood for Gwenene and whatever was bothering her. They needed to act now, before Artos did. He'd seen the shock in the other Elder's eyes, knew he'd heard the threat. He shuffled through the papers on his desk. 'Where is it?'

'Where is what? Denoris, did you hear me?'

He stopped shuffling papers, fixing her with a glare. 'Yes, I heard you. Now, where is the page from Davies' diary?'

Gwenene's mouth came open, her blue eyes sparking with anger. 'Don't you want to know what happened?'

'You can tell me on the way. Come on.' He went to the sofa, taking her arm so she came to her feet. He knew she had let him handle her so, and he softened, slightly.

'Where are we going?'

'To the Library, then the stables. But first I need to find that paper.' He pulled her along as they left the study, heading down the long hallway towards his chambers.

'Why?'

Denoris stopped. 'What?'

'Why?' Gwenene raised her eyebrows, luscious mouth pursed. 'You know where the girl is. You don't need his diary, even if it is here.'

Denoris stared at her. She was right, of course. But she didn't understand. Gritting his teeth, he hauled her along the hallway once more, using his free hand to open his chamber door. The bed had been made, the room tidied, and he could see the piece of folded paper on the small table near the half-shuttered window. He took Gwenene over to the bed, pushing her down so she sat, bouncing a little with the impact. Before she could speak he grabbed the paper and opened it, reading:

'*She has taken me to the Library. It is a place of great fascination, shelves full of knowledge beyond human understanding. And she has left me here. I know where she goes, but I also know what it means, that she has shared this knowledge with me. I mean to use it, to gain power and win her once and for all. I know that she loves me, she whispers it in the night, when she thinks I do not hear*—'

'Gah!' Denoris crumpled the page, throwing it onto the bed. 'You took him to the Library of the Dark.'

Gwenene shrugged. 'And? It's not like you didn't know about it. He needed something to do, after all, while you and I – well.' She laughed a little, and Denoris thought he would explode with jealousy and rage. He took her arm again, but this time she pulled back, her free hand latching onto his throat, fingers like steel. 'You drove me to him!' she hissed. 'And then you ended it. It is over, done! There is nothing more to know! Let us just take the girl and be done with this nonsense!'

'I want to know what else you told him.' Denoris spat the words between clenched teeth, pushing against her hand. 'I want his notes, I want to know what he knew, and why Alma is following his trail. Even if we get her, there are no guarantees she'll tell us everything.'

'Even if you were to give her a tallus?'

'I do not trust the boy. He may tell her what it's for. No, we need to have everything in place before we proceed.'

'Really?' Gwenene's grip tightened and Denoris coughed. The fingers at his throat softened, as did her blue gaze. 'Are you sure this is not about me? I swear to you, I humoured him only, told him what he wanted to hear. It was a game, nothing more. Do not let an old jealousy stand in the way of our plans.'

Her blue eyes were brighter, her lips parted and he found himself being drawn into her gaze, his hand sliding down her arm as he sat down next to her.

'I need to do this my way.' He took her hand in his. 'And I need to know that you are with me.'

She looked at him, all teasing gone from her gaze. 'Always.'

~

ARTOS RUSHED INTO HIS BEDROOM, BRUSHING PAST A STARTLED-looking Beran.

'My Lord? Can I help?'

'No time to talk now, Beran. Is the spare room ready, as I requested?' Artos opened the wooden chest at the foot of his bed, lifting out a set of neatly folded clothing.

'Yes, my Lord, it is. Please, let me—'

'Good. Send a message to Thorion, if you please. Tell him—' Artos paused. How could he say this, without giving everything away? He trusted Beran, but he knew the very walls had ears. Ah, he had it. 'Tell him I have gone to the hills.'

That should be enough. Thorion knew the Gate there, and where it led. All being well he would be back soon enough with Alma, and they could keep her safe.

Beran withdrew, closing the door and Artos started to strip off, changing tunic and breeches for the clothes on the bed. He had to trust they would do – it had been so long since he had been to the human world. At this he paused. He knew the town where

Alma would be, but he didn't know exactly where she would be. Tightening his belt, he dismissed the concern. What was important was that he went through before Denoris tried again. For it was obvious that was his aim, to set up some sort of sham engagement to Deryck and tie Alma to his cause. Blowing out a long breath, he went to his dressing table and opened a drawer. He took out a knife, sheathed, tucking it into his pocket. Then he picked up the folded letter from where it lay next to his bed – it wasn't finished, but it was a start, at least. Folding it a second time, he put it in his jacket pocket. Then he left the room.

A while later he passed through the Gate, sensing the crackle of the tracers as he crossed. Damn! He'd been so keen to go he'd forgotten to check the Gate. Well, it was too late now.

He emerged into a green field much like the one he'd just left, sun shining overhead. But instead of the Palace and gardens he saw a small town nestled along the bay and undulating hills, streets heading down to the water. High on the point the Castle stood, a ruin now. Artos paused, remembering a time when it had stood whole and proud.

He started down the slope towards the town.

~

'LET ME DO THE TALKING.'

Denoris strode ahead, pushing open the great wooden door to the Library. He didn't wait for Gwenene to answer. All he had asked for were the notes the girl and the half-breed had been working on. Yet for some reason, he hadn't been given them. That the *Librarian*, of all people, thought she could defy him! She was lucky he hadn't taken her to the rooms under the mountain, hidden beneath his home. Thorion – at the thought of the High King his lip curled – would no doubt have had a problem with it, had he done so.

The Library was quiet, just a few scholars at the desks,

sunlight coming through the long windows illuminating the rich colours of books and wood, the grey of stone. As Denoris entered, the Librarian got to her feet. She smoothed her hands down her skirt, her head high, while around the room the scholars gaped as he and Gwenene strode towards the desk. All at once Denoris was amused, his lips twitching. Yes, this might be fun – at least he could make her squirm a little.

'Librarian.' He nodded a greeting and the Librarian bobbed a curtsey. As she did so one of the scholars got to his feet and moved to stand behind the woman, as if guarding her. Denoris had to stop himself laughing out loud. As if one human scholar would be any match for him.

'Lord Denoris, Lady Gwenene, how may I be of assistance?' The Librarian nodded to them both.

'I have a request.' He smiled, but made sure there was no warmth in it. Let her guess how she might have offended him. He dropped the paper he was holding on the table. 'I wish to have the rest of these notes.'

The Librarian, with a hand that shook only slightly, reached out to pick up the paper. She scanned the contents, and Denoris saw her expression change.

'Well?' he said.

'Ah, Lord Denoris, you have me at a disadvantage, I fear.' The Librarian broke off as Gwenene made her way sinuously around the desk towards the hapless scholar, who watched her approach with open mouth. As she closed in on him she smiled, then moved behind him to slide one slender arm around his neck. He started to sweat, his face shiny with fear.

'Now, now, Gwenene,' said Denoris, once again trying not to laugh. 'There's no need for that, is there?' The Librarian turned to her erstwhile protector and Denoris banged on the desk, making her jump. 'Well, is there?' he repeated, letting steel slide into his voice. Funny though it was, this was no joking matter.

'Ah, no, my Lord,' whispered the Librarian, bowing her head.

Denoris nodded. 'Well, it's good to see that you recognise my rank,' he said. 'So, it is therefore a mystery to me as to why, when I asked for the notes that the girl and Caleb were working with, you chose to keep some of them from me. Can you explain to me,' he leaned forward, placing his hands wide on the desk, 'why you would do such a thing?'

Gwenene snickered, and there was a gasp from the scholar. Her arm was tight around his neck, her exquisite face close to his ear. The Librarian faced Denoris with her shoulders square.

'My Lord, I did no such thing.'

'You didn't?' Denoris raised an eyebrow as he took the paper out of her hand, brandishing it under the Librarian's nose.

'No, my Lord, I did not. You asked me for the papers, I gave you what I had. All that I had,' she went on, nodding her head forward for emphasis.

'So where are the rest?' asked Denoris. His gaze shifted past the Librarian and he grinned, unable to hold back. "Oh, Gwenene, let the poor fellow go. He will wet himself before long if you keep hold of him.'

'Oh, all right.' Gwenene pouted as she relinquished her grasp on the now ashen scholar who, trembling, collapsed in a nearby chair. She moved towards the Librarian and Denoris shook his head, catching her eye. She came to perch on the edge of the desk, the folds of her blue gown draping around her slender form. 'I know there are more pages,' she said in her husky voice. 'I saw them myself, when he was writing them.' She smiled pleasantly, but her eyes were flat and hard. 'So who has them, dear Librarian?'

CHAPTER 4
BEST LAID PLANS

The High King moved across the Foyer, cloak billowing out behind him as he nodded to passing courtiers, haste hard within him. A Channeller! A full Gift! If Alma was a Channeller, as they suspected, she would need their help more than ever, regardless of her choice to turn her back on Ambeth. It had been so long since one had been born that he needed to check the ancient records regarding the Gifts of their kind. He also needed to find Artos and decide on a course of action. But whatever they did, it had to be done quickly. They could not let the Dark get their hands on her again.

Beran came down the stairs to his right, his feet clattering on the stone steps. He stopped and looked around, obviously searching for someone. When he saw Thorion his face lit up and he raised one hand – the King, sensing some urgency, stopped.

'My Lord!' Beran came over, bowing deeply. 'Forgive me.'

'It is fine. What is it, Beran?' Thorion raised the man from his bow. 'Is Artos well?'

'Yes, I mean, he is, my Lord. But he is gone.' Beran moved closer, his voice low, dark eyes watchful. 'He bade me tell you he has gone to the hills. And asked me to ensure the second bedchamber be ready for his return.'

Thorion drew in a short breath, nodding briefly. So. It seemed Artos had chosen to act – something must have happened to push him into haste.

'Thank you,' he said.

Beran bowed once more. 'My Lord.'

Thorion nodded, leaving Beran behind as he moved into the Great Hall. It was busy as usual, lunch being set up under the windows, too noisy for a full summoning. Still, he was not without options. He went to the mosaic star set into the centre of the floor and stood there, his eyes closed, not caring who might see him. It was his right, as King, to check on his domain whenever he chose. He sent his thoughts out to the Gate in the hills and there it was – a flash of energy, a crossing made. The tracers had been replaced and he cursed inwardly. However, Artos was through and so, whatever happened, he was ahead of the Dark. It was all they could hope for, now.

Opening his eyes he nodded at a passing courtier. A flush came to her cheek and he smiled, letting his eyes slide towards blue. Leaving the Hall, he headed for the Library once more.

ROZELLE OF THE DARK RODE ACROSS THE FIELDS TOWARDS THE distant smudge of gardens and forest, the Palace gleaming like a pearlescent shell. She was alone, but unworried. She could always invoke the name of Lord Denoris; that in itself was enough to guarantee her safety. However, there were times when family duty outweighed that of her master, and so she had been to visit her parents' estate in the hills. Her father was keen to hear of her progress, that she be part of the right circles at Court. They could hardly complain about her association with Denoris, no matter what it entailed.

She slowed her horse, frowning a little. A flash of light to her right caught her attention and she pulled her mount to a halt. Four fingers of stone stood a few fields away, grey against the rising hills. The flash had come from there.

Her eyes widened and she urged her horse forward, towards the Stone Gate. The tracers! She hadn't checked them for a few days, not since replacing them – Denoris would have her hide and worse if she failed him. Cursing under her breath, she leaned low over her horse's neck as they sped across the fields, cold air streaming past them both. When they reached the stones she hardly waited for the horse to stop before dismounting, her hands held out in front of her as she closed her eyes, feeling for the tracers with her mind. She had reset them herself a week before, on the way to visit her family, crafting them so they were subtle – only the most powerful would have felt them during passage.

There it was! The signature of Light, and powerful at that. Whoever had just gone through was of the highest level – well, there were only a handful of people who fit that description, and only one she could think of with motive to leave.

Another signature appeared, fainter. A few days old. Also of the Light. But this one was coming into Ambeth, rather than leaving. She went deeper and there it was, a third passage through the Gate, returning to the human world. Rozelle's stomach dropped. She whirled and ran to her horse, her legs tangling in her riding skirts in her haste. She needed to get to the Palace, and Denoris, now.

THE LIBRARIAN'S HANDS TWISTED ON HER SKIRTS AS DENORIS waited, his annoyance rising. He was getting tired of this game.

'Well, yes, Lady Gwenene, you are right - there are more of these notes. But this Library, as you know, is for the use of all and, well, you are not the only one who has been asking for this information.'

'Who else?' growled Denoris, his voice rumbling low as he loomed over the Librarian. She swayed, placing a hand on her desk for support. Good. She should fear him. If she was keeping this information from him...

'High King Thorion has also been here, my Lord,' she whispered.

'Thorion,' breathed Gwenene, whose attention had moved to somewhere over Denoris' shoulder.

'Yes, that's what she said,' snapped Denoris, scowling at her, 'but it's not a problem. All I need to do is—'

'What is it you need to do?' came the voice of the High King, his tone courteous yet cold. Denoris closed his eyes and grimaced, belatedly understanding Gwenene's shift of focus. He turned, bowing his head to Thorion. The King stood at the centre of the room, resplendent in dark blue leather armour, his expression unreadable. He paused briefly before bowing his head in return. Denoris let out a breath and smiled, opening his arms as he moved towards his King.

'Well met, my Lord,' he said. 'I was just enquiring about some notes.'

'Enquiring,' echoed Thorion, raising his eyebrows as he looked around. The scholar, sweating and deflated, was recovering in his chair, while the Librarian was pale and trembling, still leaning on her desk.

'Well, yes.' Denoris kept his tone pleasant, trying not to grit his teeth. 'We are doing some research into the whereabouts of the Cup, as was discussed in the Council Meeting.'

'I take it you are looking for the notes on the, er, Welsh situation,' said Thorion, glancing at Gwenene, who bowed her head. Denoris nodded.

'That is correct, Thorion. Perhaps we could—'

'We?' said Thorion, his eyes narrowing slightly and Denoris

half-smiled, knowing himself bested. 'As you made very clear at the last Council Meeting, you wish to work alone. You may have them when I am finished with them,' said Thorion, his tone final. 'As to when that might be, I do not know.'

Denoris held back a roar of frustration, his fists clenching. But there was nothing else he could do. 'My Lord,' he said, bowing his head once more. He turned to Gwenene. 'Come, my Lady, let us go from here.'

He knew Thorion was watching him as he left, Gwenene trailing behind. When the heavy wooden door closed behind them Denoris picked up his pace; Gwenene hurried to catch up. Taking his arm, she held onto him as they moved swiftly through the Foyer and out through the double doors, taking a sharp turn towards the stables.

'Wait, Denoris! Stop dragging me around!' snapped Gwenene. She slowed, letting go of his arm. Denoris stopped dead and turned to her.

'I have had enough of this!' he snarled.

'As have I!' she snapped back, her blue eyes flashing fire. 'So what do we do now?'

'We get the girl. Enough of this careful manoeuvring – the time has come to act.' He marched towards the stables once more, his fists clenched. Gwenene ran after him.

'So what, we just cross over and grab her? You know why we cannot do that, why we haven't done it before! Send someone else – send Deryck again! We can't jeopardise our positions here! Not to mention Thorion will–'

'Thorion!' roared Denoris, turning around and marching back towards her. 'I have had quite enough of Thorion and his wise ways!'

'Denoris, be quiet!" hissed Gwenene, her hands on his arms. He shook her off.

'I know, I know, you do not need to tell me,' he ground out.

'Now come on. Let us go to the one person who can do this for us.'

'Etras.' Realisation dawned on her lovely face. Denoris nodded, his anger abating slightly. He could always count on her to know what he was thinking.

'Yes,' he said. 'For him there are no more consequences. Come on.' They entered the stable yard where their horses stood ready and waiting, a third horse, loaded with their baggage, being led by the groom who would accompany them. Denoris waved him away.

'No,' he said to a protesting Gwenene. 'Let us travel light, and our destination be our own. We need to act and fast. If we don't get her now, Artos will.'

Mounting his horse he wheeled it around, waiting. Gwenene, after a moment's hesitation, ascended her own mount. She smiled at Denoris, dark and lascivious.

'Let us go,' she said, her mouth curving around the words. Denoris, seeing her excitement, felt his own rise to meet it, and snarling smiled back. They spurred their mounts forward and were gone.

ROZELLE HURRIED ALONG THE PATHWAY TO THE APARTMENTS OF the Dark, running across the small courtyard to the great doors decorated with iron vines. She turned the handle, pushing the door open and rushing in, not bothering to close it behind her. Running to Denoris' apartments she banged on the door with her fist.

'Lord Denoris!' she called. 'I must speak with you!'

She knew he did not like her to arrive so, that he preferred her to wait for him to come to her, but this was just too urgent. She banged again, sagging with relief as she heard footsteps approach. The door opened and she stepped back, her mouth opening to share her news. Her heart sank as Denoris' steward appeared, looking down his nose at her.

'What on earth is all this noise?' The steward frowned at her. 'I really—'

'I need to see Lord Denoris!' She glared at the steward. 'It's urgent.'

He drew himself up to his full height, even more disapproving than before. 'I'm afraid you've missed him. He is gone to the hills, with the Lady Gwenene, and will not be back until tomorrow's meeting. Perhaps you could—'

But whatever he thought she could do would have to wait. She turned and was running out of the door before he could finish his sentence. Emerging into the courtyard, she paused, assessing her options. Then she ran for the stables.

CHAPTER 5
SPARKS FLY

Alma sat back in her chair, plastic legs scraping on the stone terrace. Above, the ever-present gulls wheeled and called, the sea shushing on the beach below. She closed her eyes, tapping into the cool energy of the nearby sea, the sun warm on her face as her newly discovered powers surged through her. She could feel waves crashing on the pebbled shore, the rhythm of the sea pulsing through her, and she imagined herself as a small fish darting through green depths. She heard a voice calling, faint over the sound of the rushing waters, and opened her eyes, surprised to find herself back in the cafe.

'Alma, where were you? Your breakfast's arrived.' Merewyn, sat across the table from her, was looking at her strangely.

'Oh!' The image of the little fish swam away as Alma came back to reality.

Merewyn grinned. 'I thought you were sleepin'. What were you doing, anyway?'

Alma laughed, feeling a bit freaked out. 'Er, I was in the sea, with the fish.' She picked up her tea and took a sip. As she ate her breakfast she started to feel better, more grounded. Though she needed to watch herself, really – she couldn't go drifting off whenever she wanted.

'So what was so urgent you needed to see me this early?' Merewyn's voice broke into Alma's thoughts. She sounded grumpy, but her hazel eyes were twinkling. Alma grinned. It *was* early, but she hadn't been able to wait. Reaching into her bag she pulled out a piece of paper covered with writing.

'Well, I decided to take a look through mine and Caleb's notes last night, you know, after we went to the hills and everything.'

Merewyn's blonde eyebrows rose, but she didn't say anything.

'Right.' Alma cleared her throat. It was getting easier to say Caleb's name, but it still hurt. 'So, there were a couple of things I found. Here.' She pushed the paper across the table to Merewyn, who picked it up.

'Okay?'

'Well, I just wrote down anything that seemed important, so, I don't know, does any of it make sense to you?'

Merewyn started to read, her finger moving down the page.

He keeps mentioning five pointed stars, are they significant somehow? I mean, they're all over the place here, so maybe it's a link to Ambeth?'

'He?'

'Davies. I'm sorry it's all a bit haphazard, but his notes were all over the place.'

Merewyn laughed. 'Don't I know it! He had a filin' system that seemed to consist of piles of paper all over his office, yet he knew where everythin' was. Woe betide me if I ever moved anythin' or tried to tidy up!'

Alma nodded. 'I forget that you knew him,' she said. 'It's kind of weird, still, you know?'

'Yeah, I guess.' Merewyn crinkled her nose, not seeming too worried. 'Anyway, you're right. Five pointed stars *are* important.' She turned her wrist over to show Alma her tattoo. 'That's why I have one on my wrist. They are neutral, neither Light nor Dark, and an ancient symbol of protection. Interestin' that Davies kept goin' on about them.' She took a sip of her drink, staring out across the view. 'He loved this place, you know. Was so proud of his town and its history. It was a shame what happened to him. And now here we are, lookin' for his secrets after all these years. It is a strange thing, all that time.'

'Well, let's hope we find them,' said Alma. 'Then perhaps he can rest.' She paused, unsure what to say against the old sorrow she could sense in her friend. 'D'you think it might be something to do with the shape of the Castle?' she asked, finally. 'Like, you know how old churches were done in a cross shape? Is the Castle a star?' She looked up at the ruins, one hand shading her eyes from the bright sun. 'I dunno.' She shrugged, feeling disappointed. 'I just feel like, somehow, it has something to do with this.'

'Well, maybe it does,' said Merewyn. 'It's usually a good thing to trust your hunches.'

Alma nodded. 'Yeah, Meredan said that to me as well, once.'

Merewyn smiled. 'Let's see what else you've got.' She bent her head and kept reading.

The Castle in question was built by fairies, according to this guy. I can't think of any castle I've been to where someone says this. But then, they probably thought he was nuts. I think fairy might mean someone from Ambeth, so this must be the link. God knows they all seem a bit unreal at times.'

Merewyn laughed.

'What?'

'Oh, just the bit about the Castle being built by fairies.'

'Yeah, I thought that was kind of weird and cool at the same time.'

'He was right, you know.'

Alma's jaw dropped. 'Wait, what do you mean?'

'Well, Thorion told me once, that the Castle here was built by a Lord of Ambeth as his stronghold. He had a human consort and wanted a place to be with her. And it's not the first time Ambeth has been described as Fairyland. So Llewellyn, for all intents and purposes, was right.'

'Huh. Poor guy. I bet no-one believed him, either.'

Merewyn's hazel eyes clouded over. 'No, they didn't,' she said, her voice soft. 'Poor man indeed.' Her mouth twisted and she returned her attention to the page.

'These ancient stones hold a secret and I will find it. That's what he said. Caleb has just reminded me that part of the prophecy reads 'in stone'. So maybe that has something to do with it? God, why are his notes such a mess!'

Alma's eyes prickled. She remembered Caleb smiling at her across the table in the Library, all the hours they'd spent together. He would have loved to have been part of this, she thought, looking up at the ruins again, high on their mound above the town. It was obviously the right Castle, it had to be! Her notes and the information she'd read, plus the fact that Davies had been here – it all added up to one thing. This was the Castle in Davies' notes. But what the hell was she supposed to do next? All this crap about being the 'chosen one' and she'd never had any idea about anything. Pain burned in her chest and she wiped her eyes, looking out to sea. She wished Caleb was with her, or even her father – at least he might know what to do next.

Her fingers were tingling, pins and needles under her skin. She frowned. There *was* something she could do. Or at least try to do. 'Um, Merewyn, what if I tried to, I don't know, sense the land? See if it can tell us anything?'

Merewyn's eyes went wide. 'Well, it's a thought, Alma. Are you sure you can? I mean, I don't know enough to help you – you really need your grandfather here.'

'Well, how different can it be from going through the Gate? I just have to close my eyes and breathe, right? It's worth a try, at least.'

Before Merewyn could protest further Alma pushed her chair

back and closed her eyes. She started breathing in and out, trying to relax, trying not to think of how silly she felt. At first there wasn't much; just the sound of the sea, the noises from the cafe, the wind blowing. She went deeper, trying to reach past the sounds of children and traffic, people talking to each other, feeling the shape of the Castle in her mind. But it wasn't working. She took a deep breath, blowing it out. She was trying too hard. Making sure her feet were flat against the ground she tried again. This time the pulse came, energy from the earth below moving through her feet to her legs and into her chest. Her eyes flew open and Merewyn jumped.

'Alma, are you—'

She held up her hand. She almost had it, could feel the shape of the Castle mound, almost like a dome, mirroring the curving blue sky above. And inside it, deep under stone, there was something. A glimmering, a cool energy that shone steady like a star, surrounded by a tangle of Dark and Light, just like she'd seen the night before. A car honked loudly in the street below and, distracted, Alma lost the thread. Try as she might, she couldn't get it back. The noise from the café took over, a group of adults nearby talking loudly, one of them on their phone. It was gone. She huffed out a disappointed sigh, sagging forward.

'Are you all right? Did you feel anything?'

Alma pulled her chair up to the table once more. 'Well, there was something,' she said. 'But then I lost it.' She shot the noisy adults a baleful glare.

'So, what did you feel?' said Merewyn, eyes wide, her hands clasped together.

'Well, there's definitely something under the Castle mound,' said Alma. 'It felt like a dome or something, like it's hollow underneath.'

'Underneath?' Merewyn looked up at the hill. 'Like, a hidden chamber or somethin'?' She frowned. 'But there's no way into the mound, at least I don't think so.'

Alma shrugged. 'Well, that's what it felt like. Maybe I need to go up there and try again.'

'It's worth a try.' Merewyn picked up her phone, elbows on the table as she tapped on the screen. 'Let me check when it opens. The times change over the summer.' She stopped tapping, waving her phone around. 'This damn signal! It's so useless sometimes! I've got nothin'.'

Alma frowned. She could see Merewyn's energy pattern, Light and Dark mixed together, but here and there the lines were jagged. Instinctively she reached out and took Merewyn's hand, holding it and rubbing it with her fingers, feeling power pulse gently through her skin.

'Whoa!' Merewyn snatched her hand back and stared at Alma. 'What did you just do?'

Alma let out a breath. 'Um, well, I could see your energy was a bit funny, jagged. So, I just, fixed it, I guess.' Alma spoke haltingly, unsure of what had just happened. She hadn't really thought about it, just done it. 'Sorry, I didn't mean to.'

'Alma, that is amazin'!' The lilt in Merewyn's voice was even more pronounced as she gazed at Alma, hazel eyes wide. 'I mean, I was a bit cranky about the phone and Thorion bein' just so *obtuse* when it came to lookin' after you, but you've taken it all away. I feel amazin'!'

'Wait, you've spoken to Thorion? You didn't say anything, did you? About me knowing about, well—'

'Oh, no, Alma, I promise you I said not a word.' Merewyn tried to look serious but failed, sinking back into her chair with a blissed-out smile on her face. Alma shook her head and refilled both their mugs from the teapot, replacing the cosy once she was done. It looked like she wasn't going to get much out of Merewyn for a little while. She sat back and took in the view, the bay curving out to the horizon, water blue like the sky above. She was still tingling with the aftermath of the energy surge, and it felt strange yet right at the same time. Her new powers were going to take some getting used to, but at the same time it felt wonderful to have something from her father, as though he had sent her a gift through the years. She hugged the thought to her, warmed by it.

'So, shall we just go up there then, after this? See if it's open?' All at once she wanted to flex her new muscles, see what her powers could do.

'Hmm, okay.' Merewyn still had her eyes closed. She looked so relaxed Alma grinned. She could wait a little longer.

A SHORT WHILE LATER THEY LEFT THE CAFÉ, HEADING ALONG the promenade towards the Castle. Merewyn was almost bouncing, her face lit up. Alma, hands in pockets, glanced at her.

'What's the big deal?' she asked, amused. 'I mean, I didn't really do much...'

'You're a full Channeller, Alma! D'you know how rare that is?'

'I don't even really know what it is,' said Alma, 'let alone how rare.' She frowned, unable to completely share Merewyn's excitement. 'But how come I wasn't able to do this stuff before? I mean, if I've always had the talent...'

'Because you didn't know you could. This is not somethin' that's part of your regular world. It wasn't 'til I told you what you could do that you realised. Although, there must have been some manifestations?'

'Manifestations?'

'Well, have you ever made anyone feel better, just by wishin' for it?' Merewyn stopped to lean against the blue-painted railings, her back to the beach, arms folded, her pixie face bright with curiosity.

Alma thought about it. 'Well, maybe one time, I don't know...' She shook her head, dismissing the idea.

Merewyn's mouth dropped open. 'Tell me, please.'

'Ah, it's stupid,' Alma looked down, scuffing her foot along the ground. But Merewyn was insistent.

'Alma, I'm not kiddin' about this stuff! Please, I promise, it's not stupid.'

Alma made a face, tucking her long hair behind her ears, the breeze lifting strands around her head. 'Um, okay, well, Mum wasn't feeling too well one time. It was just before my eighth birthday and I was worried,' she laughed a little, 'that she would have to cancel my party.'

Merewyn grinned. 'Go on.'

Alma thought for a moment. 'Well, she was lying on the couch and I remember sitting on the floor next to her, taking her hand...'

She had *been worried about her mother. Eleanor had been lying on the sofa for hours, but when anyone asked her if she was all right she just turned away. Alma had thought she saw tears on her mother's cheek and her own heart had broken, wanting to make Eleanor happy. So, when she got the chance, she'd crept up to sit next to her, taking her mother's cool hand in her own small ones, leaning on the side of the sofa as she'd wished with all her might that she would get better.*

'And so, what happened?'

'After a few moments she sat up and kissed me on the cheek, said she was feeling much better. Then she got up and went on with things as normal.'

'So, d'you see—'

'Maybe I helped her? I don't know.'

'If only your father had lived, he would have shown you how,' said Merewyn, looking sympathetic.

'Yeah, but he didn't, did he? I'm only realising now, how much I missed out on not knowing him. But it would have meant Dad would never have been with Mum and that would have made him unhappy, so... ugh, I don't know. This whole thing is so annoying sometimes.' Alma put her head down, her good mood of before gone.

Merewyn was quiet for a moment, then her face twisted in what looked like regret. 'You need to tell Thorion. And you need to do it now.'

CHAPTER 6
HER STORY TO TELL

Alma's mouth dropped open, ready to protest, but Merewyn went on. 'Either you do, or I'll have to. I'm sorry,' she said. 'But you can't be walkin' around with all this power and him not know about it.'

'What?!' Alma folded her arms. 'No way. Not yet.'

'You can't hide from this!'

Alma recoiled. She wasn't hiding! After all the crap she'd been through for Ambeth. Her temper started to rise.

Merewyn spread her hands, her tone conciliatory. 'I don't want to make you angry—'

'Well, you are.' In fact, she was furious. About everything: her father, the weird powers; all of it was too much.

'If he doesn't know he can't protect you. The Dark will find you and—'

'Oh, I'm sick of all this!' Anger thrummed through her, and she felt like she might explode. 'Sick of worrying about the Dark, of being frightened. Why can't I just be me?'

'Because of that!'

Merewyn pointed at Alma's hands. They were tingling, her

fingertips buzzing and she looked down in surprise to see them glowing, along with her bracelet stone. 'Merewyn, I–'

'Alma, I'm sorry, but it needs to be told. You can't keep this a secret for much longer!' Merewyn moved closer, her face pale, small fists clenched at her side. 'Just look at you, you can't even control–'

'I can control it! And, you're not the one to tell him! It's up to me!' Alma felt tears starting in her eyes, hot and angry. She took in a shaking breath, trying to pull back the tingling in her finger- tips. The glow lessened as she focused on it.

Merewyn spoke, breaking her concentration. 'Then choose. You cannot deny who you are anymore!'

'Ugh!' Turning on her heel, Alma started to run. Forget the Castle, forget her new powers, forget everything! She just wanted to get away. Even though deep down she knew she was overreact- ing, at the same time she wanted to scream all her frustration and sorrow and anger to the skies. She raced up the road to her grand- mother's house, feet pounding, breath sobbing in and out. When she reached the house she stopped at the front door, hands on her thighs as she bent over to get her breath, wanting to compose herself before going inside. After a few moments she straightened up, wiping her hand across her face. Opening the door she went in. The hallway was shadowy and cool, the pale green wallpaper striped with light from the kitchen. Meg was in there, bustling about, her shadow passing across the light every so often.

'That you, Alma?'

Well, who else would it be? Alma scowled, about to make a retort, then thought better of it. 'Yes.'

'I thought you'd be out longer. I'm off shopping, would you like to come with me?'

Shopping, thought Alma. That was what normal people did, people who didn't have to worry about strange powers and dead fathers and the gathering Dark. Wander around some shops, look at pretty things, maybe even buy something. Shopping, decided

Alma, was exactly what she needed to do. 'Er, yeah. Sounds good. I just have to get something.'

'Oh, no hurry. I was planning on leaving for the bus in about twenty minutes, okay?'

'Fine.' Alma headed upstairs to her room, climbing the white painted treads to the third floor. She flopped onto her bed and stared at the ceiling, her mouth tight against the anger welling in her, anger at herself as much as with Merewyn. Holding her hands up she turned them this way and that, but there was no sign of the strange light or tingling. Damn! She knew Merewyn was right and that she needed to speak with Thorion. But this was *her* talent, *her* powers, from the father she had never known. It should be her choice what she did with them, who she told about it. She was angry about her father as well, the more she thought about it. About the hurt her mother still carried, about the missed chance to know him. How different her life would have been if he had lived. But then she thought of her dad, of the love in his brown eyes as he talked to her, the way he adored her mother. And her little brothers who, though they drove her mad at times, she couldn't imagine being without. God, this was all so hard! She rolled onto her side and hugged her pillow close, staring at the square of blue sky visible through the open window.

She *couldn't* tell Thorion. She didn't want to. Not yet. Not until she'd spoken to Artos. And there was no way she was letting Merewyn do it either. It was her story to tell when she chose. She knew what that meant, though. One way or another, she had to go back to Ambeth. The only other option was to never speak to Merewyn again, to ignore everything that was happening and turn her back on the place like her mother had, consigning it to fantasy, to a box under the bed. But she was far more involved than her mother had ever been, plus there was the small matter of the gathering Dark. Besides, if she did that, Merewyn would have to tell Thorion anyway and then they'd all be looking for her. Blowing out a big sigh she rolled onto her back, reaching in her pocket for her phone. Maybe there was a way around this. Because, like it or not, there was something about the Castle, and she was starting to get an idea of what it might be. Scrolling through, she found Merewyn's number and started to type.

MEREWYN SAT IN HER GARDEN UNDER A SHADY TREE, A MUG OF tea going cold on the small table next to her. She hoped she hadn't blown it. But what the hell else was she supposed to do? A full Channeller? She couldn't remember ever knowing one, even in her long life. And here Alma was, running around the place with power just coming out of her fingertips. Merewyn couldn't leave her unprotected – now that the encounter with Deryck had awoken Alma's powers the Dark would find her, one way or another, and her bracelet wouldn't be much help against their combined might. Sighing, she folded her arms and leaned back, looking up at the golden green leaves dappling patterns overhead. Her phone beeped and she jumped. She grabbed it, relief flooding through her as she saw a text from Alma.

I'm sorry I ran off. But u can't decide this for me. No-one tells Thorion until I do, until I speak to Artos. So here's the deal. We find the Cup, then we tell them. R U in?

Merewyn grinned.

I'm in, she texted back. *But u knew that already. So r u saying u know where it is?*

She waited a moment then her phone buzzed in her hand.

And u won't speak 2 Thorion?

Merewyn raised her eyebrows.

I swear on the Light I won't say a word.

Her phone beeped once more.

We need 2 visit the Castle. This afternoon good 4 U?

Huh. Shaking her head, smiling, Merewyn texted back.

Pick you up at 3.

Dropping her phone on the table she picked up her tea, sitting back as she took a sip. Bleurgh. It was stone cold, but it didn't matter. Everything was fine, better than fine. Getting up she went into the house, the door swinging shut behind her as she entered the kitchen, tipping her tea down the sink. She put the kettle on to boil again, her mind on the day ahead. She still needed to talk to Thorion, she knew that, but a promise was a promise. She would keep her word to Alma, tell him only what he needed to know. Now she had to prepare for the afternoon's work. Closing her eyes, she checked the Gate tracers. They were still set, still unchanged. Good. She only needed an hour or so, but she'd be offline for that time so they needed to hold. Not that she was expecting anyone to come through.

Opening the fridge, she reached for the milk, making a face when she saw there were only a few drops left. No matter. She'd pick some up later. Now, she had work to do. Picking up her keys and bag, she headed out the door.

ARTOS HEADED DOWN THE HILL, WIPING HIS BROW. IT WAS SO warm he shrugged off his jacket, rolling up his shirtsleeves. Taking the road, he stayed close to the grass verge until the pavement began. Picking up his pace, he kept going until he reached a crossroad where he stopped, trying to get his bearings. He was among the houses but still high up, the town stretching down to the blue water below. The Castle was ahead of him to the right and he squinted, shading his eyes with his hand. A honking noise made him jump. A huge metal shape rushed past him, honking again, and he stepped back, his heart pounding. Was that a... car? Surely it hadn't been that long since he was here! Shaken, he started walking again, taking care to stay off the road. Deep down, he was starting to doubt his wisdom in coming through alone. He should have talked to Thorion or

Meredan about what to expect – they at least had been across within the last fifty years. Still, done was done, and he needed to make the best of the situation. Turning a corner, he headed downhill once more.

~

ALMA WANDERED ALONG THE BUSY SHOPPING STREET, BLINKING at the energy patterns appearing all around her. Children glowing golden, couples twined together. She stepped back abruptly, moving away from a well-dressed woman whose energy was dark and murky.

'Are you all right?' A hand touched her arm and it shocked her back to reality, the energy lines disappearing. Her grandmother was standing in front of her, looking worried.

'Uh, yeah. Tired, I guess.' She smiled, trying to shrug it off, but Meg tilted her head, blue eyes shrewd.

'Cup of tea?'

Alma nodded. All at once it was what she wanted more than anything. Meg led her into a nearby café, bright checked table-cloths and dried flowers in little vases on the small tables. They took a seat and a waiter came over, smiling, his black apron pristine. Meg ordered tea for them both then, once the waiter had gone, focused on Alma. 'So, what's going on?'

What's going on? So much Alma could barely get her mind around it. She stared at her grandmother, not knowing what to say. Then she thought of something she could discuss.

'Well, just before she left, Mum told me. About my father.' It was abrupt, but it was the only way she could get the words out, energy lines appearing all around her again. She sat back, hands to her temples, screwing up her eyes as she fought to control it. Okay, Merewyn was right. She needed help. She could feel the energy in her mind, as though it all came to a single point and she found that if she focused on it she could control it, like holding the reins of a horse. She realised Meg was talking to her and opened her eyes. 'Sorry, what?'

'I said, Alma, it was time, really. Are you all right with it?'

Her grandmother was looking worried and Alma took a deep breath, feeling more and more in control. Okay, she could do this. Their tea arrived, steaming in the pot, china cups clinking as they were set down on the table. Meg poured, pushing a cup across to Alma who added milk and sugar, stirring it well.

'Um, well, I guess I already kind of knew,' she started.

Meg raised her eyebrows.

'Well, Mum mentioned it when she gave me the bracelet. And I overheard you both, a few years ago, talking about him. But I didn't know his name or anything. And now I do.' Her hand went to her bracelet as she stared down at her tea, watching the steam swirl above the cup, the little bubbles of milk going round and round.

'He was lovely.' Alma looked up to see Meg smiling. 'But so is Graham.'

'Oh yeah. I mean, it doesn't change anything, not really. Dad's still my dad.'

'I know. And I could not have asked for more for my Eleanor, that he took such good care of her. But your father, your real father—'

'Galen.'

'Yes, Galen. He loved her, and you, so very much. It was such a waste, what happened to him.'

Alma nodded, the sting of tears as always when she thought about it. She figured this was how things were going to be for a while. Picking up her cup she took a sip. 'That's what Mum said as well.' She took another sip. 'She still loves him.' Might as well get it out there. She waited for her grandmother's reaction.

Meg paused. 'Yes, I know,' she said finally. 'Love like that, you only feel it once in a lifetime. Like two halves of the same whole.' Alma's mouth dropped open. 'Oh yes,' Meg continued, nodding.

'But there are other kinds of love and I know she could not do without Graham. They've been friends since they were children, you know.'

'Really? That long?' said Alma. Her chest was sore with emotion, her control on the energy lines slipping. She took another deep breath, another gulp of tea. Bloody Ambeth. She glanced over at a nearby table where a group of teenage girls were laughing and chatting, bright plastic shopping bags around their feet and for a moment she felt the weight of everything that had happened pressing on her and it was almost too much. 'Ugh.' It was half a sob, half a groan and she tried to muffle it, but the tears started to fall. She picked up her tea again, drinking and sniffling, eyes blinking.

'Oh, Alma, I didn't mean to upset you.' Meg dug in her purse, pulling out a pack of tissues that she handed to Alma, concern on her lined face.

'No, no, it's all right.' Alma put down her cup and took the tissues, pulling one out and wiping her eyes while Meg topped up her cup. 'It is, really,' she went on, though her throat still felt choked up. 'So Mum knew Dad when they were kids, hey?'

'Oh yes,' said Meg. She grinned. 'He was always hanging around, always ready to defend her if anyone bothered her. Not that she needed it – she's fiery enough, just like you.'

'Really?'

'Ha, yes.' Meg laughed. 'I can still remember her throwing a bucket of water over Graham and another boy, Tom Pritchard I think it was. He'd been chasing her, pulling her hair and Graham had stepped in. But before he could do anything she'd grabbed the rainwater bucket and thrown it over Tom, drenching Graham as well. Oh dear, I did laugh.'

Alma smiled. 'And he still wanted to be her friend after that?'

'Oh yes. He's had eyes for no-one else, his whole life. So she's very lucky.'

'She said that too,' said Alma, starting to feel better. She drained her teacup, setting it down with a clink in the saucer.

'More?' asked Meg, lifting the pot, but Alma shook her head.

'No thanks. But, um, thanks, for listening.'

Meg smiled at her. 'Like I said, any time you want to talk to me, I'm here. Now,' she said, sitting back in her chair, 'do you think you could manage a few more shops?'

Alma nodded. 'Sounds great.'

ARTOS CAME TO THE COTTAGE HE KNEW BELONGED TO ALMA'S family. He remembered an older house in this spot, thick stone walls and a low roof, deep-set windows winking in the afternoon sun. The newer house was an improvement, he supposed, taking in the three levels, the white painted window frames. Still, he had liked the warm smoky rooms, the way the timbers had groaned against winter storms, the thick walls keeping the worst of the weather out. It was a long time ago, though, when his visits to this world had been far more frequent.

Right, enough wallowing in the past. Time to get on with the present. He walked up the path to the door, standing on the step. He put his hand to his mouth. Then he rang the doorbell.

CHAPTER 7
NEGOTIATING ROUGH WATERS

Denoris rode hard towards the mountains, urgency within him. It was time to act. Beside him Gwenene matched his pace, bent low over her horse's neck, long dark hair streaming out behind her, delicate profile pale against the green slopes.

He had always liked women with dark hair, though none had touched him, none until her. She had come to him one night in the gardens, her blue eyes gleaming in the moonlight, her skin like pearl. Walking with him through the maze of hedges she had taken advantage of the shadows to kiss him. Then she had started to run. Intrigued, he had followed as she drew him deeper into the gardens, her blue draperies drifting behind her. Finally, he'd caught her, taking her in his arms. He'd not been gentle with her that night, but she had met him all the way and they had been together ever since. No matter who else they amused themselves with, they always came back to each other. As he watched her ride, her slender hands on the reins, excitement grew within him at the thought of being alone with her. If only she would give him a child.

The ground began to rise beneath them, their horses' hooves thundering as they entered the pass leading towards Etras' stronghold, a castle set high among the crags. Pointed towers of grey stone rose above a solid keep, black flecks swirling around one of the towers. The faint shrieking of winged Watchers could be heard, growing louder as they drew near.

'Are you ready?' Denoris pitched his voice to carry above the sound of their approach. Gwenene glanced at him briefly, but did not slow her pace.

'I am.'

A few moments later they arrived at the towered gatehouse. 'The Lord Denoris and Lady Gwenene, to see Lord Etras!' Denoris bellowed, his voice echoing around the stones. There was an answering shout, and a moment later the great wooden doors swung inwards. Their horses' hooves clattered against the cobbles as they passed under the archway, emerging in a small courtyard, Etras already striding out to meet them.

'Well met, my friends!' He was tall and well-muscled, his dark beard shaped around his strong jaw, shoulder length brown hair brushed back from his brow. He and Denoris had been friends since they were boys and had shared many adventures. Unfortunate proclivities aside, Denoris knew he could always count on him.

'Well met,' he called, dismounting and handing his horse to a waiting groom.

'What brings you here? It has been long since I have seen you both.' Etras helped Gwenene down from her horse and swept her into a bear hug, swinging her around as she laughed, kissing her cheek as he set her down.

'I know, old friend, and for that I apologise,' said Denoris, coming over. 'It's good to see you.' Etras smiled and hugged him, a brief clap on the back. Above them the Watchers shrieked, leathery wings flapping as they entered their tower. Gwenene tipped her head back to look.

'Useful things, those,' she observed.

Etras nodded. 'They are, Lady. Eyes to see where I no longer can, they keep me informed of much in Ambeth.'

'And beyond?' asked Denoris, intrigued.

'Yes, they can pass our borders with ease,' said Etras. 'But come, you must both be needing refreshment after your journey, and I have much to offer.' His gaze lingered on Gwenene a moment longer than necessary and Denoris frowned.

'Well then,' he said. 'What are we waiting for?'

He went to take Gwenene's arm, but Etras beat him to it, leading them through another large archway and into a second courtyard, towards a pair of large timber doors flanked by human guards. 'You are looking well, my Lady,' he said. Denoris could see his hand sliding down Gwenene's back.

'Thank you. As are you,' she replied. 'The mountain air must agree with you.' She tossed her head and smiled, though Denoris knew she was annoyed as Etras pulled her closer, her blue eyes flashing sparks. He suppressed a sigh. Etras had always been like this, unable to withstand temptation, whether willing or not. It was what had got him into his current predicament, though it seemed exile had not chastened him in any way. He wondered whether they'd done the right thing, coming to him. Perhaps it would have been better to let old dogs lie. But they were here now, and may as well see it through. Darkness knew his options were becoming fewer, and if Etras could help him, it would be worth a few hours' annoyance.

The guards pulled the double doors open, timber scraping across the cobbles. They entered a large Hall, a fire burning in the massive fireplace at one end. A long wooden table, well-polished, sat at the centre of the room. Windows set high in the stone walls let in the last of the afternoon light as Etras led Denoris and Gwenene to a group of comfortable chairs set near to the fireplace. Gwenene went to remove her cloak but he took over, his hands covering hers, fingers caressing her as he undid the clasp. She bore it with good grace, though she glanced at Denoris as Etras took her cloak with a flourish, hanging it carefully over a nearby chair. They each sat down, Denoris frowning at Gwenene who shook her head at him slightly. He sighed inwardly, knowing he needed to keep hold of his temper.

'I have missed you, old friend,' he said, leaning back in the leather armchair.

Etras, who was pacing in front of the fire, stopped, frowning. 'So why has it been so long since I've seen you?' His fierce expression relaxed into a smile. 'I thought you would have come sooner, see how your army is progressing.'

Denoris raised an eyebrow. 'And how is it coming along?'

'Well enough. Galardin take time to make, as you know, and there are not so many humans in these parts.' He stopped as a serving girl, her dark hair tucked up under a kerchief, entered the Hall. 'Wine for my guests, and quickly!' he barked. The young woman jumped, performing a hasty curtsey before running off. Etras turned back to his guests. 'I cannot take too many of the staff,' he went on, lowering his voice. 'They do begin to ask questions.'

Gwenene snorted and Denoris shot her a warning glance. She sat back, a faint smile on her lips. The wine arrived, blood red in a glass flagon, white in a frosted silver jug, with three goblets. The young woman set everything down on the nearby table and went to pick up one of the jugs, but Etras waved her away. She left quickly, looking over her shoulder with frightened eyes as she scurried from the Hall. Denoris watched her go, interested by her reaction. Etras, meanwhile, picked up a goblet, offering it to Gwenene.

'Red or white, my Lady?'

'Oh, red, definitely.' Gwenene smiled as she took her glass.

'And you, Denoris?'

'White.' He took the goblet and sank a long draught, finding he needed it. The wine at least was excellent; he couldn't fault

Etras for that, though he was surprised he could keep such a good quality cellar in exile.

'So why has it been so long? You still haven't answered me, Denoris.' Etras poured himself a drink and went to stand near the fire. 'Last time I saw you, you promised to visit regularly, and yet here it is, a year gone nearly, and this is the first I see of you.'

Denoris tried not to frown. Really? The solitude must be getting to Etras – he sounded more like a complaining old woman than the proud warrior he knew of old. He took another mouthful of the exquisite wine, shrugging as he answered.

'Things have been... difficult of late, and there has been much that has taken my time.'

'I heard about your boy,' said Etras. 'Killing Thorion's son. What was he thinking?'

'He was not thinking.' Gwenene glanced at Denoris. 'He was distracted, by the girl.'

'Ah yes, the one of the Prophecy. Is it true what I've heard, that she is Galen's child?'

'It's true,' nodded Denoris, taking another long draught, emptying his glass. Etras raised his eyebrows, coming over to refill it.

"Tis a shame you did not kill her mother as well as Galen. It would have saved us a lot of time.'

Denoris sighed. As if he hadn't thought of that, a thousand times over. 'Well, it has come to me these days that we cannot change the Prophecy, that it does read true. I could have managed things better, I suppose, but how can I change what is destined? No, Etras, I could not have done so then, nor can I now. Alma is the one who will find the Regalia, and that is what brings us here.' He took another drink and leaned his head back, feeling weary. Another young woman appeared, this one blonde, carrying a jug of fresh water that she placed carefully on the table.

'Did I ask for this?' Etras shot the girl a harsh glance and she trembled. 'Bring food for my guests, and quickly!' The young woman bobbed a curtsey and left the Hall, Etras watching her go. Denoris glanced at Gwenene again. She nodded.

'We need your help, dear Etras.' She put her goblet down and stretched, slender arms over her head.

'I'm always available to help you,' said Etras. 'It's lonely here, you know, in the mountains. Perhaps you can help me too.' He moved closer, running the back of his hand gently along Gwenene's cheek as she leaned back in her chair. Denoris' mouth dropped open. What the hell was Etras playing at?

'What of your wife?' He allowed a slight edge to creep into his voice. 'For I had heard you were married.' Gwenene flinched and Etras stepped back, his hands raised.

'She passed away, a month or so ago. In childbed, the child gone too. She was human, obviously not strong enough to carry my seed.'

'I am sorry to hear of it,' replied Denoris. 'It's a shame we have no more solace to offer you than friendship, is that not right, Gwenene?' He raised his eyebrows and she met his gaze, her face unreadable. 'Still, you seem to have an abundance of serving women,' he went on, eyeing the plump curves of yet another young woman who had come in, bearing a tray of food. 'Surely they can be of assistance, should you feel... lonely.'

Etras stared hard at Denoris then laughed, loud and hearty. 'True, old friend. But you cannot blame a man for trying, not with someone as alluring as your Gwenene.'

Gwenene's eyes flashed blue fire at this and she sat up, but Denoris motioned her to silence.

'No, I cannot blame you, my friend, to be tempted by such beauty. I trust though, that I will not have to worry about it happening again. Otherwise I fear this could be a very short visit.'

'Oh, Denoris, enough!' snapped Gwenene. 'Both of you,' she said, looking at Etras, who had the momentary grace to look ashamed. 'We are wasting time! Tell him, Denoris, tell him why we are here, what we need from him.'

CHAPTER 8
WISHING LUCK

'Oh God.'

Deryck hung his head as a familiar group of girls came into the Great Hall. Beside him Ellery giggled, clapping a hand over her mouth as Deryck shot her a fierce glare.

'Sorry,' she said, 'but you've made your bed there.' She giggled again, and nudged nudged Deryck, wanting to cheer him up. 'Surely it's not that bad. She seems nice enough, and she obviously likes you.'

Deryck put his head in his hands. 'She's all right, I guess,' he said. 'But I just don't want her around.'

Ellery frowned. This was not like her confident brother. 'In the old days you would have just told her so,' she said. 'What's changed?'

'You *know* what's changed,' he said. 'Now I know what it's like when you want someone, and, well, I don't want to hurt her feelings. I don't know...' He ran a hand through his blond hair.

'Oh, Deryck.' Feeling sorry for him, Ellery refilled his glass and topped up her own. Musicians struck up a lively tune, couples coming to dance in the centre of the room. Stars were visible through the stained-glass windows and soft light from hanging lanterns illuminated the scene, gleaming gold above the dancing pairs. It was a lovely evening, Ellery thought, looking around for Tomas. She couldn't see him, but she could see Lissa. She nudged Deryck again. 'Heads up, she's coming over.'

'Oh no.' Deryck lifted his head as Lissa approached, a bright smile on her face.

'Well, maybe you shouldn't have slept with her,' hissed Ellery. 'You're going to have to dance with her, at least. And that's the last of the wine,' she added, as he drained his glass. He shot her a dark look before standing to greet Lissa.

'Oh, Deryck,' she squealed, 'isn't it the loveliest night? Hello, Ellery.' Ellery raised her glass, lips closed tight over her laughter. Deryck gave her a pleading glance as Lissa grabbed him by the arm and dragged him out to the dance floor. She threw herself against him, hugging him tightly, her head on his shoulder as they swayed, other couples dodging around them.

Ellery laughed out loud, unable to hold it in any more. She finished her wine, feeling dizzy as it went to her head. That was the last for her as well, she thought, shaking her head at the servant carrying another full jug. 'Could we have water, instead, please?' He nodded, moving away. She felt a gentle hand on her shoulder and looked up to see Tomas. He was smiling, dressed in a green tunic and breeches, his long brown hair tied back.

'Would you care to dance?'

'I'd love to,' she said, standing up. Ooh, she really was dizzy. She took his arm and he led her to the dance floor, swinging her into the dance. He turned out to be a good dancer and Ellery was content to let him lead, relaxing into his arms. Dear Tomas. He'd been so good to her that day in the gardens, when she'd thought her world ended, and when he'd stepped in to help her save Deryck from a beating. As they passed her brother and Lissa, Tomas raised his eyebrows. Ellery laughed.

'I know,' she said. 'But he's on his best behaviour tonight, I promise.'

'He'd better be,' replied Tomas. 'Patric is still cross about his sister, and I know the others were keen to keep going with the fight.'

'Well, they'll have more to contend with if they try it again.' Patric and his friends were stood together on the edge of the dance floor, watching the dancers, including Deryck and Lissa. 'He's hardly drunk anything.'

'Let's not worry about it.' Tomas smiled, his brown eyes gleaming in the lamplight. 'It's nice dancing with you, Ellery.'

'Thank you for asking me,' she said. 'I like dancing with you, too.' It *was* nice, she thought, giving herself up to the moment, enjoying the sensation of being twirled around the room, Tomas's hand warm on her back. The music stopped and so did they, moving apart to bow and curtsey as was custom. Another song started and Ellery was about to move back into Tomas' arms when she felt a tap on her shoulder.

'May I?'

She turned to see Deryck, Lissa standing behind him with her arms folded, her expression mutinous. Ellery frowned, and he widened his eyes at her. 'Will you dance with me, sister?'

'Er, of course.' She suppressed a sigh. 'You don't mind, do you, Tomas?' He shook his head. 'Or you, Lissa?' Lissa made a noise that sounded like *humph*.

'Oh, come on,' muttered Deryck, taking her hand and swinging Ellery out into the dance before Lissa could protest any more.

'Well, thanks,' said Ellery. 'What was that about? I was having a nice time with Tomas.'

'I'm sorry, really I am. I just, I couldn't dance with her again.' His brows drew together.

'It's fine.' It wasn't, but she understood. People were glancing at them as they moved around the room, and she lifted her chin. As they passed Patric and his friends he hissed at them.

'Dancing with your sister. A safer option, tonight.'

Ellery turned to glare at him, missing a step as she let go of Deryck but he pulled her back to him, bringing her into the dance once more.

'Don't worry about them,' he said. 'I really need to talk to you. What am I going to do about her?' He jerked his head and Ellery followed the movement to see Tomas had asked Lissa to dance, squiring her past them with a wink at Ellery. She blew him a kiss. 'Thank you,' she mouthed, and his face lit up in a smile. Then they were gone into the mass of dancers.

'It's like that, is it?' asked Deryck.

Ellery blushed. 'No, I mean, I like Tomas, he's lovely. Oh, I don't know. Anyway, what about your problem?'

Deryck made a face. 'I can't be with her anymore.'

Ellery thought for a moment. 'Why did you approach her in the first place? I mean, you must feel *something* for her, right?'

'I guess,' he said. 'I mean, she's nice and everything. But she's not... and then I wake up and I think I'm with... *her* and realise I'm not and the pain just comes back again.' He looked so distressed Ellery's heart bled for him.

'You need to talk to her,' she said. 'You saw how angry Patric was. You can't keep using her and expect to get away with it.'

Deryck hung his head, then gave Ellery a pleading look. 'You couldn't–'

'No, I could not,' said Ellery. 'It has to come from you. Either you make her official, or you break it off.'

'Then I'll have to break it off,' muttered Deryck. 'Because there's only one person I wish to be with.'

'I'm sorry,' said Ellery, meaning it. 'I really am.'

'I know,' he said. 'And thanks, for listening at least.' The music came to an end and he heaved a big sigh. 'Well, wish me luck,' he said, letting go of Ellery. She leaned in and kissed him on the cheek.

'Good luck,' she whispered. Lissa arrived, dragging Tomas

behind her and letting go of him to attach herself to Deryck once more.

'Shall we dance again?' she gasped, gazing up at him adoringly.

'Um, no, Lissa. I think perhaps we should go outside for a while.' Deryck managed a twisted smile as Lissa pressed against him, giggling her delight.

Ellery slowly shook her head. 'You're going to need it.' Taking Tomas's hand she entered the dance once more. They danced together for several songs, the music getting livelier until Ellery, laughing and breathless, asked Tomas to get her a drink.

'Of course,' he said, leading her back to their table. She sat down, fanning herself with her hand, watching the couples whirling around the room, all glitter and spark under the great lanterns. Tomas returned a few moments later, holding two cool drinks. He handed one to her and she took a sip, relieved to find it was cordial, sweet and refreshing.

'Thank you,' she said. 'That's just what I needed.'

Tomas grinned, sitting down beside her. 'Me too.' He took a long draught. 'Couldn't face any more wine tonight.' Ellery smiled at him, happy to be sitting there, his warmth so close to her in the booth. Tomas smiled at her, then his focus shifted to somewhere over her shoulder and his expression changed. 'Uh-oh.'

Ellery turned to see Lissa coming into the Hall. She was sobbing loudly, running over to her group of friends who surrounded her, clucking and whispering. A few moments later Deryck came in. He looked around, raising a hand once he saw Ellery. He seemed subdued and, as he came closer, she could see a red mark on his cheek. Uh-oh indeed.

'Are you all right?' she asked, as he came to sit down with them, sliding back in the small booth against the wall, as though he didn't want to be seen. 'So you talked to her, I guess?'

Deryck nodded, his face twisting. 'Yes, and she was none too pleased.' He raised his hand to his cheek, his expression wry. His eyes narrowed and he looked past Ellery. She turned to see Patric, his face like thunder, coming across the room, his two friends behind him.

'What have you done to my sister now?' he said, fists clenched at his side. 'What, is she not good enough for you to make official?'

Ellery tried to intervene. 'Patric, I'm sure Lissa is just—'

'Let me handle this,' said Deryck. Heaving a sigh, he got to his feet and faced Patric, his shoulders back and arms at his side, palms open. 'It was not right of me to use your sister in such a way, and so I have ended things with her.'

He sounded reasonable enough, but Patric was obviously not impressed. Without another word he stepped forward and took a swing at Deryck. Ellery gasped, her hand to her mouth, while beside her, Tomas half rose from his seat. But Deryck easily blocked the punch, trapping Patric's arm and moving in close, his forearm hard on the other boy's throat, forcing his head back.

'Don't make this worse than it is, Patric,' he said, green eyes glittering. 'I'm trying to do the right thing here.'

Patric's face was red and he struggled to speak. Deryck moved his arm back slightly, easing the pressure.

Patric coughed, glaring at Deryck. 'Let go of me then, and let's talk.'

'Talk?' Deryck looked at Patric's friends.

'Yes.' Patric ground out the word and Deryck released him, moving back out of range of another punch. The other boy shook himself, tugging at his tunic with one hand as he warned his friends back with the other. Deryck folded his arms, waiting.

'So what's wrong with my sister?' Patric's tone was belligerent, but he kept his distance.

Deryck frowned. 'Nothing,' he said. 'I swear to you, I meant no harm. It's just, my heart belongs to another, that's all. So I did not wish to lead her on any further.'

Ellery was shocked and so, she could see, was Patric. He took a moment to recover, much of his bluster gone.

'And what of the time you spent with her?'

'It was her choice to be with me.'

Patric stared at him, then nodded. 'Fine. I will give you that. But I tell you this, Deryck. If you so much as touch a hair on her head again I will have you.'

Deryck said nothing. He was sober and Ellery could see Patric knew that, knew what it meant. His friends were also glancing nervously at each other. At least Deryck's reputation as a fighter was worth something here, she thought. Drunk, he might be taken down by three of them. Sober, he was a much different proposition altogether.

'Watch yourself.' Patric gave Deryck one last glare before he and his friends turned and walked away. Deryck seemed to sag slightly, his shoulders dropping as he turned to Ellery.

'Come on, sit down,' she said, patting the seat next to her. 'D'you want something to drink?'

Deryck shook his head. 'No thanks. I think I might go now. Tomas, will you see my sister safely home?'

'I will,' said Tomas. Ellery got to her feet, kissing Deryck on the cheek. It was still pink where Lissa had slapped him.

'Oh, Deryck,' she said. 'Are you sure you don't want me to come with you?'

'No,' he said. 'I think I need to be alone. Besides, I don't want to spoil your fun.' He smiled at her, his handsome face lighting up. Then he was gone, striding through the Hall and out into the Foyer, disappearing into the night.

~

'WHAT CAN I DO FOR YOU?' ETRAS FROWNED SLIGHTLY. 'MY powers are diminished here, under this so-called exile.' He spat the last word and Denoris glanced at Gwenene before answering.

'Do you remember, all those years ago, Gwenene and her lap-dog?'

Gwenene gasped and Denoris grinned, enjoying her discomfort, payback for his own. Etras began to laugh.

'I do,' he chuckled, 'and I see you do also, Denoris. Still, after all these years, do you resent the time he spent with your lady love?'

Denoris lost his grin. 'I do not like to share.'

'And you made him pay, as I remember.'

'Well, he did steal something of mine, other than Gwenene's affections, so I was hardly going to let that pass, was I?' Denoris leaned forward to pick up a piece of succulent roasted chicken, brought by yet another serving girl, tearing it apart with his fingers before starting to eat. Once again it was good, tasty and cooked to perfection, the meat coming easily from the bone.

Gwenene snorted. 'He was just a human,' she started, her tone dismissive, but Etras chuckled.

'Yet he held your interest for quite a while, did he not? He must have been skilled in some way, to distract you long enough to steal Denoris' book.' His tone was insinuating and Gwenene squirmed, her face growing red. Denoris threw his head back and laughed.

'Well, Etras, it seems that "my affections" may not have been the only thing he took from here,' she snapped, her blue eyes flashing. 'And if the two of you would stop laughing for long enough maybe we could discuss it!'

'Oooh-ho ho!' laughed Etras, hands up in mock surrender, while Denoris, wiping his hands on a napkin, chortled. Intercepting another glare from Gwenene, he decided to back down. They had given her a hard enough time.

'Gwenene is right. It seems the girl, Alma, is now on Davies' track in Wales.'

'But, why?' Etras frowned.

'Because she thinks he stole the Cup,' said Gwenene. 'And, well, I must say he was obsessed with it, always going on about it.'

She reached for the wine jug, refilling her glass before sitting back.

'Really?' Etras raised his eyebrows. 'But surely we would have—'

'You had other things to do, if I remember right,' snapped Gwenene. 'You have no one to blame but yourselves if this is true.' She took a long drink, her ivory throat moving as she swallowed.

Denoris picked up another piece of chicken. 'So, this is what we need,' he began, tearing the roast bird apart.

CHAPTER 9
WINE AND REGRET

'I think maybe I should go now, Tomas,' said Ellery. It was getting late and people were starting to leave, though there were a few still dancing. She reached for her cloak, fastening it around her neck.

Tomas looked disappointed for a moment, then nodded. 'I understand,' he said.

She knew he meant it. He was so lovely, she thought. If only her life weren't so messed up at the moment she might—

'You okay?'

Ellery realised she'd been staring and sat back, her cheeks hot with embarrassment. 'Oh, sorry.' She looked down, completely confused. 'Um, I guess I really am tired.'

Tomas got to his feet, offering her his arm. 'Then let me take you home.'

'Oh, you don't have to worry,' she started, feeling awkward.

'Ellery.' He waited until she looked up. 'I'm not offering because your brother asked me to. I'm offering because I want to.' He smiled, a strand of long brown hair falling in his face where it had escaped his ponytail and she got to her feet, reaching up to gently tuck it behind his ear. He blushed, ducking his head.

'Thank you.' She took his arm, glad he was there for her. They exited the Palace into darkened gardens, the night cold and frosty. Ellery pulled her cloak around her and huddled close to Tomas. He hesitated a moment, then put his arm around her, holding her against him.

'You don't mind, do you?' She shook her head, not minding at all. He was pleasantly warm despite the chill evening, and she nestled into the curve of his arm as they walked the shadowed paths together. When they reached the garden outside the apartments, pale lanterns hanging in the trees, she realised she didn't want to go inside yet. Tomas still had his arm around her and, as they stopped, he turned, pulling her into an embrace. Her heart pounding, she put her arms around his neck. He bent his head to kiss her and she kissed him back, feeling his mouth curve as he smiled against her. A few pleasant moments passed before she pulled back.

'Tomas, I should go in.' But her hand was still on his face, feeling the warmth of his cheek, the soft stubble along his jaw. He didn't let go of her.

'Really?' he said, his voice soft. 'For I would rather stay with you, Ellery.'

She took in a breath, tears starting in her eyes at his tender tone. 'Oh, Tomas,' she said, her voice shaky. 'I would rather stay with you too.' She realised it was true. She also knew it wasn't going to happen. She couldn't bring Tomas into the mess of her life, not until she figured out what she was going to do.

'Then stay.' He leaned in to kiss her once more, his breath warm on her face as his lips moved across her cheek, to her neck, his hand brushing her hair aside. She closed her eyes, tears prickling against her lids, as she wished things could be different.

'I can't,' she whispered, putting her hands against his chest and pushing, gently, so he would let her go. He stared at her. 'It's complicated,' she said. 'But I want to see you again, if that's okay. Please.'

'What's going on with you?' He didn't sound angry, more worried than anything and her face twisted in her efforts not to cry. It took her a moment to answer.

'My life is uh,' she managed to get out. 'It's just, my father is so...' She looked down and he reached out to pull her close again.

'Ellery,' she felt his lips against her hair. 'You can tell me anything. Come on.' She almost broke, then. Lifting her head, she tried again.

'I like you so much,' she started, her hands resting on his waist. 'It's just, there's a lot of stuff going on in my life at the moment and I can't get you involved.' He nodded, his brown eyes full of concern.

'I knew there was something going on when I saw you in the garden the other week. Are you sure you can't...?' She shook her head, her eyes bitter with tears as she glanced towards her front door and he nodded. 'I get it. But I'm here for you, whenever you want.'

'Oh, Tomas.' Ellery's voice caught and she swallowed against the lump in her throat. 'I want to keep seeing you. Can we take it slow, that's all. I'm trying to figure things out, I just need time.'

'You can have all the time you need,' he said. 'As long as I can still see you.' His arms wrapped around her and she leaned against his chest, holding him tight. She lifted her head and they kissed once more, intense. He let her go, one more soft kiss.

'I should go,' he said, touching her cheek. 'But I'll see you soon?'

She nodded, watching him walk away in the cold darkness, her hand to her lips as though she could keep the kiss there, hold on to the sweetness of it for a moment longer. When she could no longer see him she turned to go inside but stopped short when she saw a figure sitting on the bench against the wall, his head in his hands. It was Deryck and she blushed, hot with embarrassment that he'd seen her kissing Tomas. Then she took in his shaking shoulders and concern replaced her blushes.

HELEN JONES

'Are you all right?' she said, putting her hand on his shoulder. He looked up and she could see his cheeks were wet, golden hair tangled around his face.

'Ellery.' His voice was raspy. 'I didn't hear you coming.'

'Oh, Deryck.' Ellery's heart clenched as he wiped his eyes. She sat down next to him and he huffed out a choked sob, rubbing his face with the heel of his hand. She put her arm around him and he leaned his head on her shoulder; she could feel him shaking and turned, putting her other arm around him, comforting him just as he had done her. Once he was calmer she released him, getting to her feet.

'Come on,' she said, tugging gently on his arm. 'You're cold. Let's go inside.' He let her pull him up from the bench, her arm in his as she opened the big doors and they entered the hallway. It was dark and quiet, the door to their father's study standing ajar, a glow indicating the fire was still burning. Deryck tried to pull away from her, but she stopped him, holding onto his arm.

'You need to talk about this,' she said. 'Let's sit for a while. It doesn't look as though Father's here, and I'm sure he's left some wine in there. Please, don't be alone.' His face was all shadows and angles and she waited, then saw him nod. Releasing him she took off her cloak, hanging it on one of the pegs then following him into the study. The room felt cosy, less menacing without their father's dominant presence and Ellery sank down on the sofa, her emotions in a whirl, her happiness about Tomas tempered by her worry about Deryck. He sat next to her, sagging forward, head down.

'Hey,' said Ellery, rubbing his back gently, hating to see him that way. He turned to her.

'You're right,' he said. 'I shouldn't be alone right now. I do need a drink though.'

'Shall I call for something?'

Deryck shook his head, his mouth curving in a half smile. 'No need,' he said, and she raised her eyebrows. 'I know where father keeps the good stuff.' Getting to his feet he walked over to the shelves, pressing on a carving. A panel slid open, revealing several bottles of wine along with some crystal glasses. Ellery grinned.

'Nice work, brother.' She tucked her feet under her as she relaxed back, lulled by the crackling fire, the heavy silence of wood and thick carpet. She hugged herself, thinking of Tomas, as Deryck brought a bottle and two glasses over, placing them on the low table before sitting down in the chair opposite. He uncorked the wine, releasing a soft fragrance of berries and honey, and filled the glasses, the wine gleaming like rubies, clear and red against the crystal.

'You're right, it is the good stuff.' Ellery reached for her glass, but Deryck held out his hand, stopping her.

'Let it breathe first.' He smiled, though his eyes were still red. 'Trust me, it's worth the wait.'

Ellery bit her lip. 'Will Father be cross if we drink it?'

'Don't worry, I'll take the blame.'

She sat back again, taking in the dark circles under Deryck's reddened eyes, the more prominent cheekbones. She had never seen him like this before. 'So Deryck—' she began, but he cut her off abruptly.

'Let it rest, just for a few minutes, El. Let me get my thoughts together.'

They sat in companionable silence, Ellery closing her eyes and leaning her head back. When Deryck spoke she opened her eyes in surprise, realising she'd almost drifted off to sleep.

'I'm glad that I finished things with Lissa. And you already know how I feel about Alma.'

Ellery blinked a couple of times before nodding, still leaning her head against the back of the sofa. She was so comfortable. Then she realised Deryck was waiting for a response. 'Um, yes, I know.'

'I never loved anyone before,' he went on, sounding reflective.

'And now that I do, well, I can't deal with it, that she's gone. That I ruined it.'

Ellery's brows drew together. This was something else she'd never seen, her brother so taken by one girl, so broken up by his actions. But she wanted to know, had been wondering for a while. So she sat up and asked, knowing he'd understand what she meant.

'Um... why did you do it?'

'Caleb?' He huffed out a breath and leaned forward to pick up his wine, taking a long drink. Ellery said nothing, just waiting. Eventually he answered, wine red on his mouth. 'It was the Dark energy. You don't know what it's like, when it starts to connect with you, 'cause you're half-human.' Ellery nodded, not offended. She wanted no part of it. Deryck went on. 'But it takes over everything – I mean, I can manage it better now, I guess.' His hand went to his throat, hovering over the stone there before he dropped it down, his face twisting. 'Plus I was jealous, I suppose. I don't know – the whole thing's a blur, really. Except for her.' His voice dropped almost to a whisper and Ellery felt a pang of guilt, remembering how she had called the Dark Hunt, chasing Alma through the woods. All she had wanted to do was please her father, not even thinking of what it would have done to her brother if they'd caught her. She reached for her wine, taking a sip.

'Oh!' She looked at the glass in amazement. Flavours exploded on her tongue, warmth running through her. Deryck grinned.

'Told you,' he said, taking another mouthful. He sat back, his grin sliding away and Ellery knew she needed to explain, that it was important he knew how she felt.

'That day,' she said, thinking hard, wanting to be careful in what she said. 'Well, it all seemed so clear at the time, what we were doing. What Father wanted.'

Deryck nodded. 'I know,' he said. 'And I know you didn't know about Alma, that you couldn't have–'

'I would have taken her,' she said, meeting his eyes with her own. 'I would have ridden her down like an animal. Like he wanted. And now I'm so glad I didn't, that she got away.'

Deryck blew out a long breath. 'So am I,' he said. 'Even though I can't have her, at least I know she's safe.'

'But for how long, Deryck? You know Father wants her. What can we do?' She drank some more wine, feeling it go to her head, bursts of berry and honey running riot in her mouth. It was so good she kept drinking, sliding down in her seat.

'What can we do?' Deryck echoed her words, looking thoughtful, running a hand through his hair. 'Get drunk, I guess.' He laughed, raising his glass to her and she giggled, returning the gesture. 'I'm trying not to use my stone as much,' he went on, leaning back in his seat, long legs sprawled out.

'Good.' Ellery drank more of the fabulous wine. She finished her glass and Deryck refilled it, topping up his own as well. ''Cause you need to stay strong.' She wagged her finger at him.

'It's hard. I mean, how are you doing with yours?'

'Um.' She looked down at her chest, at her necklace. Even though her head was starting to spin, she knew she couldn't tell him her secret, her plan to defy their father and have a fake necklace made. 'Well, I'm just trying not to use it either. It makes me feel so weird when I do, anyway.'

'Right.' He nodded. 'Sounds like a good thing to do.'

'I'm glad he's not here.'

Deryck raised his eyebrows. 'Who – the Dark Overlord?' Ellery burst out laughing, lying back on the couch and shaking with giggles. Deryck laughed as well, starting to look more himself as he leaned back in the deep armchair. 'It's a lot easier when he's not around, especially with how he's been lately.' His expression grew sombre. 'I wonder what he's doing?'

'Who cares?' said Ellery, drinking more wine, still laughing. Taking the bottle, she topped up Deryck's glass. 'Tonight, we don't have to worry about it.'

CHAPTER 10
A TRIP INTO THE PAST

Gwenene shifted in her chair, the cushions moving against her back. Etras was staring at her again. She smiled, even though the heat in his eyes made her feel sick. She wasn't used to his games anymore, to constantly feeling on edge when he was around. If only Denoris would get to the point!

'We need the girl,' he said, as though reading her thoughts. Thank darkness for that! The plates before them were empty except for bones, and Etras had called for more wine. Another serving woman brought hot towels, expertly avoiding Etras' roaming hands as she dispensed them. But she was not to escape that easily. As she handed the towel to Etras he took it and, wiping his mouth, grabbed her arm with his other hand. 'Catrin, wait,' he rumbled, emerging red-faced. She bowed her head, her expression resigned. He gave her back the towel, then ran his hand across the top of her breasts where they showed above her bodice. 'Come to me later.' The young woman nodded, not looking at Etras. He let her go and she bobbed a curtsey before leaving hastily. Gwenene looked away. She had lost enough serving girls to Etras to know what would happen later.

'Right then.' He rubbed his hands together as though nothing had happened. 'What is it you want me to do?' His mood was markedly improved.

'We want you to cross over, to get her for us,' said Denoris. He paused and shook his head. 'I must say, Etras, your methods are as direct as ever.' He gave the other man a look of grudging admiration. 'So if you were to apply the same, er, methods to capture our prize, we would be most grateful.'

'And what will you do for me?' asked Etras, smiling broadly. 'A night with your Ladyship, perhaps?'

'Honestly, you have a one-track mind!' Gwenene glared at him. 'I cannot imagine how you get anything done!'

'Oh, I get things done just fine,' he said, leering at her. She folded her arms and sat back, glancing at Denoris whose jaw had tightened. He was going to hit Etras in a moment, she was sure of it. Perhaps it had been a bad idea, coming here. It was a moment before he spoke.

'Perhaps, when you get us the girl, we'll be in a position to go to Thorion and intercede for you,' he said. 'Artos, in particular, will be willing to do almost anything to ensure she isn't harmed any more than she needs to be.'

Etras raised his eyebrows. 'Thorion will never overturn my exile,' he said flatly.

'Well, perhaps you shouldn't have killed his lover.' Gwenene was at the end of her patience with both men, hating seeing Denoris so meek. Etras' brows drew together and he scowled. Denoris darted her a warning glance. But honestly, did he expect that she would put up with this nonsense? Still, she knew what this meant to him, that they wouldn't both be here if things weren't getting desperate, so she sat back, trying to look conciliatory.

Denoris went on. 'Etras, you know I stood for you when you went before the Council, and I'd be prepared to do the same again if you get Alma for me. Thorion is different these days. The loss of his son hit him hard, I think. Do not doubt me on this, I will do all I can and, if we hold the girl and the Regalia, we'll have the power we need to do it.'

'And can I have the girl, once you're finished with her?' asked Etras. Gwenene snorted, unable to help it.

'No!' Denoris rubbed his hand over his face. 'No, you cannot. And I would appreciate if you did not... harm her in that way. She is promised to my son.' Etras raised his eyebrows. 'It's not a bad match, for she is Galen's daughter after all. And he cannot seem to get over her.' Gwenene held her breath.

Etras stroked his beard, pacing in front of the fire. He stopped, turning to them both. 'All right,' he said. 'I'll do it.' He gave a great shout of laughter. 'What do I have to lose, after all? I need a bit of adventure. Ha!' He pointed at Denoris. 'I will go through and get the girl, bring her back and you'll speak to Thorion, get this ridiculous exile lifted.'

'And you'll deliver the girl to us, unharmed?' Denoris stood, holding out his hand to Etras.

'Unharmed. Fine.' Etras sighed out the words as though mightily inconvenienced. He took Denoris' hand and shook it. 'So, what's your plan?'

'She's in the town where we caught Gwenene's lap-dog, all those years before. Go through the Stone Gate, find her, and give her this.' Denoris held out a small velvet pouch, which Etras took. He started to undo the ties. 'Do not touch the stone!'

Etras reached carefully into the bag, pulling out a long silver necklace with a black stone suspended from it, red glints at its heart. He pursed his lips in a soundless whistle. 'A tallus? These are—'

'Expensive? I know, believe me.' Denoris shook his head. 'But they have an effect on half-humans like nothing I've seen. Ellery is completely incapacitated under her stone. I could do anything to her and she would just smile.'

'Really?' Etras grinned, the necklace swinging from his hand, the silver chain glittering. 'I'd like to see that.'

'Well, you won't,' snapped Gwenene. 'And Denoris, really? You said you weren't going to give her a tallus!'

'Well, she'll be married to my son shortly, so it only seems right.'

'Married? You said nothing of this – Artos will have your head and rightly so if you force her!'

'There will be no need to force her. Once she's wearing the stone, she'll be happy to marry my son. And why shouldn't she be? She loved him, once. Darkness knows it's a better match than any half-breed could hope for, Galen's daughter or not. Patience, my dark dove.' The words were tender, but there was a thread of anger in his voice. 'You have no need of the power they hold. Otherwise, I would have given you a tallus too.'

'And who are you to decide? I can get one myself if I want one!' Gwenene half-rose from her chair, ready to leave and damn them all and their plans.

Etras began to laugh. 'Far be it for me to interrupt your lovers' quarrel, but what am I to do with the girl once I have her?'

Denoris stared at Gwenene for a moment before turning to Etras, and she could almost swear she saw pleading in his green gaze. 'Put the necklace on her and explain to her that she'll be marrying Deryck, and that you're taking her to him. She'll agree to anything once it touches her skin.'

'Anything?'

'I swear, Etras, if you cannot control your urges I'll ask someone else to do this and you can rot here for another ten years!'

Denoris had had enough, Gwenene could see. She waited, wondering how Etras would respond.

'Forgive me.' He stopped laughing. 'I won't harm a hair on her head, I promise.'

Gwenene wasn't sure Etras could be trusted, but they were fast running out of options. She rose from her chair in a rustle of garments. 'So you'll do it, then? Just as we've asked?'

'For you, Lady, I will,' he said, all gallantry once more.

'Good.' Relief coursed through her that it was done and they could leave. 'There is a Council meeting tomorrow. Denoris and I need to be there, to be seen. All the Elders will be in attendance, so it's the perfect time for you to bring the girl in and the announcement can be made.'

'But I'm in exile. And,' Etras shook his head, 'you would do this? Walk in to a Council Meeting with Galen's daughter? It would mean war, surely.'

'Your exile is only due to Thorion's ruling. Once we have the girl, the power shifts to the Dark. There will be no war.'

Etras put his hands on his hips, frowning. Then his expression cleared. 'So I'll be free?'

'You will.' Gwenene wasn't sure about that, but didn't care. Let them sort it out later.

'I knew I could count on you, my oldest friends.' Etras came to Gwenene and lifted her hand to his lips, his mouth moving on her skin. She snatched it back, trying to contain her disgust.

'Indeed,' said Denoris, catching Gwenene's eye. 'When you have the girl, put the tallus on her and bring her through the Gate. Do not waste time, though – if the girl has anything of her father in her she may have some resistance to the effects of the stone. Oh, and make sure you destroy that talaith she wears. Overnight should be long enough for her to be in thrall to the tallus, ready for you to bring her to the Great Hall for tomorrow's meeting.' Etras nodded, one hand rubbing his beard. He smiled, a flash of white teeth and Denoris clapped him on the shoulder. 'So we are agreed? We can count on you for this?'

'Agreed, old friend. I shall ride for the Stone Gate tonight.'

'Thank you,' said Denoris. 'Now, my friend, if you will forgive us we must leave now – I'm sure you've enough to do, getting ready for your journey.'

Etras looked stricken. 'But you will not stay longer? Let us drink together a little more.'

'I'm afraid we must leave, dear Etras,' said Gwenene, unable to take another moment in his company. She retrieved her cloak, fastening it around her neck. She had to suffer one more embrace, Etras' hands moving on her so that she squirmed and wriggled away from him, laughing even while her hands curved into claws beneath her cloak, wanting to scratch his eyes out. Then Denoris was there, taking her hand as they went out to the courtyard, keeping her close to him as though he knew her thoughts.

The air was cool, the stars bright, as they waited for their horses to be brought around. Torches lit the courtyard, gold against the violet light. Etras held out his hands, arms wide.

'Please, stay longer. Wait here for me to come back. I'll get the girl, then we can celebrate together, drinking as we used to do.' Etras sounded almost wistful.

Gwenene shook her head. 'I'm sorry,' she said, secure in the curve of Denoris' arm. 'I am weary tonight. But once this is done, once we hold power in Ambeth, there will be plenty of opportunity for us to drink together once more.'

'And the sooner you go, the sooner this will happen,' added Denoris. There was a clatter on the cobbles as a groom arrived leading their horses. Gwenene mounted quickly, needing no assistance.

'We will see you again,' she said, relieved to be out of his reach.

'Farewell, old friend, and thank you. I await your return.' Denoris clasped Etras by the arm in farewell and mounted his own horse. Gwenene waited, her horse moving beneath her as though it could sense her restlessness, her desire to be gone.

'Thank you,' said Etras, 'for coming to see me, and for this adventure.' He laughed again, the sound echoing around the stone yard. 'I will get your girl and see you tomorrow.'

Denoris and Gwenene turned their horses, Denoris raising a hand in farewell as they rode towards the gates and the passage beyond. As the gates clanged shut behind them, Gwenene heaved a sigh of relief.

Denoris laughed. 'Was it that bad?'

'I would rather sleep in a hedge than spend one night in his Hall!' Gwenene looked balefully back at the fortress, a dark hulk against the navy-blue sky.

'I agree,' replied Denoris, his laughter gone. 'He is getting worse. It must be the solitude – he's been apart from social niceties for so long he's forgetting how to behave.'

'Forgetting! Humph!' She urged her horse forward, wanting to be clear of the place. Denoris came up beside her. Moving his horse closer, he reached out his hand.

'I would not have suffered him to lay another finger on you,' he said, his green eyes warm. Gwenene slowed down. She was still angry, but she couldn't resist him when he looked at her so. Her mouth, almost against her will, curved in a smile as she took his hand.

'Thank you,' she said. 'Now let us go home. I want to scrub the feel of that place from me.'

'I can help, if you like.' Denoris quirked one golden eyebrow at her and Gwenene let go of him to spur her horse forward once more, whooping in delight.

LATER SHE LAY AWAKE IN THE DARK, AMONG THE COOL SILKS OF her chamber. Beside her Denoris slept, a warm arm flung across her. He had been more tender than usual, and she had thought she would sleep easily. But thoughts of the past ran through her mind, chasing sleep away. She sighed, giving into them.

CHAPTER 11
GOLDEN GREEN

The Estate of Lord Denoris, Ambeth
  (Midsummer's Eve, 1927 - Human Realm)

'I STILL DON'T KNOW WHY WE ARE NOT ATTENDING THE FESTIVAL *Ball.'* Lady Aeres sat straight in her high-backed chair, long red-gold hair pinned back from her beautiful face. 'We go every year.'

Gwenene, seated on the nearby sofa, leaned her head on her hand, feeling as though she might die of boredom. Why Denoris had bothered to ask her here she didn't know. They'd had no time together, Aeres demanding his attention constantly. She hadn't seemed too pleased to see Gwenene when she'd arrived. The feeling had been mutual.

Denoris went to his wife, lifting her hand to his lips. 'I thought it would be nice for us to have some time together alone.' He kissed her hand before letting it go.

'And yet we are not alone.' Aeres glanced at Gwenene, narrowing her eyes slightly. Gwenene met the other woman's gaze, raising one eyebrow. 'Forgive me, Lady Gwenene, I do not wish to offend. I just find my husband's, er, whims difficult to understand at times.' A faint line appeared between Aeres' brows and she raised a hand to her temple.

'The Ball is boring, my dear,' said Denoris. 'All the same people, year after year.'

'Did we not meet at the Ball?' Aeres smiled at her husband, blue-green eyes lighting up. Gwenene looked away, suppressing a snort.

'Indeed we did, my Lady. I remember it well.'

Gwenene fiddled with a fold in her silvery skirts, pulling at a loop in the fine embroidery until it came loose, not wanting to watch Denoris flirting with his wife. Aeres continued. 'It was a glorious night, as I remember. You danced with me twice—'

'And later, we walked in the gardens.' There was innuendo in his voice and Gwenene's stomach turned. She knew what Denoris liked to do on his walks.

'Would it not be nice to do so again?'

'This year the Lady Gwenene and I have Council matters to discuss.'

Gwenene looked up, wanting to see how Aeres would take this. She was staring at Denoris, her face even paler than normal. 'And this means I cannot attend the Ball as well? It seems unfair—'

'So you would go alone?' Denoris raised an eyebrow. Moving around his wife's chair, he trailed his hand along her shoulder, picking up a loose red-gold curl, his green eyes full of heat. Gwenene wanted to take her drink and throw it at the pair of them. Oh yes, challenge him, Aeres! You more than anyone should know how it excites him. She picked up her glass, draining it, closing her eyes against the sight of them both, sick with jealousy as she heard Aeres sigh. She should just leave them to it, really she should. There were others who wanted her; why, she could snap her fingers and half the Dark Court would be at her feet.

There was a muffled protest from Aeres and Gwenene opened her eyes to see Denoris straightening up, Aeres half twisting away from him. She had one hand to her head, her brow furrowed as though she were in pain.

'Are you not well, my dear?' Denoris asked, all courtesy. Aeres took a moment to answer.

'Now that you say it, I think perhaps I have a headache.' Her frown deepened and Denoris looked annoyed.

'Shall I make you a drink? Perhaps that will help. For you know I wish to visit with you later. Celebrate our anniversary, if you will.'

Aeres' eyes widened and she sat back in her chair, glancing at Gwenene.

'In-indeed, my Lord?'

'Indeed, my Lady,' smiled Denoris, wolfish. Aeres folded her lips and took in a breath before standing, her silk gown draping elegantly around her.

'Well, if that is the case, I shall leave you both for now. I wish to rest for a while.' There was a high colour in her cheeks and she gave her husband a mildly accusing look before sweeping from the room, not waiting for either of them to answer.

'Oh, Denoris,' Gwenene tried not to laugh as the door closed behind Aeres. 'I don't know why you don't just set her aside so we can be together. It must be so very tedious for you.' She admired his muscular form, silhouetted against the brightness of the sunset as he went and poured himself a drink. Making another, he brought it over to Gwenene, taking the seat opposite hers. He regarded her indulgently, though there was a hardness to his eyes that did not fool her.

'You know I cannot leave her, not yet,' he said, before taking a sip of his drink.

Gwenene frowned. 'But we cannot continue like this forever. Just imagine how it would be, the two of us together, the things we could accomplish.'

'And will you give me a son?' asked Denoris. 'For you know Aeres was chosen as a suitable mate for me, that she will bear me a child one day hence. It has been foretold.'

'Hmmph.' Folding her arms, Gwenene looked out through the long windows, across rolling green lawns to the ocean beyond. The sky was fire, red, gold and orange fading to blue. 'Is it so important to you? Another child?'

'I have no children left, you know this.'

She turned back to him. 'And what of it?'

Denoris tilted his head, holding up his hand so she stopped talking. 'It seems we have a visitor.'

Gwenene drew her brows together, unsure at first what he meant. Then she realised. 'You set tracers? At the Stone Gate?'

Denoris nodded, one corner of his mouth lifting in a snarling smile.

'Tut tut.' Gwenene grinned, waving a finger at him. 'King Artos will not be happy with you.'

Denoris laughed, his head going back to reveal his strong golden throat and Gwenene took in a breath. If only Aeres would leave him.

'I have need of a new Galardin,' he said, interrupting her musing. He took another drink. 'They are not so easy to come by these days. The village residents guard the forest gates too well now, and there are not so many humans who follow the old rituals anymore.'

'So this is the Council matter we need to discuss?' She arched an eyebrow and he grinned.

'That, and other things.' The expression on his face changed and he stood, placing his goblet down before coming to lean over her. Her head went back and she sighed as he caressed her face, her neck, his hand warm on her skin. She met his green gaze.

'And what will you do for me, if I bring the visitor back to you?'

His golden hand tightened on her neck and her breath caught in her throat. He bent to kiss her, his lips moving sensuously on hers.

'You know I must be with Aeres tonight,' he murmured. 'But I can assure you, I will show you my gratitude when I am done with her.'

Gwenene drew in a sharp breath, feeling a prickle of hurt at his words. 'Then I shall go, and leave you to your task,' she said, the lightness of her tone disguising the annoyance she felt. If she did not desire him so much…

~

LLEWELLYN DAVIES LAY ON HIS SIDE, RETCHING AND HELPLESS, overwhelmed by dizziness. He felt as though he'd been turned upside down, so great was his disorientation, land and sky swinging around him. Panting, sweating, he finally managed to get to his knees, one hand to his head as he took in his surroundings. He frowned. It looked much the same as where he'd come from – a curving bay and sea below, green hills around him. But then he saw a great white building set in sprawling gardens where the town should be, the dark massed woods stretching to the horizon and he knew he'd done it. Lifting both hands to the purpling sky he cried aloud his elation, hardly able to believe it. He sat back, tears in his eyes. They would have to believe him now.

Looking around, he saw a great house some distance away, windows catching the setting sun, mountains beyond stretching to the sky. Something white moved on the slope below and he watched, fascinated, as it came closer. The stone in his hand started to burn like fire and he gasped, dropping it. He scrabbled in the grass in a panic until he found it, using the scrap of leather to pick it up and place it safely in his bag. He looked up, his breath catching in wonder as he saw what drew near. For, riding the whitest of steeds, her silver draperies rippling against its velvety flanks, was the most beautiful woman he had ever seen. Her raven hair floated in tendrils around her exquisite face, and her large blue eyes were fixed on him with an expression of sympathy. She reined in her horse and he swallowed. Here, surely, was what he sought – a faery queen, a being from another realm. Realising he was still on his knees he struggled to his feet, managing to perform what he felt was a reasonable bow as the magnificent woman dismounted and approached him, a smile on her face.

'Are you lost?' she asked, her voice like a peal of silver bells, clear against the warm evening air.

'Well, th-that is,' stammered Davies as she moved around him, one slender white hand trailing down his arm. 'I mean, I do not know where I am, so I suppose that would make me lost.' He laughed and she looked at him curiously.

'And this does not worry you?'

'Why should I be worried?' said Davies, a little breathlessly, for she had come to stand in front of him, her hands sliding over his chest to his shoulders, her glorious face just inches from his. She laughed softly, her expression intrigued. Sliding her hand down his arm, lingering on the muscles there, she reached his hand and gently opened the fingers. Her *perfect brow furrowed for a moment as she took in the burn mark on his palm.*

'And what is this you have done to your hand?' she said. Bringing it to her mouth she kissed the mark softly. Davies took in a breath, licking lips that were suddenly dry.

'Hmmm.' She sighed as she moved even closer, her eyes on his mouth, her hands once again on his body. She started to undo the buttons on his shirt then stopped, looking at him with a hurt expression.

'Do you not like me?' she breathed.

'What? Yes, yes, of course. You're the most beautiful woman I've ever seen.' Davies was thoroughly bemused and not a little aroused.

'Well then,' she smiled, 'what are you waiting for?' And with that her lips were on his and she was pushing him down to the green grass – before Davies could move she was on him, and he was lost.

Later he lay in the cool of the meadow, stars wheeling above him in the dark night. His faery queen's hair twined around him, her hands caressing him as he met her every need, obeyed her every command. She cried out like a bird and, a moment later, so did Davies. As she relaxed down into his arms he couldn't believe his good fortune. Turning onto his side he gazed at her, one hand coming up to her face, hardly daring to touch her beauty, afraid she might disappear. She smiled at him lazily, stretching like a cat and he summoned up courage to speak to her. Ridiculous that he should fear to do so but, even after what they'd just done, he was unsure of his place.

'My Lady–'

She stopped him, a gentle finger on his lips. 'My name is Gwenene,' she whispered, her warm breath scented like apple blossoms, her skin soft against his.

'I am Llewellyn,' he replied, and she raised one eyebrow.

'A strong name,' she murmured, her slender fingers brushing his hair from his eyes. 'A kingly name, even.' She laughed then, as though at some joke only she knew. 'And what of your second name?' she went on,' for I know you humans like to carry the name of your father. Tell me.' Her tone was imperious, but her smile softened the words.

'Davies,' he said, looking deep into her blue eyes.

'Well, Llewellyn Davies, I shall tell you a secret,' she said. 'I was sent here to claim you for another, who wished to do you harm.' Davies' eyes widened and he tensed, all at once realising how vulnerable he was, how far from home. 'Oh, do not worry. I shall not let him harm you.' She kissed him, blossom soft. 'For I have decided,' she went on, 'to keep you for myself.'

'Is-is that so, my Lady?' whispered Davies, hardly daring to breathe.

'Yes,' she smiled, pushing him onto his back and bending close for a kiss. She lifted her head, her dark hair falling around them both, blotting out the stars.

'And-and what do you wish of me?' asked Davies.

'Why, I wish for you to be mine. To love me, and only me. I will do you no harm, I promise.'

'I think I already love you,' gasped Davies.

'You think?' she asked archly, her hands moving up to his throat. Strong and supple as steel they were, though a moment before they had been as soft and light as silk. She kissed him again, her hands tightening slightly. 'You are a long way from home, Llewellyn Davies, and I think it best you do as I say, if you wish to get back.' Her voice was silvery, her face exquisite in the moonlight. Davies stared at her, fear and desire tangling in his chest.

'I love you,' he managed to say, and, in a way, he wasn't lying. 'And I will do as you ask.' He had no choice, really, and she knew it, as surely as if she held a knife to him.

She released him, her hands sliding down his chest, her nails scratching him lightly so he shivered. 'Well then, Llewellyn Davies, I shall let you go home to your world. I might even come and visit you there – it's been a while since I stepped into the mortal realm.' She smiled and Davies relaxed slightly. Her embrace grew more sensual and she moved against him, his hands caressing the smooth skin of her back. Teasing him she rubbed against him, nipping and biting and he groaned, deep in the night. 'But you must promise me something.'

'Anything,' gasped Davies, who was so far gone now that he would have given her his eyes, should she have asked.

'That you will return. If you do not – well, you don't want to cross me.'
Davies cried out his assent as she settled on him, and she smiled.

❧

'YOU DID NOT COME BACK LAST NIGHT.' DENORIS ENTERED THE
sitting room to see Gwenene curled up in a chair, reading. Her dark hair
was held back with jewelled pins that glinted in the light streaming
through the windows, illuminating the book she held in one pale hand.

'No, I did not,' she said, not looking up, 'and what of it? You were
otherwise occupied, as I understood it.'

Denoris folded his lips, sighing. He'd had a difficult night with Aeres,
who was not always disposed to his advances, and the last thing he needed
was Gwenene arguing with him as well. He sat down, taking the chair
opposite hers.

'So where is the human?' He folded his arms and leaned back, waiting.

Gwenene laid down her book carefully. She smiled. 'I sent him back
this morning. But not before claiming him for myself.'

'Oh? And what of my desire for a new Galardin?'

'What of it?' she snapped, her smile gone, blue eyes flashing fire. 'I had
needs as well. And I chose to put them before yours.'

Denoris snorted. 'Is that so?'

'Yes.' She frowned, her tone final. She picked up her book again and
Denoris stared in disbelief. He stood and went to her, taking the book and
throwing it aside, leaning over her with one hand on either arm of her
chair. She glared at him, all curve and heat. If he did not desire her so
much...

'I told you I would come to you, once I was finished with Aeres,' he
said, not hiding the anger in his voice. Let her hear how she had displeased
him.

But Gwenene was not easily cowed. Lifting her lip in a sneer, she shot
back. 'Can you see why, perhaps, I would not be interested in that?'

Denoris breathed out hard, trying to control his rage at the thought of
her with someone else. Straightening up, he walked over to the door and

turned the key. Gwenene stared at him, still curled in her chair. He felt the slow coil of desire twist as he went to lean over her again, pushing her against the soft chair. But she pushed back, not willing to submit.

'It was my right to claim him, if I wished,' she hissed, 'and I enjoyed it.'

Denoris, held back only by her hands on his chest, grinned. 'It is of no matter,' he said. 'Another human came through last night and I have had her brought here. She'll do for my purposes.'

'So why,' spat Gwenene,' are you chastising me for my choice?'

'Because I have already claimed you for myself, and I do not wish to share you,' he replied.

'I have to share you,' snapped Gwenene. 'And, as far as I can see, I am free to spend time with whomever I wish.' Her breath quickened, her hands hard against his muscled chest.

'And,' replied Denoris, his eyes never leaving hers as his hand came to rest on her breastbone, his fingers curving around her throat, lust flaring in him. 'Who do you wish to be with now?'

Gwenene swallowed, her blue eyes furious. Clenching her teeth, she bared them at Denoris and he growled deep in his throat, his hand moving lower and making her gasp. He knew he had her, then, as her hands left his chest to slide around his shoulders, pulling him near. He bent his head to kiss her.

LATER HE WALKED ALONG A DARK CORRIDOR CARVED DEEP INTO THE hillside below his manor, earth and damp stone muffling the cries of those unfortunate enough to find themselves held there. He had left Gwenene curled up in her chair, sated and half asleep. The scratches on his back were still sore, the red droplets blooming on the white linen of his shirt a love token. Truly, she was like no other.

About half way along the passageway he stopped, using the key at his belt to unlock a heavy wooden door with a small barred window. It swung open, scraping across the stone floor. Inside the tiny cell, the only light a small candle on a shelf, sat a young woman, her dress dirty and wrinkled. Her face was stained with tears and her hair was coming loose from its *carefully coiled bun. On seeing Denoris she sat up, her eyes widening. He smiled, coming to sit next to her on the low wooden bench.*

'Hello,' he said, taking in her sweet face, the brown eyes with long lashes, the trembling pink mouth. A lock of dark hair curled around her neck and he lifted it gently, bringing it to his lips, smelling the faint scent of perfume that lay below the fear.

'Who-who are you?' breathed the girl.

'I am Denoris,' he replied, his hand caressing her cheek, lingering on the petal soft skin. 'And who are you?'

'My name is Beryl,' replied the young woman, gasping as he moved closer, running his nose along the edge of her jaw, kissing her neck just below her ear. He felt her sigh and relax against him, her small hands coming up to rest lightly on his shoulders.

'Beryl,' he murmured. 'A jewel of a name.' She laughed against him, then gasped again as he removed the remaining pins from her hair so it uncoiled down her back, running his fingers through the silky length. He considered for a moment taking her but, as footsteps approached, thought better of it.

'Well, sweet Beryl, welcome to my home,' he said. Her lips parted and he leaned in to kiss her. She was wide-eyed in the flickering darkness, half in love with him already.

'What will you do with me?' she asked. 'I am hungry...' Her voice trailed off as four figures entered the small cell. Denoris gently removed her hands from his shoulders and stood, reaching out to caress her cheek one last time.

'Do with you? Why, dear Beryl, I shall do nothing with you. It is my helpers who will do all the work.' He stepped aside. 'Do not worry, you'll be fed once they are finished.' Beryl shrank back as the four advanced on her, the tools in their hands glinting in the guttering light from the candle. Denoris walked out of the cell, closing the door behind him. As he walked down the corridor he heard the screaming begin. Aroused, he went to find Gwenene.

CHAPTER 12
SHOW ME YOUR WORLD

Wales, August 1927

NIGHT WAS FALLING AS LLEWELLYN STEPPED THROUGH THE GATE *once more, the stone warm in his hand. She had explained it to him, that he did not need the power of the Feast Days now he had the stone, and could travel as and when he pleased.*

And oh, it pleased him.

All thought of the university had left him, the shouting lecturers and their dusty halls a distant dream. All he knew now were green gardens under a golden sun, and his beloved, fierce and sweet, like nothing and no one he had ever met before.

As he came between the stones she was waiting for him. Once he could stand he smiled at her.

'I am yours.'

WALES, SEPTEMBER 1927

. . .

'*LLEWELLYN.*'

She stood silhouetted against the sky, her beauty fierce as the sun setting behind her, the Gate stones tall either side of her. His heart leapt to see her, to hear her speak his name.

'My Lady.' He stepped forward, bowing, and heard her laugh.

'Show me your world.' Her cool hands came around his face as he straightened up, her lips close to his. 'I want to know how you live.'

'As you desire, beloved.'

The words slid from his tongue, longing thrumming through him as she kissed him, the world seeming to wheel around him, so great was his pleasure. He had waited all day in a fever of anticipation, half wondering if he'd dreamed the whole thing. But his faery queen was here, real and soft in his arms, and he could hardly believe his luck. She released him, and he smiled.

'Let's go home.'

AMBETH – THE GREAT HALL
(Human World - October 1927)

LLEWELLYN APPROACHED THE DOUBLE DOORS TO THE GREAT HALL, Gwenene on his arm. She had dressed him in midnight blue velvet, her own glorious form clothed in flowing silk of a lighter blue. He'd protested at first, feeling strange in the elaborate clothes – he still wasn't entirely at ease, sweating under the layers of fabric. But upon entering the Hall he stopped, his discomfort forgotten. The stained-glass windows, the crafts-manship of stone and timber, created a space surpassing any he had ever seen before. And the people! They were all around him, devastating in their beauty. All at once he was glad of being dressed like the others, not wanting to attract any more attention than he already was. Gwenene tugged on his arm and they started through the crowd. Faces came and went around him; two handsome red-haired men, alike almost as twins; a slender woman with dark skin and elegant bone structure, dressed in *green to match her eyes. As the crowd parted he saw a tall blond man, obviously of power and status, standing with a beautiful woman, her red-gold hair twined intricately around her head, her gown of green and gold the perfect foil for her ivory skin. Gwenene headed straight for them and Llewellyn swallowed, his throat dry. He bowed deeply, an amused Gwenene waiting for him to stand straight before introducing him.*

'Llewellyn, I would have you meet a close friend of mine, the Lord Denoris.' Denoris nodded his head, his expression cordial, though his eyes were green ice. Llewellyn felt his spine prickle. 'And his wife, the Lady Aeres.' Aeres, blue-green eyes shining like jewels in her lovely face, extended one pale slender hand and Llewellyn took it, bowing once more. Yet for all her beauty there was an air of sadness about Aeres and her gaze, when it settled on Gwenene, was distinctly cold.

'It's a pleasure to meet you both.'

Gwenene laughed, taking him by the arm and leading him away. The other couple had said not a word, though Denoris' eyes followed Davies as he moved through the crowd. He met his gaze for a moment, troubled, then Gwenene was in front of him, her hand on his cheek as she forced him to look at her.

'What's wrong?' she asked, though she sounded more annoyed than concerned. She turned to see Denoris still watching them and moved closer to Davies, twining her arms around his neck, pressing her body to his. 'Don't worry about him,' she whispered, her blossom-scented breath soft on his face, her mouth distractingly close. 'All you need to worry about is me. Come, let me show you something.'

Taking his hand, she pulled him through the crowd towards one end of the room. A carved dais housed two thrones, and beyond them an alcove glowed golden in the grey stone wall. As they moved between the thrones, his eyes widened. Lying on the shelf of the alcove were two items, a sword and a cup. Both were of silver metal studded with jewels, exquisitely made and shining with their own light. Davies felt his face slacken with awe as he took them in, his gaze drawn to the delicate curves of the Cup.

'But... this is a wonder,' he said. 'Surely, it cannot be.' He turned to

Gwenene who was smiling, her face lit by the golden glow. 'Gwenene, what are these things?'

'They are the sacred Cup and Sword, Llewellyn.' Her voice softened as she gazed at the items, her hand loose in his.

'The sacred Cup...' he breathed. His eyes grew wider. 'But, what is such a treasure doing here?'

'Here? What on earth do you mean? They've always been here,' said Gwenene, a line appearing between her dark brows.

Davies shook his head. 'Not always,' he said, still hardly able to believe it. 'This once graced our Lord's table, then rested in my own land for many years before disappearing.'

Gwenene shook her head, frowning, jewels gleaming in her dark hair. 'No, Llewellyn, this is nonsense. Come, let us go and dance.' Music had started, a lively beat, and all around couples were moving to the dance floor. She pulled at his arm, but he couldn't take his eyes from the Cup.

'I will get it for you,' he whispered, reaching out a trembling hand to touch it. 'Let me give it to you, my Lady, and together we can return it to its rightful home.'

He turned to her, seeing confusion in her eyes. Did she not know? She tugged on his hand and he followed her, though he kept turning to look back at the glowing alcove. He thought of Christ, dark browed and pale faced, drinking at his final supper from that very cup and wanted to fall to his knees, to weep at the mystery and sorrow of it all. He felt Gwenene's hands on him, his back hitting the hardness of stone as she pushed him up against one of the pillared arches, but his eyes were dazzled and he couldn't see. Her hand touched his face and he blinked, looking at her strangely as though he didn't know who she was. Sighing, she kissed him, her hand moving low to grasp him in a sensitive spot. It was like having cold water thrown over him. He gasped, shaking his head as though to clear it.

'Dance, did you say?' he managed. She smiled, but then her mouth tightened, her head turning. He turned as well to see Denoris moving past, Aeres in his arms as he gazed affectionately into her eyes. Davies frowned. Gwenene shrugged, smiling, exquisite as she touched his face once more.

'Actually,' she said, 'I have a better idea. Shall we go to my chambers?'

She moved against him, giving him no doubt as to what she meant and he took in a breath, the fierce desire she always inspired in him coming to the fore.

'Yes,' he murmured, bending to kiss her. 'A capital idea.'

WALES, DECEMBER 1927

THE NIGHT WAS COLD, BUT UP AHEAD THE TOWN HALL GLOWED *with light, spilling out of the windows in long rectangles onto the snowy ground. The faint thump and squeal of a jazz band could be heard, drifting on the frosty air and couples hurried from all directions, keen to get inside. Davies, dressed in his best dinner suit, was almost bursting with pride and excitement. On his arm, her dark hair pinned up into the bobbed fashion of the day, was Gwenene. She hugged his arm close, holding her fur coat to her throat with her other hand.*

'Oh, I can't wait to get inside,' she pouted, red painted lips looking black in the half-light. 'It's freezing! Are you sure you wouldn't rather stay in, by the fire?' She raised her eyebrows and he grinned, ducking his head. Tempting as her offer was, there was no way he was missing this chance to show the world that she had chosen him. 'Or we could go to Ambeth,' she went on. 'My chambers there are warm, and winter has not arrived, as yet.'

'We're going to Ambeth in a few days,' he said, smiling at her. 'It'll be warm inside, I promise, and you can take off your coat and show them all how beautiful you are in your new gown.'

'It is rather gorgeous, I suppose,' allowed Gwenene. 'All that lovely beading! So kind of you to get it for me.'

'It was my pleasure.'

She looked at him through her lashes, pressing even closer. 'It will be, you mean. I don't believe I've thanked you properly yet.' Her voice was a husky promise and a thrill went through Davies at her closeness, her perfume swirling through his senses, making him giddy.

Reaching the door they went in, stamping their feet against the cold. Davies took Gwenene's coat from her, standing back in admiration as she did a little shimmy, the colourful beading on her dress making rainbows in the small hallway. Taking off his own coat, he removed two engraved invitations from the pocket before going to the cloakroom window, where the girl in attendance was staring at Gwenene with her mouth hanging open.

'Two to check, please,' he said, handing over the coats.

'Oh!' Startled back to herself, the girl took the proffered jackets and gave him two tickets. He tucked them in his pocket, then turned and offered his arm to Gwenene. As they moved away she winked at the cloakroom girl, laughing outrageously. A pompous gentleman in a tight dinner suit, whose eyes lit up when he saw Gwenene, stopped them at the entrance to the main ballroom.

'Invitations, please,' he said, holding out his hand. Llewellyn gave him the engraved cards and the man examined them, then handed them back. 'By Jove, Davies,' he said, leaning in. 'She is a looker.'

Llewellyn smiled. 'She's a beauty, indeed.'

Gwenene smiled at him, ignoring the glares from the other women in the room, her feet tapping to the lively beat. 'Oh, I love this human music,' she said, beaded fringing bouncing on her frock. 'It's just so, I don't know, invigorating! Do you like it?' She ran a pointed finger along the front of the doorman's suit, which looked in danger of bursting its buttons as she shimmied against him.

'Er, well, that is, yes, yes I do, I like it very much indeed!' the man replied, eyes popping as she danced around him. Kicking up her heels, she threw back her head and laughed.

'Oh, come on, Llewellyn!' She held out her hand.' Let's dance.'

'Wait!' They both turned to see a young man approaching with a camera and flash. 'A photo, please, for the local paper? No way I'm missin' a pic of you,' he said, looking Gwenene up and down. As she moved towards him Davies grabbed her arm, wanting to be in the photo too. He smiled at her, still unable to believe his luck. Pop! Off went the flash and she screamed, throwing herself into Llewellyn's arms.

'*What was that?*' *Her blue eyes were panicked and he sought to calm her down, feeling her heart pounding.*

'*It's all right, my love. Just a camera, a thing that takes pictures instantly.*' *He glared at the photographer who, having spotted his next target, beat a hasty retreat.*

'*A... camera?*' *she said, fear on her face changing to intrigue, her quick mind obviously taking it all in. She shook her head, earrings glittering. 'Interesting. You'll tell me about it later.' Her feet started tapping once more, the band on the stage swinging into yet another infectious rhythm, brilliantined hair shining under the lights as they entertained the crowd. 'Oh, I do love the human world! So much to see. Shall we dance?'*

'*We shall,*' *he said, looking at her with all the love he had in his heart as he led her onto the dance floor, seeing the glances from the other men, the stares from the other women as she started to move, graceful and abandoned and more beautiful than anything he had ever seen before.*

AMBETH – THE LIBRARY OF THE DARK
   (*Human world - January 1928*)

'WHAT DO YOU THINK?'

Gwenene smiled, her silk gown swirling around her as she raised one graceful arm towards the shelves of books.

'*It's – I'm amazed.*' *Davies looked around with wide eyes at the comfortable room, at the deep leather sofas set in small groups near the windows, inlaid wooden tables and chairs the perfect place to sit and study. And the books! Carved shelves reached almost to the ceiling in the double height room, long ladders on rails allowing access to the higher levels. It would take him years to even scratch the surface. He stood there, hands on hips, the scholar in him buzzing with excitement as he leaned his head back to take it all in.*

'*So, you like it?*' *She came to stand behind him, her hands on his shoulders as she leaned against him. She was almost as tall as he was and he could feel her breath on his ear as she spoke. 'For I have to go somewhere, my Llewellyn, and I thought you might like to stay here a while, do some reading.'*

'Oh?' He turned, taking her in his arms to kiss her. She responded before gently pushing back, her hands on his chest.

'Yes.' She smiled, though he thought he glimpsed something else in her eyes. But as soon as it came it was gone and she was out of his arms. She went over to the shelves, beckoning him to follow her. 'But before I go, let me show you a secret.'

Intrigued, he came closer. She stopped at a carved section, her slender fingers moving across the carving to rest on a single curled leaf. She pressed on it and a drawer, long and thin, popped out of the woodwork, so finely made it was almost invisible to the eye when closed. Inside was a large square object wrapped in a velvet cloth. He went to pick it up, but she stopped him, one hand on his chest.

'This belongs to Denoris,' she said. 'It is a treasure of our people, and he doesn't know I'm showing it to you. It is a token of my... esteem for you, that I am doing so.' She stared hard at him, as though willing him to understand what she was saying. He nodded, unsure what else to do, but knowing it was a significant moment. She went on. 'So, if you do come in here to look at it, you must replace it exactly as you found it, for if he were to know you were looking at it, that I had shown you...' Her mouth twisted. Lifting the object out of the drawer she handed it to Llewellyn. 'Take it now, have a look. I think you'll find it interesting.'

He took it carefully, holding it with both hands. 'But what if he comes in here while I'm looking at it?'

'He won't.' Gwenene kissed him, feather light. 'And I'll be back soon.' She moved away in a rustle of silk, glancing over her shoulder as she left the Library. He stood there with the book in his hands, jealousy at where he knew she was going and intrigue at what he held fighting within him. Realising he had no other option, he went to a nearby table and sat down, pulling his chair close as he unwrapped the velvet to reveal a book. His eyes widened.

. . .

LATER, GWENENE ENTERED THE GREAT HALL, RUBBING AT HER HIP *as she walked. She sighed. A solitary figure stood at the alcove, brown hair rumpled, his hands clasped behind his back. Llewellyn.*

She'd been away longer than expected, Denoris needing more from her than usual so she ached all over, despite the warm bath she had taken afterwards. And now this. She didn't understand it, Llewellyn's obsession with the Cup, but she'd known she would find him here. Coming up behind him she touched his shoulder. He turned, his face lighting up. Sliding her arms around his waist she leaned against him, wanting to be soothed as he held her close, feeling his solid calm energy. Eventually she lifted her head.

'Come on,' she said, her voice catching in her throat. 'Let's go to bed.'

CHAPTER 13

LOVE AND LOSS

Ambeth – Palace of The Elders
  (Human world - April 1928)

GALEN LEFT THE GREAT HALL, ENTERING THE LANTERN-LIT FOYER. *He rubbed the back of his neck, feeling weary. Something was up. Things hadn't been right for a while, the repercussions of the Great War in the human world and the loss of the Crown in Ambeth still resonating. The energy seemed to have settled somewhat, but he and Gwion had their work cut out for them, trying to restore the balance to landscapes ravaged by loss. What he needed, he decided, was a drink and a good night's sleep. About to take the stairs to his chambers, he paused. A familiar blond figure walked past, heading for the outer doors. Galen frowned. He was tired, but this needed to be said.*

'Well met, Denoris,' he called.

The other Elder turned. 'Well met, Galen.' He nodded his head, cordial enough, though his green eyes were watchful.

'Did you enjoy your evening?' Galen walked over to him. He kept his manner neutral, but inside he was reaching out, seeing if he could sense any change in the energy of the Dark Lord.

Denoris laughed, unexpectedly. 'I did,' he said. 'The band were entertaining, for a change. And you?'

'Yes, they did well enough. Human musicians seem to possess a talent that we do not, an ability to lose themselves in the making of good music.'

Denoris snorted. 'At least they are good for something. Although,' he went on, folding his arms. 'I have made some interesting visits to their world in recent times.'

'Oh yes?' Well, this confirmed his suspicions. 'And have you discovered anything worth sharing with the Council?'

'Oh, I don't think there's any need to worry,' said Denoris.

'I do,' said Galen. 'The Balance slips daily, despite all we do. This new century has been one of unparalleled suffering for humans, and I want to know why. Why, once the Crown went missing, did revolution and war take over?'

'But it is also a time of innovation,' Denoris replied, his voice smooth. "The machines they can make! It's extraordinary, the way they come up with something new every week.'

'But at what cost?' Another voice joined the conversation and Galen turned to see Gwion coming across the Foyer to join them, red hair shining gold in the light of the lanterns, silver grey armour moulded to his tall muscled form. He nodded at his brother before turning his attention back to Denoris. 'They ravage the earth like never before, battles that were once between tribes now taking place between nations.'

'If I didn't know better, I would think the Dark were meddling again,' said Galen.

Denoris reddened. 'You think because your father is High King, it gives you the right to speak to me this way!'

'Indeed I do not,' said Galen. He raised his eyebrows. 'Though it seems I have hit a nerve.'

Gwion put his hand on Galen's shoulder. 'Perhaps, brother, it's time for us to investigate, spend more time in the human world. Though there will be nothing for us to find, is that right, Denoris?'

'You tell me,' said the Dark Lord, his tone challenging.

'Maybe I will,' said Galen.

Denoris bared his teeth. 'You dare to try and read me, as though I were one of your humans?!'

Galen smiled. 'What on earth do you mean?' he asked. 'I'm merely passing time, discussing issues of importance with a fellow Elder.'

Denoris shook his head. 'Do not play games with me, Galen. Your touch may be subtle, but it doesn't mean I cannot feel you in my mind. You do not know who you are dealing with.' His green eyes narrowed and he leaned forward slightly, hands clenching into fists.

'We know exactly who we are dealing with.' Gwion moved closer to Denoris, mirroring his stance.

'Is that so?' the Dark Lord said, his soft tone in contrast to the fury twisting his handsome features. 'Well, if you're finished, I'd like to be on my way.'

'You're free to leave whenever you choose, Denoris.' All at once Galen was tired of the game. 'In fact, Gwion, I think I may be weary of all this myself. Shall we go drinking instead?'

'Sounds a much better way to spend the evening, brother.' Gwion shot Denoris a fierce look before heading for the stairs.

'Until next time, then.' Galen nodded at Denoris and turned away. He knew Denoris was watching him, could almost feel the heat of the Elder's glare on his back, but he didn't care. Wine, and much needed sleep, waited. Laughing, he followed his brother up the stairs.

THE GREAT HALL LAY DARK AND DESERTED. GUARDS STOOD AT their posts outside in the Foyer, the entrance doors barred for the night. No one heard when a door opened slowly at the back of the Hall and a dark figure crept in, looking around nervously as it inched along with its back to the wall. The moon shone bright through the tall windows, muting the colours of the stained-glass and mosaic floors, but the figure had no time for the beauty of the night. Its focus was on the alcove glowing golden against the shadowed stone wall. It stood for a moment gazing at the Sword and Cup, reaching out to run one finger along the curving silver bowl.

Clasping the stem of the Cup the figure lifted it from the niche. Immediately the light decreased and the figure froze. But nothing happened and after a moment it moved again, placing the Cup carefully into a small cloth bag. The figure stepped away from the niche and, keeping close to the wall, it moved quietly back towards the door and went through. Then it, and the Cup, were gone.

~

GALEN WOKE SUDDENLY. DREAMLESS SLEEP TO WIDE AWAKE, A BURN *of uncertainty in his chest. Something was wrong. He reached out with his mind, but there was nothing apparent in his chamber or the rooms beyond, though he could feel his brother was also awake. The urgency grew within him, tightening his muscles, making his mouth dry. He felt Gwion's approach before he heard him banging on his bedroom door.*

'Galen?'

'I am awake,' *he managed, half-choked by nameless fear. He sat up, swinging his legs over the side of the bed, then went and opened his chamber door. The room beyond was still dark, just a glow of embers in the fireplace. Gwion was there, bare-chested, his red hair tangled, the same fear in his grey eyes.*

'What in the Light is it? Is it Denoris?'

Galen shook his head. 'It is something larger than anything he could devise.' *He frowned, the urgency pressing hard against the confines of his skull, his head starting to ache.* 'It is everywhere. Something has changed.'

Gwion nodded, his hand coming to his brow, his face twisting. 'What time is it?'

'Early.' *Galen went to the window and opened the shutters, letting in the cool morning air. The sky was pale, half-lit, the sun only just rising over the shadowed gardens. It all seemed calm, nothing untoward that he could see. He closed his eyes, gripping the stone sill as he concentrated, trying to find his way to the source of the change. But it was no use. All he could feel were endless eddies as though a stone had been dropped in water, reverberations in the energy surrounding them all.*

'It's the Hall.' Gwion snapped out the words. Galen opened his eyes, turning to his brother.

'What?'

Gwion's eyes were closed, a line between his brows, lips pulled back from his teeth. Galen thought he saw a tear on his brother's pale cheek. Gwion opened his eyes. 'The Hall. That's where it has changed.'

Before he finished speaking Galen was moving. He pulled two shirts from the chest at the foot of his bed, shrugging one on and throwing the other to his brother. Leaving his bedroom, he took his swordbelt from the hook next to the fireplace, buckling it on.

Gwion needed no urging – he was a step behind Galen, reaching for his own sword. They left the room, running down the stairs toward the Great Hall.

~

ARTOS WOKE IN THE DARK OF EARLY MORNING, ALONE. THIS WAS how things were for him now. His sons had love affairs, as did others of the Court, but he had not the heart for such things since his beloved Nerys had passed, long years ago.

But there was something different about this waking, a feeling as though he had just lost her once again, a bittersweet ache of unbearable loss spreading through him. He felt tears, wet on his cheeks and frowned, wiping at them. Had he dreamed of her?

Then he woke fully, and realised. As High King, he was tied to the energy of Ambeth, could feel when things went awry. And something was terribly wrong.

CHAPTER 14
SLIPPING FURTHER

Galen was first into the Foyer. Dawn light poured through the dome over-head, reaching pale fingers into the shadows between the pillars. Two guards stood, as was always the case, at the door to the Great Hall. When they saw Galen they snapped to attention.

'My Lords, is all well?' The closest guard approached, one hand to her sword, frowning. She looked him up and down. Galen knew he was dishevelled, his hair still loose, but he had no time.

'Tell me, has anyone entered the Hall this night past?'

'No, my Lord.' She shook her head, turning to her fellow guard as though for confirmation. He also shook his head.

'Let us in, if you will.'

'But do not follow until we call you,' added Gwion, moving past Galen and through the door, which the closest guard had unlocked. 'And call for the King. Now!'

Galen followed his brother into the Hall. Coloured shimmers of dawn light fell through the stained-glass onto the mosaic floor, sparking colours from the great lanterns. But the alcove...

'The Cup!' he cried, running for the thrones and the alcove beyond. He got there first, Gwion just behind him, falling to his knees with a horrified

groan when he saw that only the Sword remained on the stone shelf. He heard Gwion cry out as he sank down next to him.

'What is this?'

Galen turned to see his father approaching. He had also dressed hastily, it was obvious, his tunic unbelted, his silvery hair unbrushed. Galen reached out to him.

'Father...' He choked, unable to speak against his pain. But Artos had seen. The colour drained from his face and he reached out blindly, leaning on one of the thrones for support. He clung to the carved wood and metal before straightening up and turning away as though unable to bear the sight.

'Guards!' he roared. Immediately the two guards ran through the doors into the Hall, skidding to a halt as Artos advanced on them both, eyes like ice in his white face. 'The Cup is gone! Mobilise the troops, search the Palace and gardens! Check all the Gates! It must be found!' The guards, shock on their faces, bowed and departed quickly.

'Father, we must assemble the Council.' Gwion pushed himself to his feet. 'They must be told.'

Galen also stood up, feeling as though the floor were dropping away from his feet. The Balance was already out of alignment. How in the name of Light were they to maintain it without the Cup and Crown? He ran a hand through his hair, unable to process what had happened. His father had already moved to the centre of the room, positioning himself over the five-pointed star set into the mosaic, tapping into the power of the stones below. He closed his eyes and Galen felt the pulse of power as he sent out the news. Once finished he came over to them both, sorrow deep in the lines of his face.

'My sons.' His voice broke and he stopped, rubbing a hand over his face, broad shoulders bowed as though under a heavy weight.

'Father.' Galen came to him, his heart breaking, as did Gwion, each taking an arm to support their father, moving him to a nearby bench where they sat down. A servant hurried into the Hall, stopping with a hand to his mouth when he saw them.

'Wine, and quickly,' said Galen, worried about his father. Artos shook his head.

'Water, if you please. I need to keep my wits about me.' The servant bowed and ran off. 'This is a dark day for Ambeth,' Artos continued. 'We cannot rest until we find the Cup. Tell me, can you feel anything?'

Gwion looked at Galen who nodded, reaching to take his brother's hand. They both closed their eyes, their senses ranging out beyond the borders of their land, sensing the Balance, feeling the inexorable slide as it started to tip, the increase in chaos as Darkness surged in power.

'What is this?' A desperate voice cut into their focus. Galen faltered, feeling Gwion lose hold of the thread as he opened his eyes. A dishevelled Thorion stood there, still buckling on his sword as he stared at them all, eyes full grey. 'Is it true? Has the Cup gone?' Artos stood and went to him, though Galen knew he had no comfort to offer.

'It is so.' The King laid a hand on Thorion's arm. More Elders were arriving, the noise level in the Hall rising as they realised their loss. Adara, immaculate in silk and brocade, came over to them.

'I cannot believe it.' Her golden eyes were full of tears and Gwion came to his feet.

'My Lady.' He hastened to her, taking her slender hand in his own to kiss. 'Neither can we. It is a dark day for Ambeth, and the world beyond.'

Adara gazed at Gwion, her lips trembling and Galen, still connected to him, felt his brother's mingled pain and longing at seeing her so. 'I know,' she whispered. 'I can feel it. Such a terrible thing. What are we to do?'

'We will find it, I'm sure,' said Gwion, still holding her hand.

'And the Balance?'

'Is slipping further,' he said.

She began to sob and Galen knew his brother was restraining himself from taking her in his arms to comfort her. Why, Galen didn't know – surely on a day such as this he shouldn't worry about revealing his feelings. But instead it was Thorion who put a gentle hand on her arm. She turned to him, seeming almost bewildered.

'Thorion, it is too much...' She put her hand to her head, grimacing. Gwion clenched his fists.

'Come, Adara,' Thorion said. He was still visibly shaken. 'Sit with Galen, and I'm sure Gwion will be able to arrange a drink for you.'

Gwion reached out to her, then let his hand drop. 'Be not distressed, my dear,' he said. 'We will prevail, I know it.'

Adara sat down next to Galen, watching Gwion as he crossed the Hall, threading through the increasingly agitated Elders. Galen could feel her turmoil, see the pattern of light energy twisting within her.

Thorion rubbed a hand over his face. 'So, what happens now?'

Galen got to his feet, leaning on the wall for support, trying not to look at the alcove. 'I don't know.' He paused, fighting the howling emptiness threatening to consume him. All around him patterns of Light and Dark flashed in and out, the high emotion in the room making it more difficult to control. He swallowed. 'We find it. Gwion and I were already looking for the Crown.'

'We were.' Gwion returned holding a drink for Adara, which he handed to her. 'You all right?' he added in a low voice to his brother. Galen nodded, managing to regain control of himself.

'Thank you.' Adara had stopped crying, but her expression was troubled as she scanned the room. It was in uproar, Elders in groups talking and gesturing, crying out their sorrow at their loss. Several were on their knees.

'Anything?' murmured Thorion, and she glanced at him. Galen raised an eyebrow. But she shook her head, golden curls waving around her flawless face.

'Nothing unusual; sorrow, pain, confusion, calculation. No, the one who did this is not here.' She sighed, taking a sip of her drink. Artos called them all to attention, his voice ringing out above the noise, silencing the crowd. Adara took Gwion's offered arm as they moved to stand in the circle formation, the Sword gleaming alone at the end of the room.

'GWENENE, I WOULD SPEAK WITH YOU.'

She stopped, her stomach clenching. Denoris. She'd studiously ignored *him during the Council Meeting, shocked by the loss of the Cup, a thread of worry in her mind as to where Llewellyn might be.*

'My Lord Denoris?' She turned, trying to control her reaction to him, her heart beating fast. He was equally affected, she could see by the glow in his green eyes as he looked at her. He moved close enough she could feel the warmth of him, though he didn't touch her.

'It has come to my attention that you have been sharing our knowledge with your human lover.'

Gwenene went cold. Surely he didn't know about the book? She licked her lips before answering and his eyes widened. 'What of it? He's an intelligent man, and a fine lover.' She tossed her head, defiant as she held his gaze.

His jaw clenched. 'Is that so? I wondered why I had not had so much of your time as late.'

His voice was velvet, but she could hear the tension in it. He was armour clad, leather taut across his muscular frame, and she swallowed. About to touch him, she glimpsed Aeres standing nearby with two other courtiers, watching them. Hurt bloomed in her chest.

'I'm surprised you noticed, my Lord. You've been busy yourself.' She raised her chin.

'You know why—' He restrained himself with a visible effort, blowing out a breath through his nose. 'Just take care, my Lady. There are things in our Library not meant for his eyes.'

Inside Gwenene sagged with relief, but she made no outward sign, knowing Llewellyn's life, and possibly her own, hung in the balance. 'He is human, Denoris.' Her mouth curved around his name so it came out as an endearment, despite her best efforts. 'How much can he understand?'

He gave her a searching look, then nodded. 'I suppose you're right, as always.' She smiled, allowing him that reward, and his face softened. 'Will I see you later?' His hand came up as though to touch her, but she shook her head.

'I'm meeting Llewellyn,' she replied, trying to keep the shaking from her voice. His expression changed, his hand dropping back to his side. 'And it looks as though you are required elsewhere.' She inclined her head and Denoris turned to see Aeres coming towards them both. He moved away

from Gwenene towards his wife, taking her hand to kiss, his other arm going around her waist as she smiled at him. Gwenene watched them for a moment, then turned and made her way from the Foyer, heading for the stables, tears on her cheek as cold as the pain in her heart.

~

LLEWELLYN SAT IN THE GRASS NEAR THE STONE GATE, HIS HEAD IN his hands, fear deep within him. He had *to do this. There was no other way. In his heart he knew that Gwenene, for all her words of love and passion, belonged to Denoris yet he could not let her go, was hopelessly in her thrall and had been since the moment he saw her riding towards him. The only way he could see to compete was to steal power, to make himself a worthy opponent for the Dark Lord. And a worthy guardian of the Sacred Cup.*

It had been so easy, once he'd figured it out. He'd studied the Castle for years, thought he knew every stone in its ruined walls. Then he'd made the crossing, met Gwenene and been exposed to the knowledge and power that lay in her realm. When she'd shown him the book of skylore he'd been fascinated by the diagrams, stars and planets wheeling through the heavens, tiny writing detailing deductions and conclusions based on their findings. Left to his own devices in the Dark Library he'd started making notes, working out the formulae, but as he'd leafed slowly through the pages he'd seen something that stopped him in his tracks. A drawing of a castle on a mound set at one end of a curving bay, a sky full of stars above connected by arcs and equations, indicating they had been mapped from the building below. The legend next to it, curling script dark on the page, read 'The stronghold of Iorweth', but he'd known what it was, where it was. It was his Castle and, picked out in gold at the base of the mound, was a star. He'd known what that meant too; he'd seen the maps in the Library, the markings for the Gates between this world and his own. There was a Gate in the Castle mound.

So he'd gone back to his own world and spent days and nights feverishly climbing the mound, examining every square inch of it in the hope of finding the entrance. But nothing. Finally, delirious, he'd collapsed one night onto the cold grass, rolling over to lie on his back under the wheeling stars, so like the image in the book. All at once he'd felt small, insignificant, pinned down like an insect against the curve of the earth. He'd thought of the ancient Lord who had built the place, the Faery King, his mind ranging free as he'd drifted in and out of consciousness. Then it had come to him, the only possible answer. The entrance had to be somewhere in the Castle itself.

Sitting up, he'd made his way through the dark ruins, staggering down the hill to the quiet streets below. At home he'd slept for the first time in days, waking to eat breakfast made for him by small blonde Merewyn, smiling at her as he'd left the house, whistling jauntily. Returning to the Castle he'd set about his task with renewed vigour, painstakingly examining every stone until he'd found the way in and, finally, the Gate.

And it was to the Castle, his beloved Castle, that he had brought the Cup. Returned to Wales, to where Joseph of Arimathea had brought it all those centuries ago, at least according to the old stories. And now he, Llewellyn, had returned it once more. Emotion welled through him, tears pouring down his face and he rubbed his eyes with both hands, sniffing and gasping as he fought for control.

He had to go through the Gate and act as though nothing was wrong, that nothing had changed. He knew the Cup was missing; he just needed to act suitably surprised about it. Not that he imagined anyone would suspect him, but Gwenene's blue eyes did not miss much. Swallowing, he got to his feet, pulling the travelling stone from his pocket and holding it out. It began to glow and, taken by its magic, he crossed over, expecting to see Gwenene waiting on the other side.

But something was wrong. As he came through the Gate he was seized by strong arms. Unable to move, gasping from the disorientation of the crossing, he hung there, brown hair falling forward over his eyes as the guards held him tight.

'Who are you?' one of them growled.

'Er, I am Llewellyn,' he managed, aware he needed to be careful, despite his dizziness.

'And he is with me,' said an icy voice. Llewellyn lifted his head to see

Gwenene, a vision in blue on the back of her white horse. The guards let him go and stepped back, leaving him to fall to his knees.

'Our apologies, Lady Gwenene,' said one of the guards, 'but we need to check everyone who enters and leaves Ambeth.'

'I'm aware of the situation.' She moved her horse closer to the group. 'And I can vouch for this man.'

Llewellyn managed to get to his feet, hating her seeing him so weakened by the crossing.

'Come on.' She rode up, extending one white hand. He took it and she pulled him up in front of her, her strength as always surprising. Sliding an arm around his waist she kicked her horse into a canter and they were soon far from the Gate, riding across the green meadows towards the gardens.

'I presume you're wondering what all that was about,' she said into his ear, her breath warm on his neck. 'Well, it seems someone has stolen our Sacred Cup. I've just come from an emergency Council Meeting. There will be no courtly dances or music tonight, I fear. We'll have to make our own fun.' Her hand moved lower and he jerked in the saddle, almost falling except for her arm holding him. Laughing out loud in surprise and relief, he started to relax. There was no way anyone would be watching him now, he was sure.

Later they lay together in Gwenene's chambers, both of them sated for the time being.

'You are a... surprising lover,' she purred, her body soft against his.

'I am?' He frowned, not sure what she meant. She laughed, low in the firelit room, silken sheets gleaming, her long hair spread across the soft pillows. Her hand came up to his chest, playing with the dark hair there as she looked up at him.

'What I mean, my Llewellyn, is that you are holding my interest. Which is something not many can do, you know. Truly it was a blessing I spared you, that night at the Gates.'

He ran his hand along the curve of her hip, enjoying the satin skin under his fingers. 'Is that so, my Lady?' he asked, flirting with her, teasing her in a way he only felt safe doing when they were alone. She indulged him, fluttering her lashes, kissing him, playing along. All at once Davies *was filled with love so strong he couldn't bear it. He rolled over on top of her, pinning her underneath him as he kissed her, her hands grasping at his arms. He looked deep into her eyes, one hand coming up to caress her cheek.*

'Then come and live with me! Be mine, come to my house and I'll continue to love you as you wish. Your every desire will be mine.'

She held his gaze a moment then, so quickly he wasn't sure how, she escaped from under him and moved to lie across his back. He could feel her soft curves against him, her breath tickling him.

'I cannot leave Ambeth,' she said. But she didn't say no and so Llewellyn, heartened, continued.

'It won't be forever, I know that. You are longer lived than I and I know there will come a time when you will tire of me, when I'm an old man.'

'And what will you do then?' she whispered, sliding off him to lie on her side. He turned to face her.

'I shall walk into the sea, let the gods take me.'

A troubled look crossed her face. 'Let me think about it.'

Llewellyn grew angry. After all he had done for her! Would do for her, if she would let him. 'Well think quickly, for I would like an answer.'

At this she came back to him, blue eyes flashing sparks. 'What? Do not think to control me, Llewellyn Davies! There is no-one alive can do that. Be very careful.'

Llewellyn gazed at her, his anger gone to sadness, reaching out to smooth her hair. 'I do not wish to control you, Lady. I wish only that you be mine.'

'And what,' asked Gwenene, pressing herself against him, 'is it about this situation that makes you think I'm not?' She kissed him, her mouth hot, teeth sharp as she bit him. He moaned, giving himself up to her, utterly and completely hers.

H_E WOKE JUST PAST MIDNIGHT. G_{WENENE} LAY NEXT TO HIM, moonlight lighting one delicate cheekbone, limbs soft against the tumbled sheets. Kissing her lightly on the brow, he slid from the bed. Taking care to *keep quiet he dressed quickly, holding his shoes in his hand as he let himself out, closing the door behind him. Stone walls rose tall around him, lanterns spaced at intervals the only light on his journey and he held his breath at each corner, not wanting to be found. But he reached the Library door without incident, lifting the latch and pushing it gently so it opened sound-lessly, gliding over the smooth slates of the floor. Inside the armchairs were deserted, the room lit only by the moon coming through the long windows.*

Making his way to the section of bookshelf containing the hidden book, Llewellyn muttered a prayer under his breath as he pressed carefully on the carved leaf. The drawer slid open soundlessly and, licking dry lips, Llewellyn lifted the book out, wrapping it tightly in the velvet cloth before putting it in his bag. He didn't mean to keep it for long, only a few weeks, just until he'd mastered the power he knew had to lie within its pages. Closing the drawer he turned and left the Library, remembering to close the door behind him. It wasn't until he was out in the gardens beneath the stars that he allowed himself to breathe.

Sitting on a nearby bench he put on his shoes before starting for the Long Walk and the fields beyond. He knew it would take him a while to get to the Stone Gate, but he'd be there well before sunrise and through before, he hoped, anyone thought to look for him.

CHAPTER 15

I AM YOURS

Gwenene woke to an urgent hand shaking her.

'Llewellyn, stop it,' she grumbled, pushing out at the offender, who caught her hand and held it tight. She opened her eyes, startled, to see Denoris leaning over her.

'I am not Llewellyn,' he growled. 'But I would be interested to know where your lover is hiding.'

Gwenene sat up, reclaiming her hand. She looked around. Llewellyn was gone, that much was apparent – his clothes were missing from the chair where he'd left them, as was his bag. Outside the sky was still dark, only pale moonlight coming through the slats in the shutter to light the room.

'But... I don't understand.' She frowned. 'He should still be here.'

Denoris, moving across the room, opened her cupboard and pulled out a gown. 'Put this on.' He threw the dress so it landed on the bed.

Gwenene pulled it to her, anger at his highhanded manner starting to spark. She'd get dressed when she was damn well ready. 'Denoris, what is going on?' She stood, still holding the gown, but clothed only in her long dark hair.

'What is going on?' Denoris advanced on her. 'He has stolen my book of

skylore, that's what's going on!' He stopped, taking in her gleaming figure, his eyes moving the length of her.

'What?' Gwenene felt a lurch of shock, her anger turning to fear. Denoris would know that she had shown it to him, that she was the only one who could have done so. She wondered how he would punish her. He reached for her, pulling her to him, kissing her fiercely. She gasped, pressing against him as she kissed him back. He let her go, his breath coming hard as he brought up his hand to cup her face.

'You are mine,' he said, green eyes intent on her. 'And I will share you no longer, do you understand?'

She stared at him, fear and anger and desire fighting inside her, exquisite pain at his words. 'But I have to share—'

'No,' said Denoris. 'I have to be with Aeres, you know why. But you are the one that I want for myself. Will you do this, for me?'

Gwenene stared at him before nodding, slowly. A smile spread across his handsome face. 'Good,' he said, still holding her close, his hands warm on her skin. 'Now, my Gwenene, we need to find your lap-dog and get my book back.'

'But, I still don't understand,' said Gwenene, playing with the blond hair at the nape of his neck. 'How do you know...?'

'Do you think I would leave such a thing unguarded? I put a trap spell on the book, so I would know if anyone moved it from the Library. The spell went off two hours ago and I tracked it to the Stone Gate. It can only be him.'

'Does it matter?' she murmured. 'You'll get it back, eventually. Stay with me.' She moved against him, caressing his muscular arms.

'There will be time for that, don't worry.' His hands were on her, leaving trails of heat upon her skin. 'But first your lover needs to be dealt with. I warned you, did I not, about sharing our knowledge with him.'

Gwenene stopped caressing him. She stepped back. 'What are you going to do?'

'We,' Denoris raised his eyebrows, 'are going to get the book back. You've been there, haven't you? You'd know where he would hide?'

'Well, I've only been to his house.' Gwenene thought fast as she slipped *her gown over her head. Happy as she was that things were restored with Denoris, there was a part of her that was troubled by what she knew was to come. Denoris did not forgive, and for one who had not only stolen her affections, but also one of his possessions...*

'Denoris.' Her voice was huskier than usual, and she cleared her throat before she spoke again. 'Kill him quickly, please?' Her voice rose on the last word and Denoris tilted his head. His back was to the light and she couldn't see his face, so she took a deep breath and waited, hoping his desire for vengeance would only mean one death. Not that she wouldn't fight him, if need be. He came towards her, still in shadow, until he was close enough to take her face in his hands again. She tensed.

'You do not want him to suffer.' It wasn't really a question, and Gwenene thought before answering, wanting to get it right.

'No,' she said finally, deciding to be honest. 'Will you do this, for me?' Echoing his words from before, she saw him smile, the moonlight behind him changing his golden hair to silver, green eyes gleaming. He kissed her again.

'You are mine,' he murmured against her mouth. Again, it was not a question.

'I am yours,' she breathed, relaxing.

'Then let us go,' he said, releasing her. "Etras waits for us, with horses.' And with that Gwenene knew Llewellyn's fate was sealed. Etras was a Tracker – wherever Davies had gone, Etras would find him. She felt a pang, for a moment, almost of sorrow, but it passed as Denoris took her hand. Desire was building in her, her dress sliding against her skin as they left the room, together once more.

LLEWELLYN REACHED THE STONE GATE, HIS BREATH COMING HARD with fear and exertion. Looking behind him to make sure he wasn't being followed, he brought his travelling stone from his pocket and held it out in front of him. It took a few moments for his breathing to slow enough to allow the magic to work. Finally, the stone began to glow and he stepped

through the Gate. He was dizzy and shaking yet filled with unspeakable relief to see his small town, a few lights shining in the pre-dawn darkness. Staggering down the hill he made his way home, moving through the darkened town jumping at shadows, his heart pounding so much he could barely breathe at times and had to stop, gasping, to lean against a wall. Finally, he reached his house, but there was no rest for him there, not yet. He knew they'd come after him so, pausing only to gather a few items, he left quickly, planning to make it to a safe house, somewhere he'd never taken Gwenene – a small stone cottage hidden in the mountains, it had belonged to his family for years. There he would stay and learn from the book, living off the provisions he'd stored there, water from the clear mountain stream nearby to sustain him. He was starting to regret his decision to take the book but, steeled by thoughts of Gwenene, he kept going. Reaching the road leading out of town he started to run for the hills.

'HOW CAN YOU BE SURE DENORIS ISN'T INVOLVED?' GALEN STOOD UP and went to the window, leaning against the sill with his arms folded, unable to hide his frustration any longer. He glared at the assembled Elders, all of whom were still visibly shaken. The shutters behind him were open, letting cool morning air into his father's chambers, but it did nothing to ease his anger.

'I sensed nothing from him, other than his usual mix of calculation and self-love.' Adara was sitting on the sofa, her rose silk gown in folds around her. 'And he's jealous about something – probably that poor human Gwenene has been dragging around.' Her nostrils flared as she spoke, her distaste evident. Thorion glanced at Gwion, raising his eyebrows.

'We've been keeping an eye on that situation anyway,' he said.

Adara nodded. 'I tell you,' she went on. 'None of the Elders are involved or, if they are, they're concealing it even from themselves.'

'We cannot blame Denoris for everything that goes wrong in Ambeth,' said Gwion. 'I believe Adara – not one of our Elders would do such a thing!' He went to sit next to her and she smiled at him.

Galen's mouth tightened and he looked away. For all that Adara said, he couldn't escape the feeling that Denoris was somehow involved in the loss of the sacred objects, and had been from the start. As much as he loved his brother, he didn't need Gwion's feelings distracting him and clouding his judgement.

Artos, his face seeming more lined than usual, sat in an armchair, his broad shoulders hunched forward. 'Then we need to do more!' He slammed his hand down on the arm of the chair. 'I will not have it that our sacred things are not safe in our Great Hall! It is preposterous that the Cup should disappear from under the very noses of the guards!'

'Have they any more to say?' Thorion was standing near the fireplace, legs apart and arms folded, eyes storm grey.

'I have had the ones on duty disciplined but only mildly. They swear up and down they saw not a thing, and the Lady Adara has vouched for their honesty. What more can I do?'

'So how, by the Light, does someone enter a locked Hall, the very seat of our power, and no-one notices!' Galen's voice rose, echoing around the room. Adara put a hand to her head, grimacing and Gwion glared at his brother.

'Peace, Galen,' he said. 'We are all upset. Shouting won't help the situation.'

'Neither will soft words!'

'What about the doors to the gardens?' Adara was frowning, obviously in pain and Galen, seeing her distress, relented. He could feel power coursing through him, tingling in his fingers and he took a breath, pulling it back.

'Again, we had guards in place, running patrols, and the doors were sealed, just as they always are when not in use – I cannot understand it.' Artos rubbed his face.

'Forgive me.' Galen went to pour himself a glass of wine, then waved the jug at the assembled room. There were no takers, and he put it down again. 'Maybe the Seers can help,' he went on. 'I will go to them, if needs be.'

'Yes, a good thought, Galen,' said Artos, though worry still sat in his ice blue eyes. 'And Gwion, you and Thorion will check the Gates to see if it has passed through. Meredan can also help, his tracking skill will be invaluable.'

'What can I do?' asked Adara, golden eyes dark with concern.

'You've done enough already, my dear, but if you wish you can stay and keep an old man company,' said Artos, smiling at her. 'I have need of your gentle counsel.'

Adara flushed the same colour as her gown, bowing her head. Galen caught Gwion's eye and smirked. Gwion glared at him and Thorion, catching this byplay, laughed, drawing all eyes to him.

'Er, well, I suppose Gwion and I should get started,' he said, looking slightly embarrassed. 'I have a map of the Gates in my chambers. Shall we go there and get it first?'

'By all means,' said Gwion, rising from his seat. He turned to Adara. 'I look forward to seeing you, Lady, on my return.'

She smiled up at him, holding his gaze with her own. 'As do I, Gwion.' They stared at each other until Thorion cleared his throat.

'Shall we?'

'Oh!' Adara blushed again. 'Of course. I look forward to seeing you all and, all being well, the Cup.'

'I'm leaving,' said Galen, unable to bear any more. He bowed to his father and left the room, heading along the passageway to the stairs. But before he reached them he heard his brother call out.

'What the hell was all that?'

CHAPTER 16
AN END TO GAMES

He turned to see Gwion coming along the hallway, Thorion one step behind. Gwion was frowning and Galen's jaw clenched. He didn't need this.

'What?'

'All that anger! You fair had sparks coming off you! And the Lady Adara—'

'I cannot help being angry! Our Cup is gone and you are mooning about—'

'Peace.' Thorion came to stand with them, one hand on each of their arms. His eyes were dark and his expression stern. 'We need you both to focus. And work together.'

Galen shook off his hand. 'I don't—'

'You're right. I'm sorry.' Gwion shot Thorion a warning glance. 'Galen?'

Galen shook his head. He could feel himself crackling with energy again, as though he needed to run to the hills and scream out his pain and sorrow, releasing it. But he also knew how dangerous it would be for him to do so. He pulled it back, with an effort. 'I'm sorry too. Truly.' He rubbed his hand over his face. Gwion was pale and he knew his brother would have felt the backlash of the energy surge. Thorion had his arms folded, waiting. 'Truly, my brothers.' He touched Gwion on the arm. 'Peace?'

Gwion glared at him. Then a half smile curved his mouth and it was as though they were boys again, arguing over nothing. 'Peace.'

'Thorion?'

Thorion was still frowning. Then he laughed, and clapped Galen on the back. 'Control yourself, will you? You will have us all off balance if you don't.'

Galen nodded. His anger had subsided, leaving only ashes of sorrow, their loss resonating deep inside. 'I must go to the Seers now. Will I see you tomorrow?'

'You will.' Thorion nodded. 'Safe travels, brother.'

'And to you.'

Gwion hugged him, sharp and fierce. 'We will find our way through this,' he said. 'Together. We cannot let Ambeth fall.'

Galen hugged him back. 'I know. And we won't.'

~

GWENENE, DENORIS AND ETRAS STOOD ON THE HILL OVERLOOKING the small town. Lights were starting to blink on, golden sparks in the early morning darkness, the sun a faint gleam over the ocean. Behind them the Stone Gate hummed with the power of their crossing, darker stone shapes against the mountains beyond.

Etras closed his eyes. When he opened them he grinned, turning to Gwenene and Denoris. 'I have him. He's gone to the town.'

Denoris held out his hand. 'Lead on, my Lady. I'm sure you know the way.'

Gwenene frowned. Denoris waited. She took in a breath and shook her head a little.

'I do.'

They started down the hillside, the three of them like figures from legend, Denoris in dark armour, muscled arms bare, his golden beauty *stark against the dark hillside. Gwenene's blue gown flowed behind her in the breeze, as did her dark hair as she took Denoris' hand. Etras strode along behind, tall and bearded, kinglike in posture, eyes fierce in his strong boned face. Together they moved towards the town.*

~

MEREWYN ARRIVED AT LLEWELLYN'S HOUSE JUST BEFORE DAWN, letting herself in with the key under the mat by the side door. She went to the kitchen first, tutting as she saw how little remained in the pantry. How was she supposed to prepare breakfast for the man! She left the kitchen, her lips pressed together in disapproval as she headed for the small study. She could light the fire at least – it was a cool morning and he might appreciate a warm room to start work in. But on entering she found the room in disarray. It was never tidy, but this was different. Drawers had been left open, books pulled from the bookcase and the small safe was open and emptied of its contents. Had they been robbed? She stood for a moment in the centre of the room, breathing deep as she reached out with her mind. But all she got was Davies, and a sense of urgency around him, that he was going somewhere. Opening her eyes, she frowned. Davies' notebooks were missing. Normally they sat on a pile on his desk, easily accessed should he have some revelation or need to refer to something, though he hadn't done so as much of late, more concerned with spending time with Gwenene. Merewyn had been keeping an eye on them just as Thorion and the others had asked, taking care to stay out of the Dark Elder's way on the odd occasion she came to visit.

She started to tidy up, returning books to their shelves as she thought hard. Where would he be going, and why such hurry?

She stiffened. Three were coming, had just passed through the Stone Gate. The books dropped from her hands, fear starting through her. She ran from the room, letting herself out of the side door into the early dawn light. Not bothering to close the door behind her she hurried up the street towards her house, a tiny cottage set back from the road, the large tree in the front garden almost obscuring it from passers-by. Running up the path to her front door she went inside, closing and locking the door behind her. Not wanting to trust to chance, she also sealed it with a charm. Going into the small sitting room she took a silver bowl and jug from the wooden cupboard against the wall. Setting them on the table, she filled the bowl from the jug, the liquid gleaming like pearl. Taking a deep breath, she sent the summons, gazing into the bowl. Within a few moments, the handsome face of Thorion appeared.

'What is it?' he asked, forgoing his usual courtesies.

'They are here,' gasped Merewyn. 'The Dark. I don't know what they want, but they are comin'. And Davies is gone, I think to the hills. You must tell the King.'

Thorion frowned. 'How many?'

'Three. I felt them cross over, about half an hour ago. They'll be here soon. What am I to do?'

'Stay where you are,' said Thorion. 'Do not leave your house for any reason. We will come to you.'

Merewyn nodded. 'Thank you,' she whispered, then the contact was broken.

∾

AS THEY ENTERED THE TOWN OUTSKIRTS DENORIS LOOKED AROUND, his handsome face sharp with derision.

'So this is where you've been spending your time, is it?' Gwenene shot him a glare and he threw his head back and laughed.

'Come on,' she snapped, moving more quickly, her skirts flowing behind her as she stormed ahead. Behind her she heard Etras. 'I don't know, Denoris, this seems a pleasant enough place. Wonder what the women are like.'

She snorted, turning down a narrow alley passing between two houses, not bothering to see if they were following her. Her temper was starting to rise. It was only a book, for Darkness sake! If Denoris wanted it back so badly he need only have asked her and she would have got it for him. But she knew it wasn't just the book he wanted, just as she knew why he was making her lead them to Llewellyn. Trying to ignore the disquiet in her stomach she crossed the road and came to a stop in front of a small red brick house, set high up with a view of the Castle and bay. She swallowed, considering, but then Denoris was there, his hands on her turning her to face him, his mouth on hers and she forgot everything. He pulled back, more tender than she had ever seen him before and her hand came up to his cheek.

'Remember your promise.' She held his gaze and he kissed her again, his lips soft on her cheek, close to her ear.

'I will,' he murmured. 'And you remember yours.' He smiled and she knew what she needed to do. She opened the small gate, black paint flaking under her hand, leading them around the side of the house where a wooden door, painted blue, stood ajar. She paused.

'What are you waiting for?' Etras tried to move past Denoris, but the Dark Lord stopped him, his hand hard on his shoulder.

'Let the lady lead us, here,' he said, giving Etras a pointed look.

Gwenene steeled herself, her resolve hardening. Llewellyn was a human, nothing more. She pushed the door open to reveal a large kitchen with a tiled floor. It was empty.

'Llewellyn!' she called, moving across the room and opening another door leading into a hallway. But there was no response. Denoris and Etras, knives drawn, followed her as she led them to the study, opening the door to reveal piles of paper strewn everywhere.

'It looks as though our bird has flown,' said Denoris. He went over to the desk, picking up a piece of paper and looking at it before dropping it.

'So what do we do now?' Etras leaned against the deep windowsill, folding his arms.

'Where would he be?'

A crash from the kitchen drew their attention. Etras went for the door but Denoris got there first, moving swiftly across the hallway, dagger in hand. He strode into the kitchen, surprising a young man by the door. He had just deposited a load of wood by the stove, dust still floating in the air.

'I-I er, I was just leavin',' he stammered, his eyes so wide the whites were visible all around as Denoris advanced on him, Etras and Gwenene bringing up the rear.

'Wait.' Denoris spoke softly, but his tone of command was unmistakeable and the boy froze where he was. Denoris came closer, looking him deep in the eyes and the boy's pupils dilated, his pale face becoming blank.

'Do you know Llewellyn Davies?'

'Yes.' The boy's tone was flat, his eyes staring straight ahead and Denoris nodded in satisfaction.

'I never tire of it,' whispered Etras, moving close to Gwenene, 'watching him control another's mind. Tell me, does he still like to play with the servants as well?'

Gwenene frowned. 'No. He has no need. Shh,' she went on, as Etras opened his mouth again. He was too close to her and she moved away. Denoris had his hand on the young man's throat as he interrogated him, though he didn't need to, the boy completely under his will.

'Does he have another house? Somewhere to go?'

'There's a place in the hills, belongin' to his family.' The lilting tone was gone from the boy's voice; it was just a flat monotone.

'Where?'

'Near to Gaerwen Farm, the Bevan place.'

Denoris turned to Gwenene and Etras. 'What should I do with him?' he asked, grinning.

'Oh, let him go, Denoris!' snapped Gwenene, already on edge. 'He won't remember anything. Come on, let's get this done.'

Denoris raised an eyebrow, tilting his head slightly. She folded her arms, huffing out a sigh.

'As you wish, Lady,' he said, letting go of the young man's throat. He turned his attention on him again. 'Rithaur.' The young man collapsed in a heap on the floor, all tangled long limbs. Denoris, Gwenene and Etras stepped over him as they left the house. Once on the street, Denoris looked up to the hills rising behind the town.

'Can you find him?'

Etras regarded him sardonically. 'What do you think?' He started up the road, long legs striding out in the lightening dawn. Denoris held out his *hand and Gwenene came to him, pressing against him and kissing him hard.*

'I am yours,' she said, her hands either side of his face, looking deep into his green eyes.

'And I am yours,' he replied. 'Now let us go, and end this game.'

CHAPTER 17
BETRAYAL COMES WITH KNIVES

Llewellyn stood in the small garden at the front of the cottage, watching the sun rise over the distant ocean, the clouds streaked red and gold. The air was clean and crisp, the last few stars winking out above him. He went to wash at the pump, gasping as ice-cold water cascaded onto his head and neck, shaking himself like a dog so droplets flew everywhere.

The cottage, just two rooms really, was built of grey stone and nestled into the hillside, the land behind rising sharply to a misty summit. He'd made it, finally, managing an hour or so of exhausted sleep before waking disoriented, taking a moment to remember where he was. He'd risen to light the small fire, then came outside to take in the mountain air and prepare for the day.

Brushing his wet hair back with his hands he went back inside, grabbing a small rough towel to dry himself by the welcome warmth of the fire. He filled the small pot hanging over it with water and set it to boil, adding dried meat and root vegetables and a handful of herbs. The scent of stew started to fill the cottage as he sat down at the small table, opening the book that lay there. Reverently, he turned the pages, making the occasional note in his notebook, one of several on the table.

There was a banging at the door and Merewyn, sitting on the edge of her armchair, jumped. She stood up, legs trembling as she went towards the door, hardly daring to breathe.

'Merewyn, we are here.'

Thorion. Filled with relief she ran the last few steps, unlocking the door and throwing it open. Thorion stood there with two other Elders, all of them armour clad. Stepping aside she let them in, throwing her arms around Thorion. He hugged her back and she felt him laughing.

'I'm so glad you're here,' she said, her voice muffled against his chest. He gently set her back from him.

'Merewyn, you are safe. Do not fear. You know Meredan, of course, and Gwion.' The other Elders smiled at her and her eyes widened, the impact of their beauty in the confined hallway a little hard to take. It had been too long since she'd been in Ambeth, she reflected as she smoothed her hands down her apron, trying to compose herself.

'Right, well, please come through.' She led them through to the small sitting room. 'Sit down and I'll just make some tea then.' She bustled off to the kitchen, wanting something to do. Putting the tea things together, she could hear the low rumble of voices, the creak of chairs as they made themselves comfortable. She leaned on the counter, her head down as she fought her fear, her worry about what might be happening in the hills. If anyone could help her it would be Thorion, so she just had to trust it would be all right. The kettle whistled, jolting her from her trance and she went to take it from the hob, telling herself as she poured hot water into the teapot that there was nothing more she could have done. Picking up the tray she went back into the sitting room and set it down on the small table. She stood there, her hands twisting in her apron, not sure what to do with herself. Thorion smiled.

'Peace, Merewyn, you are safe with us.'

She blew out a breath, bending to pick up the teapot. 'They're still here. I haven't felt them leave as yet, only the three of you comin' through. D'you know who it was?' It seemed to help, talking, though she knew she was babbling. She tried to pour the tea, but her hands were shaking so much it spilled, soaking the embroidered tray cloth. Thorion reached out, taking the teapot from her.

'It looks to have been Gwenene, Denoris and Etras,' he said, pouring the tea into the enamel mugs.

'What!? *Wh-what do they want?'* Merewyn felt sick. The three most powerful members of the Dark, here! Though she had an inkling what they might be after, and sorrow for Llewellyn flared in her chest.

Gwion leaned forward, hands loose between his thighs, tension obvious in the lines of his body. Thorion, who was stirring the tea, handed him a mug and he took it, nodding his thanks. A lock of his red hair fell forward and he tucked it behind his ear. 'We don't know, but there has been trouble in Ambeth–'

'We were already checking the Gates,' interjected Meredan, his handsome face serious. 'It was only luck, really, that Thorion was in his chambers when you summoned him. Gwion and I were already in the woods.'

'Wait, what's happened?' Merewyn couldn't take much more of this, her apron crumpled in her sweating hands. If she wasn't worried enough already! She could see that, despite their concern for her, the three of them were under strain, Meredan's normally bright smile subdued, Thorion's eyes sliding to grey and Gwion's jaw tight. So she held her tongue, waiting. Meredan's dark gold eyes met hers as he spoke and she saw a depth of despair in them that unnerved her completely. "It is the Sacred Cup. It has disappeared.'

Merewyn took a step back and collapsed into a chair, her legs unable to hold her.

'What?' She swallowed, feeling sick again.

'Gone. Taken from the Hall sometime yesterday night. How or by whom, we do not know.'

Her hand came to her mouth and she sat back, unable to take it in. The Cup missing, and now Llewellyn. She took in a sharp breath. 'You don't think...'

'Well, we did,' said Gwion, his mouth quirking into a half smile though his grey eyes were serious. 'We wondered when we got your summons, as to whether the human may have been involved somehow. But I checked the Stone Gate when we came through. He came through it, Gwenene and the others as well. But there's no trace of the Cup.'

'Still you came anyway.' She was horrified, her arms wrapped around herself as if for protection.

'Merewyn, we would not leave you here alone and frightened,' said Meredan, his voice gentle. 'When Thorion told us, it was the only thing to do. So come now, do not worry. Tell us more about this situation.'

'Right.' Merewyn took another breath, unfolding her arms and smoothing her skirt over her knees as she collected her thoughts as best she could. Her voice was shaking and she coughed a couple of times before she started, still coming to terms with her shock. Finally she managed to get it together. 'I went to Llewellyn's house this mornin', like I normally do, except the place was ransacked. His study is all in a mess and, now that I think of it, there was a lot missin' from the kitchen. That explains it,' she said, nodding to herself. 'And so I was tidyin' up, wonderin' what to do, when I felt them come through, and that they were Dark. And, I guess, I sort of panicked. I'm sorry, I really am.' She felt terrible about pulling them out of Ambeth at such a desperate time, her mouth twisting. But Thorion simply smiled at her. Dear Thorion, she thought, managing a faint smile in return, always the gentleman.

'There is no need for apologies. Something is going on here, and you were right to call me,' he said. 'Tell me, have you any idea why all three of them would come across?'

She made a face. 'Gwenene has been comin' here for a while, as you know. I've made sure to keep out of her way, but I know she's always come alone.'

'Wise of you to stay away,' smiled Gwion, taking another gulp of tea. 'She's possibly more dangerous than any of them.'

'Do you think?' Meredan raised his eyebrows.

'Oh yes.' Gwion's hair gleamed red gold in the morning light as he sat back. 'For she has Denoris' heart—'

'He has a heart?' Meredan scoffed. Thorion and Gwion chuckled.

'*Yes, for what it's worth. She has a hold over him like no other, and he's already dangerous. Add to that her intelligence and you have someone to be reckoned with. There is no-one in Ambeth who can influence him like she can.*'

'This is all very well,' said Merewyn, who had still not drunk any of her tea and was starting to panic. '*But right now the three of them are loose in the hills above this town doin' who knows what!*' She looked at Thorion. '*He is human, I know, and has his flaws, but Llewellyn is a good man. If they've come for him...*'

'*So you think they would come for him? Why?*'

Merewyn swallowed. '*Well, d'you think he might have taken the Cup? I mean, I know you've checked the Gates, but maybe he figured out–*'

'*Merewyn, the Stone Gate was clear when we came through, and the Cup disappeared from a locked and guarded Hall. Whoever did such a thing would have powers beyond– well.*' Huffing out a sigh, Thorion looked down.

Gwion nodded. '*Whatever they want him for, Merewyn, it can't possibly be that. So, jealousy, d'you think?*'

'*About Gwenene? I mean, she's definitely with him, I've heard them.*' Merewyn wrinkled her nose and Gwion grinned, glancing at Meredan. '*So maybe?*'

Meredan nodded. '*Sounds like Denoris. He doesn't like to share, and I've been surprised he's put up with it for so long. Tell me, does Llewellyn have somewhere to go?*' He leaned forward, dark eyes intent on her.

'*Yes,*' she said. '*He has a place in the hills, a small cottage. I don't know why he'd go there, but it does seem to make sense, that they would be here and he would be gone.*'

She sat back, completely overwhelmed. First Llewellyn going missing, then the Dark coming through and now the Cup gone too. Tears started in her eyes and she sniffed, wiping her face with shaking hands. Gwion got to his feet, tall in the small room. He came to kneel in front of her, grey eyes soft with sympathy. '*May I?*' He took her cold hand in his own and she nodded, feeling shy. He began massaging her skin and her fears eased, her *worry smoothing out as he worked his magic. After a few moments she took in a long breath, then blew it out.*

'Thank you,' she said, feeling better. 'I needed that.'

He smiled, patting her hand gently. 'So, what would you suggest, Merewyn? Where shall we go to find him?'

She looked around at them all, her energy restored. Now she could finally think straight. 'Perhaps,' she said, 'it might be best if some of us went to Llewellyn's house, in case he comes back.'

'And I'll track him to the hills,' said Meredan. 'I can do so without being seen – at least then we'll know what they're up to.'

'Would you like help?'

'I work alone,' he said, a flash of white teeth as he grinned at Gwion, who had asked the question. 'Right.' He stretched, muscled arms gleaming, crimson armour a spot of brightness in the small room. 'I'd better go soon – the town will be waking and I'll, er, probably stand out a bit.'

'Probably,' said Merewyn, raising an eyebrow. Gwion and Thorion laughed. Meredan got to his feet, coming over to Merewyn. She stood up and he took her hands in his.

'I will find him, I promise,' he said, amber eyes agleam in his dark face.

She nodded, squeezing his hands. 'Thank you.' He kissed her on the cheek, surprising her, then left the room. She heard the door close as he left the house.

'So,' she turned to Gwion and Thorion. 'Shall we go?'

'We shall,' said Gwion, reaching for his mug once more. 'Once I have finished this lovely cup of tea.' He smiled at her and drained the mug, leaving it on the small tray as he got to his feet. Thorion said nothing, but came to put an arm around Merewyn. She clung to him, needing his strength.

'Come on,' he said, eyes gleaming blue. 'Let's go.'

The sun was coming up as they left the house, a faint mist of dew on the garden. Herbs lined either side of Merewyn's small pathway, rosemary and mint scenting the morning air. She led them through deserted streets, the town still waking up. As they neared Llewellyn's house a young man came out through the gate. He was moving strangely, staggering and weaving as though drunk. Merewyn squinted, shading her eyes against the morning sunlight.

'Douglas?' He turned and the colour drained from his face, his mouth opening wide. He screamed and started to run, his legs tangling so he tripped, banging into fences and scrabbling as he made his way as fast as he could up the street. Merewyn, who had started to run towards him stopped, mystified. 'Douglas! Douglas!' she called again, but he was gone, lurching into an alleyway and disappearing between the houses. She turned to Thorion. 'I don't understand.'

'I do,' said Gwion, his gaze stern as he looked up the street. 'I would hazard a guess we are not the first people in armour he has seen today.'

Merewyn's eyes widened. 'Oh no...' She took off, running through the little gate and around the side of the house, Thorion and Gwion following behind.

~

'LLEWELLYN.'

The call came from outside, a silvery voice on the wind. Llewellyn stopped writing and lifted his head, unsure what he was hearing. The call came again, louder, and his heart sang in response.

She was here.

He ran to the door, unbarring it and flinging it wide. Gwenene was standing in the small yard, hair blowing like a dark banner in the wind, her blue dress, blue as her eyes, rippling around her. He smiled, holding out his arms, but she shook her head, and for a moment he thought he glimpsed pity on her face. Then the other two were on him, their hands hard on his arms, their eyes dagger sharp as they pushed him back through the door and into the cottage. Slamming him down into a wooden chair, the dark bearded one grabbed his arms and pulled them behind the chair, holding them tight so he couldn't move, no matter how he tried. The other one, the blond one, came to lean over him, but it was around him that Llewellyn looked. Gwenene came through the door and perched on the deep windowsill, the morning light shimmering around her so she seemed a mirage of impossible beauty.

'Oh, Llewellyn,' she said softly, shaking her head once more. 'What have you done?'

A rough hand took his chin, turning his head so he could no longer see her, instead forced to look at blazing green eyes in a fiercely handsome face. Denoris.

'She has asked me to show you mercy, human,' hissed the Dark Lord.

Llewellyn groaned in pain as the one holding him twisted his arms, his head going back.

'Oh, Denoris, just take the book and get on with it,' he heard Gwenene say as, unbelieving, he saw Denoris draw a dagger from his waist.

'No! No!' He started to struggle, shrieking in agony as the bearded one applied more pressure, his arms feeling as though they were being pulled from their sockets. He felt Denoris open his shirt, the cold point of the blade being placed against his chest and he screamed again.

'Gwenene, I beg you, please!' he sobbed. "I'm sorry, I'm sorry, just take the book and go!' He could see her once more, sitting on the windowsill examining her nails. She looked up, seeming almost surprised. Denoris looked over at her as though waiting for her permission. She shrugged, and Llewellyn's heart broke.

'No, I love—' But his cries were cut off, becoming a gurgle as the blade sank into his chest, Denoris driving it home with a snarl. His vision started to dim and he was vaguely aware of his arms being released, the three of them moving away from him, the bearded one picking up the book from the table. Then death came, and with it release from the betrayal in his heart.

❧

*G*WENENE *STOOD OUTSIDE WITH HER ARMS WRAPPED AROUND herself, looking back at the cottage. She thought of Llewellyn's whiskey brown eyes, of how he had loved her. Denoris came to her, smiling his wolf smile as he smoothed the hair back from her face, kissing her hard as she* *pressed herself against him. Etras laughed loudly, clapping Denoris on the back as he walked off, heading towards the distant Gate. Denoris finished kissing Gwenene, looking her deep in the eyes before releasing her.*

'Let us go home, my Lady.' He took her hand, morning sun shining on the strong contours of his face. 'For all is well in my world once more.'

CHAPTER 18

DEATH AND PEACHES

Meredan came slowly up the rise, careful to choose an angle from which he would be unseen. Treading lightly on the grassy slope he approached the small cottage. It seemed deserted, a strong smell of burning food on the wind, but he moved with caution, looking around as he crossed the paved yard, testing the air. Gwenene, Denoris and Etras would not dare to challenge him, but he had no wish to surprise them if he could help it. Reaching the front door he pushed on it gently. It opened to reveal Llewellyn, so obviously past help, lying sprawled in a chair with the hilt of a knife protruding from his chest. Meredan's heart twisted in sorrow. He went inside, carefully stepping around Llewellyn's legs to check the pulse at his neck, but there was nothing he could do.

'Ah, my friend, I'm sorry we did not get here sooner.'

Whispering a short prayer he gently closed the staring eyes and removed the dagger, releasing a small flow of blood. Llewellyn's body was just starting to cool – whoever killed him had not been gone long, and Meredan shook his head as he examined the dagger, its workmanship obviously of Ambeth. Wiping it carefully he tucked it in his pocket before taking a look around the cottage. It was almost bare, no pictures on the pale stone walls, a chair and table the only furniture apart from the ubiquitous Welsh dresser, blackened with age and smoke from the fire, holding a few dishes and a jug filled with water. Taking the jug Meredan tipped the contents on the fire and into the stew pot, which had almost burnt dry. The smoke made him cough, but at least it was out and he opened the door further to let in fresh air before moving into the small bedroom. There was a single mattress on an iron frame, a couple of blankets hastily pulled up to cover the small pillow. Otherwise the room was empty, except for a photograph pinned to the wall next to the bed. Torn from a newspaper, it showed Llewellyn and Gwenene, dressed in their best at a local dance. Meredan paused, taking in Gwenene's shapely figure, the slender legs revealed by the short skirt, the adoring look on Davies' face. She was beautiful, anyone could see that, but how was it that the man hadn't known what kind of person she was? Meredan shook his head, sighing. He checked behind the wooden door, where a couple of hooks held Davies' meagre wardrobe, then went back into the other room. Walking past the table he paused, picking up the small pile of scrawled notes. He left, breathing the clean air with relief as he headed down the hill towards the town.

*G*WION SAT BEHIND *L*LEWELLYN'S DESK, READING THE PROFESSOR'S *notes, frustrated by the random scramble of thoughts. There was something deeper here, he could feel it, a twisting in the energy of the small town. If only Galen were here they could track it to the source. But Galen was gone to the Seers colony and all Gwion had was a handful of nonsense about Gwenene – he threw it down in disgust, tired of reading about her 'white skin and jewelled eyes'. Honestly. Merewyn, busy tidying the spilled contents of the bookshelf, looked over with eyebrows raised. He smiled, wanting to put her at ease.*

'Nothing here, really. Do you know what he was working on?'

"He was an expert on the local Castle, I know that. Made a presentation a couple of years back, that it had been built by fairies or some such. Got laughed out of the university, as you can imagine.'

'Shame, since he was correct, I suppose, in one sense of the word.' Merewyn's mouth dropped open. Thorion, sitting on the windowsill

leafing through a notebook, looked up, smiling. 'It was built by one of us, and there are many who would think of us that way.'

'Ah, yes, Lord Iorweth, wasn't it?' Gwion grinned, glad of the diversion. He shuffled the notes into a pile, placing them in a large empty file box he had marked with the seal of the Light. 'I remember Father talking about coming here, a long time ago.'

'Ah, so he was right?' Merewyn was astonished. 'Ah, the poor man. He's never been the same you know, since they dismissed his findin's. I think it was what put him on this path.'

'It sounds as though Gwenene was fairly persuasive as well,' Gwion grinned. 'Such bad luck to have encountered her first when he crossed over.'

'Would he see it that way?' said Thorion. 'For all her other, ahem, qualities, she is beautiful.'

'Beauty is as beauty does,' said Merewyn firmly, her mouth set as she turned to put another pile of books into the bookcase. Gwion chuckled.

'Truer word was never spoken, Merewyn. And I can think of several who embody that quality.'

'The Lady Adara?' Thorion gave him a look. Gwion leaned back in his chair, hands behind his head.

'She is one,' he said, stretching slightly. 'If only she would notice me.' He sighed noisily.

Thorion laughed out loud. 'I will mention your interest to her, next time we speak. Perhaps I can put in a good word?' He waggled his eyebrows and Gwion grinned, pleased to see he'd got the message across. If anyone could convince Adara to look twice at him, it would be Thorion. He nodded.

'It would be much appreciated, my friend.'

Merewyn dropped the pile of books she was holding with a crash. 'This all very well,' she said, tears obvious in her eyes, 'but poor Llewellyn is still out there and who knows—' She choked up, turning away and rubbing her eyes with the heel of her hand as she bent to pick up the books she'd dropped. Gwion stopped laughing, feeling guilty. He started to his feet, but Thorion was there first, pulling Merewyn into a hug, her slight frame shaking against him.

'There is nothing more we can do at the moment. I know you are worried.'

Gwion went to Merewyn and put his hand on her shoulder. He could feel her energy was jumping and jagged and felt even worse about his moment of banter, not realising how distressed she was.

There was the sound of the front door opening and closing, footsteps in the hallway. Gwion went towards the study door, hand to his sword. It opened to reveal Meredan. Gwion heard Merewyn, who was hiding behind Thorion, heave a sigh of relief. He relaxed as well, his hand leaving the hilt of his weapon.

'Did you find him?' asked Merewyn, coming out from behind Thorion with her hands clasped. 'Is he all right?'

Meredan shook his head, his face drawn with sorrow. 'I'm sorry. I did find him but too late to help.'

'They killed him?' Fury surged through Gwion. This was all they needed, a mess in the human world with the Cup missing in Ambeth.

Meredan nodded. 'They did. At least, there's no doubt his killer was of Ambeth, so it can only have been them. I removed the blade myself. Here.' He handed it to Thorion who examined it a moment before giving it to Gwion.

Gwion wrapped his hand around the hilt and took a deep breath, his eyes closing as he felt for the energy attached to the blade. He snapped back to reality, trying to keep a lid on his anger. 'Denoris.'

Thorion bowed his head and Meredan reached out to a weeping Merewyn, holding her close. 'I'm sorry,' he murmured as she clung to him, sobbing loudly. After a moment she lifted her head, wiping her eyes.

'No, it-it's all right,' she whispered. 'It's just, he wasn't a bad man, you know? It's a shame, he had to go that way.' She managed a watery smile as Meredan released her and Gwion reached out to touch her shoulder, his heart twisting with sorrow. 'Thank you for findin' him, anyway.' She tilted her head as though hearing a distant sound.

'What is it, Merewyn?' said Thorion.

Gwion answered, feeling the pull of the Gate. 'They've crossed back. I just felt it, the energy from the Gate. You have it marked, don't you?' He *kept his voice gentle, seeing how very unsettled she still was, the sun shining on her blonde hair, her small slender stature adding to the impression of fragility as she struggled for words.*

'Yes. I thought it best, just in case. So I know, um, knew when she was comin'.'

Thorion nodded. 'That was well planned, Merewyn.' He paused, and Gwion knew what he was going to say. They needed to go. 'I think it may be time for us to leave as well. With things as they are in Ambeth we cannot take the chance of our absence being noted. Will you be all right?'

Merewyn gulped a bit, then nodded. 'I'll be fine.'

'But first,' Gwion put his arm around her and sent a soft pulse of calming energy through her as he did so, 'would you be so kind as to make us another one of those splendid cups of tea?' He winked at her and she laughed, shakily.

'Of course,' she said, colour starting to return to her face. She hurried off in the direction of the kitchen. Gwion watched her go. He was worried about her, as well as frustrated that they were here, cleaning up another of the Dark's messes when there was so much to be done in Ambeth. Still, it wasn't Merewyn's fault. Thorion came up beside him, putting his hand on his shoulder.

'That was kind of you,' he said, eyes midway between blue and grey.

'Well, she needed something to take her mind off it all. It's been a shock to her, anyone can see that. I've tried to calm her, but I don't want to push her. What the hell was Denoris thinking?!'

'Perhaps we should take her back with us,' rumbled Meredan, but Thorion shook his head. They could hear Merewyn moving about in her kitchen, the rattle of cups and saucers as she prepared the tea.

'She prefers it here,' he said. 'And I think it best. If she and Llewellyn disappear at the same time she would be under suspicion. No, I think we need to make sure she is taken care of, that she has an alibi. It is important that she stays here, you all know why.'

Meredan nodded. 'And it's important we get back, as well. At least we know Davies didn't take the Cup.'

Gwion rubbed his hand over his face, feeling weary. 'But then, who did?'

～

GWENENE PICKED UP A SMALL SILVER BELL FROM THE TABLE AND shook it, the chimes ringing out across her sitting room. Outside the sun was setting, golden light glinting off the flagon and three goblets on the table, shining on the soft velvet of the sofa. She knew Denoris was watching her, could feel the warmth of his gaze. She leaned forward to put the bell down, silk sleeves sliding on her arms. A young woman appeared in the doorway, her head bowed.

'More wine, Loren.' Gwenene motioned to the jug on the table. The young woman came to take it, bobbing a curtsey and managing to sidestep Etras' hand at the same time, which was no mean feat.

Denoris, in a rare good mood, laughed out loud as she left the room. 'She has your measure,' he grinned, looking at Etras. 'A valiant effort, but I do not think you will prevail in this instance.'

Etras laughed as well. 'Is that so?' He drained his glass and got to his feet. 'Well, let's see how well she evades me in that narrow hallway of yours, Gwenene.' He swayed slightly, giving her a lecherous wink before moving towards the door.

'Oh, Etras, let her bring the wine at least,' called Gwenene as he left the room, but it was too late. There was a gasp and squeal from the hallway, followed by the crash of the jug dropping. They heard Etras laugh, then grunt, and another scream from the maid. Gwenene raised an eyebrow, reaching to pick up a peach from the bowl on the table, soft skinned blush in her hand echoing the colours of the sky outside. Denoris reached to take it from her and she looked at him questioningly. He went to his belt for his knife, then snorted.

'What is it?'

'My knife. It appears I left it in your– in the human realm,' said Denoris. 'Shame. It was a fine blade.'

'I will get you another.' She took the peach back from him and bit into *it, juice dripping down her chin. Denoris leaned in to kiss her, licking the sweet juice from her skin as she slid down beneath him, the half-eaten peach dropping to the rug.*

'At last I have you to myself,' he said, growling a little in his throat as her arms came around his neck, the sweet scent of peaches filling the air.

'So, what shall we do now?' She laughed and he kissed her, hard, his hands moving on her possessively as she held onto him.

'Tell me again.' He lifted his head, holding her beneath him so she couldn't move. She knew what he wanted.

'I am yours,' she whispered, gazing back at him. 'Always.'

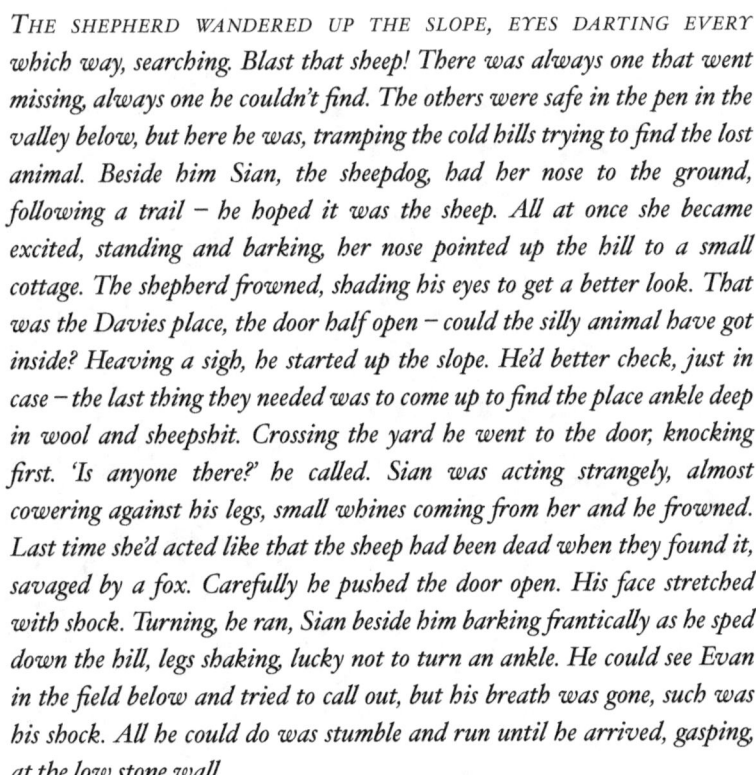

THE SHEPHERD WANDERED UP THE SLOPE, EYES DARTING EVERY *which way, searching. Blast that sheep! There was always one that went missing, always one he couldn't find. The others were safe in the pen in the valley below, but here he was, tramping the cold hills trying to find the lost animal. Beside him Sian, the sheepdog, had her nose to the ground, following a trail – he hoped it was the sheep. All at once she became excited, standing and barking, her nose pointed up the hill to a small cottage. The shepherd frowned, shading his eyes to get a better look. That was the Davies place, the door half open – could the silly animal have got inside? Heaving a sigh, he started up the slope. He'd better check, just in case – the last thing they needed was to come up to find the place ankle deep in wool and sheepshit. Crossing the yard he went to the door, knocking first. 'Is anyone there?' he called. Sian was acting strangely, almost cowering against his legs, small whines coming from her and he frowned. Last time she'd acted like that the sheep had been dead when they found it, savaged by a fox. Carefully he pushed the door open. His face stretched with shock. Turning, he ran, Sian beside him barking frantically as he sped down the hill, legs shaking, lucky not to turn an ankle. He could see Evan in the field below and tried to call out, but his breath was gone, such was his shock. All he could do was stumble and run until he arrived, gasping, at the low stone wall.*

'Up... up there,' he managed, pointing back up the hill to the cottage. 'Get the police.' He leaned over, his hands on his thighs as he tried to get his breath back. Evan stared at him and he straightened up, leaning one hand on the wall for support. 'Go, now!' he said, his voice getting louder. Evan turned and ran, grabbing his bike from where it leant against the wall, riding off at pace. Watching him go, the shepherd sat down on the wall, faithful Sian coming to sit next to him and resting her soft head on his leg. Absentmindedly he played with her silky ears as he looked up the hill to the cottage, the open door now seeming like a mouth, ready to devour all who came near.

CHAPTER 19
HUNTER

North Wales – Present Day

MEREWYN STRETCHED, UNCURLING HER LEGS AND GETTING TO her feet, feeling the blood coming back to her limbs. She was light-headed, but knew she was ready, her energy linked to that of this place. Hopefully it would be enough. There were a few people about as she made her way back down the winding path. She stopped in the small gift shop and bought a packet of fudge, the sugar restoring her depleted energy. Feeling more like herself, she headed for home, stopping to buy milk along the way. Once on her sofa, tea in hand, she reached for her phone.

R u ready now? I'll come and get u if u r. I have something planned.

The reply pinged back almost straight away. A single word.

Yes.

Merewyn finished her tea and stood up. Picking up her keys, she headed out once more.

THE DOORBELL RANG AND ALMA RAN TO OPEN IT. MEREWYN stood there, hands tucked into her pockets, her feet twisting awkwardly. 'Hey.'

'Hey.' Alma grinned.

Merewyn smiled as well, visibly relaxing. Her spiky blonde hair gleamed in the afternoon sun, the sky clear blue above. 'Are you ready?'

Alma nodded. She wasn't ready, but knew they needed to do something. She really hoped this was going to work, though she hadn't the faintest idea how to start. Still, she thought, it hadn't stopped her before.

'Bye, Gran!' she called, an answering shout coming from the back of the house before she closed the door and turned to Merewyn. 'I'm ready,' she said, slinging her bag over her shoulder. 'Let's go.' She went down the steps then stopped, looking around, mystified. 'Oh!' She turned to an increasingly amused Merewyn. 'Where's your car?'

Merewyn laughed. 'Don't panic, lazybones. I parked a short way down the road. Just wanted a bit of fresh air.'

'Right,' said Alma. 'Okay, well, lead on.' She stood aside to let Merewyn go first out the gate onto the footpath.

As they walked to the car a train went past along the seafront below, the mournful sounding horn blast floating on the warm air. Alma just caught a glimpse of the tail end of it as it sped along the coast. She took in a deep breath of sea air. Despite all that had happened and was happening, she finally felt like she was doing the right thing. She got into Merewyn's car and they pulled away, driving along streets lined with grey stone houses, glimpses of blue sea between them, doorways and gardens bright with flowers and hanging baskets. Merewyn took the winding road leading up to the Castle, small cottages along one side with low windows and doors, window boxes full of colour. She pulled in to park just outside Alma's favourite ice cream shop.

'Mmmm.' Alma took an appreciative breath as she got out of

the car, the scent of vanilla, waffles and coffee wafting through the open door. 'Perhaps we could just–?'

Merewyn grabbed her arm, shaking her head, though she was smiling. 'After,' she said, pulling Alma the last few yards to the Castle entrance. 'Let's do this.'

Big glass doors led into the modern visitor centre and inside seemed dim at first after the bright day outside, despite the large windows. A woman stood behind the counter, prices for entry to the Castle printed on the wall behind her. 'Back again?' she said, looking surprised.

'Oh yes, well, there was somethin' I forgot to look at,' said Merewyn, smiling brightly at her. 'And I wanted to show my friend too. So we'd like two more tickets please.'

'Oh no,' said the lady, flapping her hand at them. 'We close in half an hour anyway, and you've already paid once today. No, off you go, enjoy the sunshine.'

'Righto, thank you,' said Merewyn. She headed for another door to the rear of the visitor centre, Alma following behind. The walk up was steep, the path winding around the Castle mound to reveal views along the coast, mountains like layers of shadow receding in the distance, the sea glittering blue below. The beach was dotted with holidaymakers, their towels bright squares of colour against the grey stones. Alma paused near the top to take it all in.

'It doesn't seem that high, when you look at it from below,' she said, slightly out of breath. 'But when you get up here you realise, don't you?'

'You do,' agreed Merewyn. She was also panting, a faint sheen on her skin. She looked tired, Alma realised. The path began to flatten out, curving along the base of the Castle walls and leading them into a large open area. Once the Great Hall, it was now carpeted with grass and daisies, the walls that had defended the seaward side of the mound mostly gone, dense brambles now the only barrier between land and the sea. They came to a stop near the remains of a tower.

'Right,' said Alma, still breathing hard from the climb. 'What are we doing?'

Merewyn leaned one hand on the crumbling stone, wiping her hand across her brow. She looked around.

'Well, there's only a few people still here, it looks like,' she said. 'So that's good.'

Alma was intrigued. 'Why? What do you have planned?'

'Just a sec,' said Merewyn. 'Let's sit down. I want to hear why you wanted to come here.'

'Really?'

Merewyn grinned. 'Just humour me, okay?'

'Um, all right.' She went and sat down on a nearby bench, Merewyn coming to join her.

'So, why did I want to come here? Er...' Now that they were up here actually doing something, sitting on a bench talking seemed like a bit of a waste of time. Still, Merewyn appeared to need the rest. 'Well, for the view, really,' she said, looking out over the sea. 'Imagine living here, looking out at all this every day. You can see why they chose this spot.'

Merewyn grinned. 'You can,' she said, 'though I think there was more to it than just a nice view.'

Alma said nothing. She was beginning to feel increasingly awkward. Their earlier argument still sat between them and she knew she had to say something.

'Um, Merewyn.' She glanced at her. 'I'm sorry. About this morning.' She looked down, her hands twisting in her lap.

Merewyn bumped her gently with her shoulder. 'It's fine,' she said, pixie grin. 'I'm sorry too. I shouldn't have pushed you.'

Alma hunched forward, resting her chin in her hands. 'It's just, sometimes it's all too much, you know? I mean, it's been such a relief, being able to tell you about everything, but it doesn't make the pain go away, or the fear.'

'What are you frightened of?'

Alma took in a breath, then blew it out. 'Everything. I don't know.' She shook her head. 'That he just... showed up! That at any moment he could just, I don't know, appear and drag me back there!'

'D'you think he will?'

Alma thought about it. Around them the wind blew off the sea, the voices of children playing in the ruins echoing across the stones, the quieter rumble of adults talking underneath it all.

'I don't think he would want to,' she said, finally. 'I think it hurt him, that I wouldn't go back to him. But why on earth he would think I would ever...' She broke off, shaking her head. 'So, he won't come back. But his father might.'

'Alma, you know there's still a ban, don't you, on crossin' over? And you aren't just some human for Denoris to take. You are Galen's daughter. Your grandfather would not stand by and let him have you, I can guarantee it, nor would the rest of the Light.' Merewyn sounded earnest, her hazel eyes frowning.

Alma leaned back against the bench. 'There is that, I suppose,' she said. 'So you're saying I shouldn't worry?'

Merewyn was silent for a moment and Alma could see she was choosing her next words carefully. 'I just think,' she said finally, 'we should get this done as soon as we can, then we can sort the rest out. Deal?'

Alma looked Merewyn in the eyes. Fear was still in her, but she knew this was all she was going to get. She also knew Merewyn was right – with who she was, there was no way Denoris could just take her. So many things made sense now. The best thing to do, really, was to just get on with it. She held out her hand and Merewyn, smiling a little, took it. Alma shook it. 'Deal.'

~

ARTOS CLIMBED THE GREEN SLOPE TOWARDS THE GATE. HIS shoulders sagged and he stopped. He needed a minute. Sitting down heavily, he took in one deep breath after another, trying to control his anguish. All at once it was too much for him and he started crying, an iron ache in his chest. He covered his face with both hands and shook, his frustration and fear getting the better of him. If only he had thought this through! But he hadn't, and so here he was, alone in the hills and Alma at the mercy of the Dark.

After a few minutes he regained control, wiping his face. This would do no good to anyone, him sitting and crying like a child. He sighed, unable to shake the feeling of failure as he looked across the small town, wondering where Alma was. There had been no answer at the door, nor at Merewyn's small cottage, when he'd gone there afterwards. Defeated, he'd eventually headed back to the hills, knowing he couldn't wander around forever trying to find her. He needed to go back and do what he should have done before – contact Merewyn and let her know of the threat, then arrange to come through. Damn Denoris and his schemes! Now he had forced Artos into rash behaviour, and precious time had been lost. He got to his feet. It was his own fault. He knew that. He shouldn't have let Denoris needle him so. But he had lost both his sons and was an old man – he could hardly be blamed for wanting to protect the family he had left.

He felt a hand hard on his shoulder, then a sting in his ribs. He gasped in a breath, suddenly finding it hard to exhale.

'Wha–'

He heard a laugh, then. A voice spoke, one he had not heard in many years, nor had thought to ever hear again.

'Well met, King Artos.' The tone was mocking and Artos twisted away, the pain in his side making him groan. But it was nothing to the terror in his heart as he realised who was here. And who he had been sent to find.

More laughter. 'What, have you no greeting for me? I am no exile here.'

'You—'

'I– What, old man? Speak up.' Artos felt a shove and fell to his knees. Looking up he saw the tall bearded figure of Etras, a dark silhouette against the sun. Something glinted in his hand – it was a knife, Artos realised. Stained with blood. His blood.

He pushed himself back to kneeling and tried to stand, but he had no breath, no strength, hot wetness against his side. 'Do not touch her,' he managed to gasp. 'I command you—'

'You are King no longer. You have no standing here. And I,' Etras looked around, his handsome face twisting, 'I have no standing anywhere. So, what do I have to lose?'

Unable to hold himself up any longer, Artos fell forward. Etras came close, kicking him viciously in his injured side, pain like an explosion of white light. Artos screamed. Through blurred eyes he saw Etras continue on down the hill towards the town, towards Alma. He screamed again. But there was no one to hear but the sheep.

CHAPTER 20
TIMESHIFT

'Okay,' said Merewyn. 'Let's get started.' Then she stiffened, a cold feeling running through her. Someone had just come through the Stone Gate, and they were Dark. She carefully kept her face blank, trying to hide her fear from Alma. They needed to act fast. Blowing out a breath, trying to seem nonchalant, she carried on. 'We are goin' to sit and just concentrate for a minute,' she nodded at Alma, 'and then we'll see.'

Alma frowned and Merewyn held her breath, trying to still her energy, knowing Alma could see it if she chose, pick up on her agitation. It took all her will to calm down. The Stone Gate was almost an hour's walk away, so it gave them a little time at least. 'Come on.' She grinned, pushing Alma gently on the shoulder. 'What are you worried about? Nothin' can harm you, not here, I promise.'

Alma shook her head as though clearing it. 'Fine. Yep. Let's do it. Though I've no idea what you want me to do.' She tucked her red hair behind her ears, looking expectantly at Merewyn. Despite her worry, Merewyn found it hard not to smile. Alma was so like her father! She closed her eyes, trying to connect with the energy again, to make the magic work. Time-shifting was her gift, and she wanted to make sure she did it properly this time.

~

'GOOD MORNING, MY LADY.'

Rozelle nodded to the groom. 'Have you seen Lord Denoris this morning?'

The groom shook his head. 'No, my Lady. They did return late last night though, him and the Lady Gwenene.'

Rozelle bit her lip, trying not to cry. So he was back already. She was surprised she'd made it through the night. Intercepting a sympathetic glance from the groom she frowned, drawing herself up tall.

'Thank you. My horse, if you will.'

'But, my Lady, I'm not sure if she—'

'My horse!' She glared at him and he backed away.

'Of course.' He nodded, leaving.

Rozelle let out a breath, smoothing her hands down her skirt. She needed to hold herself together for long enough to get away. She'd ridden out after Denoris and Gwenene last night, until the hills got too dark to see. Unable to find them she'd returned and spent the night pacing her room, weighing up her options. They were few. She had failed Denoris, so she could either beg for mercy, or disappear for a while. She shuddered, remembering her punishment last time she'd transgressed. Her back still ached at times.

So. Exile it was. Self-imposed, of course. To her family, then out through a Gate she knew, hidden deep in the mountains. Forget the ban on crossing – she valued her life far more.

The groom returned with her horse and she nodded, mounting. Pale morning light gilded the cobbles and stone buildings, the rumpled hair of the groom. She paused, looking around at the stable yard, at the gleaming Palace and green gardens beyond, an ache in her heart. She didn't know when, if ever, she would see it again. But a life in the human world, no matter how lonely, was better than no life at all.

Spurring her horse forward she left, heading for the green line of hills and the towering mountains beyond, blinking against the mist in her eyes.

ALMA WONDERED WHAT WAS GOING ON WITH MEREWYN. SHE'D seen something cross the other girl's face, had felt her energy jump and spin. Now all seemed well again but, if she concentrated, she could see some fuzzy jagged edges to the swirling lines of light running through her. Perhaps she was just nervous about whatever they were going to do. But all Merewyn was doing was sitting still, her eyes closed, hands palm up on her thighs as she breathed deeply, in and out. Alma frowned. Merewyn's eyes snapped open.

'It's time,' she said. 'Take my hand.'

'What?' Feeling silly, Alma took the offered hand.

'Alma.' Merewyn's voice echoed in Alma's brain, as though she was speaking directly into her mind. Alma jumped, and Merewyn squeezed her hand gently. 'Stay focused, Alma. Breathe deeply and, whatever you do, don't let go of my hand.'

Alma nodded. Her heart was pounding, and it took her a moment to settle her breathing. The Castle began to grow around them, walls rebuilding themselves, the history of the ancient mound rewinding back through time. There was fire and battle, then the Castle became as new, plasterwork on the walls gleaming and fresh, roof timbers strong above them, the Great Hall standing once more. Alma gasped and sat back, her eyes wide, trying to hold it together. Again she heard Merewyn in her mind.

'This is the Castle as it was, Alma, when it was built for Iorweth, Lord of Light. I am tryin' to take us to a Feast Day.'

Figures appeared, moving quickly, blurred and somehow insub-stantial, their clothing changing with the light around them as Merewyn flicked through the days. Alma was fascinated and terri-fied at the same time, having to remind herself to breathe, to stay in the moment. The images came quickly; a woman with a large jug, a stonemason carving an ornate moulding. A woman in a long gown, crying, children running and laughing, men in mail with weapons glittering, all passing like a kaleidoscope before her eyes. The images started to slow, the clothing changing again to smooth cuts in fine fabrics and Alma recognised the attire as that of Ambeth. Candles in wall sconces bloomed with fire, a large central lantern hanging just like the ones in the Great Hall of Ambeth, green garlands appearing on the white plastered walls and twined around the dark beams above. The room filled with people, long tables appearing with benches either side, covered with cloth and laden with platters overflowing with food, servants with jugs of wine moving through the crowd. It was so like a gath-ering in Ambeth that Alma felt tears prickle at her eyes.

'We are here,' said Merewyn in her mind. 'Midwinter. And look, there is Iorweth.'

A man came through the arched stone doorway at one end of the Hall. Richly attired in an embroidered tunic belted over breeches and boots, he was tall and handsome, his long chestnut hair tied back from his smooth chiselled face, his eyes clear brown and smiling. And next to him...

Alma started in her seat and Merewyn held her hand tightly. 'Alma, don't move.' Alma heard the words in her head and tried to calm herself. But it was *her mother* walking next to Iorweth. Same dark hair, same blue eyes, same petite frame, though in this instance she was heavily pregnant, one hand curved under the swelling belly stretching the soft green wool of her gown. A silver bracelet with a green stone hung from her wrist, sparkling in the soft light. Her other hand was linked with Iorweth's, his gentle smile and loving attention making it clear who the father was.

Merewyn! She thought it, not wanting to speak in case she broke the spell but needing to say *something*. She felt the other girl squeeze her hand again.

'I can hear you, Alma. It's not your mother, but another Eleanor, a direct ancestor. She was consort to Iorweth till she died, and he loved her well. She bore him several children, some settlin' here, others in Ambeth. So you see, there's another link in your family to Ambeth, just as I told you.'

Alma blew out a breath. For a moment it was all too much and she wanted to let go of Merewyn's hand and run as fast as she could from this place with all its revelations. But instead she held on, watching the woman who looked like her mother moving around the Hall on Iorweth's arm, talking to the assembled guests, smiling and laughing.

'Okay, hold on while I take us forward,' said Merewyn in her head, and the party sped up again, Merewyn stopping things as Iorweth moved to address the crowd.

'I wish you all a good Midwinter,' he said, his voice ringing out in the Hall, 'with a prosperous year to come.' He raised his glass and the crowd roared their approval. 'And to my Lady Eleanor' he turned to smile at her '-I cannot wish you beauty, for you have that in abundance, and I shall not wish you love, for you know you already hold my heart.' Eleanor smiled at him, blushing pink, her dark hair waving around her face. 'So, I wish only that you are well, my beloved, and that the New Year will bring our child to us safely.' He raised his glass once more, as did the crowd. 'To Lady Eleanor!' he shouted. 'To Lady Eleanor!' the crowd roared back, the sound echoing in the rafters as Iorweth went to kiss his love, her hand coming up to wipe her tears, smiling.

Oh! thought Alma, her own eyes tearing up.

'Hold on, Alma, stay focused,' said Merewyn. 'I need to move forward once more, I think.' The party flickered then the Hall went dark, the crowd disappearing, the long tables now holding the scattered remains of the feast. A groan was heard and the timber door swung open to reveal Iorweth and Eleanor, though this time she was bent over, one hand to her side as she hung on to Iorweth who had his arm around her, his expression concerned.

'Come, my love,' they heard him say. 'Let us go to Ambeth, to have the child there. Our healers will take you through this safely, I promise.' He gently guided her across the room to where a door was set deep into the thickest part of the wall. Merewyn squeezed Alma's hand.

'This is it.'

Eleanor groaned again, her knees buckling so she staggered. Iorweth took her to one of the benches, helping her to sit down. 'Just a few minutes more, my love. Let me open the door and then we can go.' Making sure she was comfortable he returned to the doorway but, instead of going through, turned to face the thickness of the wall. He touched a stone about halfway down, pressing hard, and both Alma and Merewyn gasped as an opening appeared in the stone, large enough for a man to pass through. Iorweth came back to Eleanor, helping her to her feet and supporting her as they passed through the opening. They disappeared, the stone wall returning to its original appearance.

'Alma, did you see that?'

I did, she thought back, turning her head slightly.

'Okay, I'm going to move us forward again. I'll do it as quickly as I can, but you need to hold on 'til I'm finished.'

Once again images flickered around them as the Castle moved through time, siege and fire and eventual destruction taking their toll until the Castle appeared as it was in the present. Merewyn let out a long shaking breath and released Alma's hand, flexing her fingers, which looked white and pinched. Alma's hand was numb and she rubbed at it, wincing at the pins and needles as her circulation returned. She felt strange, dizzy, the sort of feeling she got if she slept too long in the middle of the day, a heavy disoriented sensation.

'Um, that was...' She trailed off, not really sure what she

thought. Merewyn nodded, putting a hand to her head and squinting as though she had a headache. The sun was still shining above them, the same few tourists wandering through the Gatehouse and around the walls. Alma looked around slowly, trying to orient herself in the present. Such a fascinating history; no wonder Davies had been so interested in the Castle.

Merewyn. She thought it at first, then realised the other girl couldn't hear her any more. Oops. 'Merewyn,' she tried again, speaking aloud this time.

'Hmm?' Merewyn was leaning forward, elbows on her thighs as she massaged her temples.

'How come you took us back so far? How come you didn't just take us to when Llewellyn was here?'

Merewyn turned her head. She looked terrible, pale and drawn. Alma looked for her energy patterns and was surprised to see how depleted they were, shining only faintly. 'Oh, Merewyn,' she said. 'Give me your hand again.'

The other girl held out her hand, wincing slightly as Alma took it in both of hers. Rubbing it gently she tried to access her power, feeling the pulse through her feet moving through her and into Merewyn, seeing the other girl's energy starting to shine more brightly. After a few moments Merewyn sat back. Alma let go of her hand.

'Wow, thanks!' Her eyes were sparkling, colour back in her pale cheeks. 'I feel amazin'! You know, your uncle could do that, did it for me once, a long time ago.'

'Well, I'm glad I could do something.' Alma grinned.

'Now, in answer to your question, well, Llewellyn spent so much time here it would have taken us much longer to get to the point where he found the doorway into the mound. We don't even know if we found the door, you know? But it seemed to me that Iorweth chose this mound for a reason, and so he would know where the Gate was if anyone did. And a Feast Day seemed to make sense.' Alma nodded. 'Plus, I wanted you to know about your family, so that's why we went back to Iorweth. Once I found out he built the Castle, I researched them in the Great Library, and that's when I found out about Eleanor as well.'

Alma looked out to sea. So her ancestors had lived here. Well, that was amazing and weird and almost too much to think about all at the same time. She shook her head. She was going to have a *lot* to think about later, she knew that, but for now they needed to act.

ARTOS WAS FADING. THE WET PATCH ON HIS SIDE WAS BIGGER, his pain abating as the world grew dim. He knew he had to get back through the Gate and find help. Placing his hand flat on the green grass he closed his eyes, concentrating. He had only a fraction of his sons' powers, but hoped it would be enough.

A faint pulse came through the palm of his hand. Then another. His breath faltered and he lost it, grimacing. He tried again, waiting for the pulse, riding it, like a heartbeat from the depths of the earth. He focused as best he was able, trying to send the energy to the wound in his side, using the last of his strength to do so. His pain increased, the sharpness of it clearing his muddled senses, the pulsing in his hand growing slightly stronger. He closed his eyes, gritting his teeth, feeling his skin crawl and tingle as it knitted together.

Panting, he collapsed back. The wound would hold, for now. Hopefully it was enough to get him through the Gate.

Pushing against the ground he managed to get to his knees, then to his feet, staggering the few steps up the hill to the Gate. He leaned on the great stones, breathing hard, the air humming around him. With the last of his strength he pushed against the stone, felt the crackling flash of energy as he crossed through.

Then everything went black.

~

ETRAS WALKED ALONG THE ROAD LEADING TO THE TOWN, remembering when he'd last been there, all those years before. A fine lark, that had been, and thanks to Denoris - now he could thank him for another adventure. As he reached the town outskirts a car roared past, honking as a young man leaned from the window, screaming something unintelligible. Etras stepped back, trying to hide his shock. He needed to keep focus. Get the girl, bring her back and he would be restored to his rightful status again, no more waiting in the silent hills, surrounded by unwilling humans with all their limitations. He jumped again as another car went by in the opposite direction. Gritting his teeth, he pressed on, checking the coil of rope at his belt, his knife, now cleaned and sheathed, hanging next to it. Another car came up beside him, slowing down as the driver wound down their window.

'Are you goin' to a festival?' asked a lilting voice. Etras turned to see a young woman looking at him with curious eyes, her corn yellow hair in a long braid. There were two more young women in the car with her, also eyeing him. Raising an eyebrow, he moved closer.

'No, I seek a friend.'

'Oh, sorry, it's just, your costume, it's so amazin', I thought, we thought,' she gestured to her friends, 'that there might be somethin' on.'

'Because we're bored,' said the girl in the passenger seat, leaning forward so he could see her soft cleavage, brown against her pink tank top.

'My costume?' Etras looked down at his dark brown leather armour, boots and cape and realised what they meant. Damn. He hadn't thought about it in his haste to get through the Gate. But the women didn't seem worried. He could smell their perfume, sweet and musky, beguiling his senses as he moved closer still.

'Could we be your friends?' The driver smiled and he felt a

familiar stirring in his loins. He tilted his head. A few minutes with them wouldn't hurt. And perhaps they knew the girl, could lead him to her.

'Perhaps.'

The third girl, the one in the back, slid over and opened the car door, slender freckled arm against the dark grey upholstery.

'Hop in,' she said, 'and we'll give you a ride. Where're you headin'?'

'I have no particular destination,' he said, 'but I will happily accept a ride.' He got in the car, armour creaking as he wedged his tall frame into the back seat, the girls all looking at him. The one on the passenger side in the front bent forward, reaching down before turning to offer him a bottle.

'It's cider,' she said, in response to his questioning look. 'Pear flavour.' He nodded approvingly, taking a sip.

'Thank you.' He raised the bottle to her as the car started to move.

'So why are you dressed like that?' The girl next to him slid close, dark curling hair around her freckled face. She ran a hand across his leather breastplate. 'Not that I don't like it or anythin'.' She giggled and he snapped his teeth at her, laughter rumbling in his chest.

'It is what I wear when I hunt.' He put his arm around her as he took another swig from the bottle, enjoying the sweet taste.

'And have you found what you were huntin' for?' she asked, reaching up to steal a kiss, mouth soft against his beard.

'Easy, Carolyn, leave some for the rest of us,' said the girl in the front seat, flashing her eyes at him as he lifted his head.

'Oh, don't worry,' he said, meeting her glance with a scorching one of his own. 'There's plenty of me to go around.'

CHAPTER 21
KEEPING SECRETS

'Deryck, Ellery, well met!'

Ellery, trying to lace her boots, looked up to see her father coming through the front door. He was armour clad as usual, his blond hair damp and pushed back, black cloak billowing behind him. He went over to Deryck and clapped him on the shoulder. Deryck winced, one hand going to his head, but Ellery felt too sick to care.

She stood up from the bench, fastening the ties on her cloak and bobbing a curtsey, wishing her stomach would stop roiling. She and Deryck had stayed up late talking, finishing most of the wine. It had seemed a good idea at the time, but now she was paying the price, her head clanging like a steeple full of bells, acid sickness in her stomach. She knew Deryck wasn't much better, his pale and sweaty face when she'd knocked on his door earlier give-away enough. And now here was their father, beaming at them both. She really didn't need this.

'Deryck, today is a very good day,' said Denoris, rubbing his hands together. Ellery tried not to curl her lip. 'I'll have news for you later that I think will cheer you.'

'Oh really, Father? And what is that?' Ellery saw Deryck swallow, a faint sheen on his brow. She couldn't help him; it was all she could do to keep herself together.

'I can't tell you yet.' Denoris smiled, wagging his finger at his son and Ellery made a face. God, what had got into him? He'd obviously spent the night with Gwenene, a bite on his neck that hadn't been there yesterday just visible above the armour. She felt even more unwell at the thought. If she didn't get out of here soon she was going to disgrace herself.

'Father,' she said faintly, and he turned to her, still smiling.

'Daughter!' He came over and put his hands on her arms, regarding her fondly before leaning in to kiss her cheek. 'You are looking well.'

Really? Ellery had to stop herself raising her eyebrows. Besides, it would hurt too much anyway. 'Th-thank you.'

'And you are wearing your tallus. Good to see. Keep working with it.'

'Oh! Um, right, yes, of course I will.' She looked down at her necklace. Ugh, that was a bad idea, her head spinning even more. Thank darkness she'd remembered to put it on, though it lay outside her dress, not touching her skin.

'Er, Father, we were just going outside.' Deryck walked carefully over to Ellery and took her arm. She could smell the wine on him, knew she must be the same and blenched. Surely their father would notice. But Denoris just nodded, turning towards his study.

'Fine, fine.' He waved a hand in their direction. 'But remember, Deryck, I need you here later, after the Council Meeting. Do not be gone long.'

'Yes, Father.' Deryck tugged Ellery along, both of them emerging into the gardens. Ellery breathed in the fresh air, gulping as she tried to overcome her nausea. Deryck let go of her, his face twisting.

'Remind me not to drink with you for a while.'

Ellery looked at him, outraged. 'Oh really? Can't keep up-urgh.' She turned away, running behind the nearest bush where she vomited. Coughing and spluttering, a moment later she heard Deryck doing the same. Sheepishly she came out from behind the bushes to see him stumble out from behind a tree, wiping his mouth. He caught her eye and grinned, though it was more of a grimace. Staggering over to a nearby bench he sat down, closing his eyes. Ellery went to sit next to him.

'If that was the good stuff,' he murmured, 'I don't know why I feel so terrible.'

'Ugh, don't talk about it,' said Ellery, her hand on her stomach. He opened one green eye to look at her, long legs stretched out in front of him.

'You know, we could use our stones.'

'No! No way.' She put her hand to her head, which was pounding with pain. But there was no way she was touching her stone. Deryck put his hand on her arm – it felt unpleasantly warm, even through the fabric of her dress and she looked down, not wanting him to see how she felt, her fear at the thought of using her necklace. His hand tightened slightly.

'C'mon, Ellery, I'll look after you. It's the only thing that will make us feel better. Otherwise we'll be like this all day.'

At this Ellery paused. She'd planned to visit the jeweller later, had thought the Council Meeting would be the perfect time to go, no need to explain to her father where she was going. But the only place she felt like going at the moment was back to bed. She bit her lip.

'It's just, it takes me over.'

He took her hand. 'I'll be here with you. And it can't be that bad. Look, watch me.' With his other hand he went to his neck, untangling the chain from his hair to pull the stone out. He held it in his hand, closing his eyes and taking a deep breath. Immediately colour came back to his face and he sighed, smiling a little. She felt his hand cool in her own, the clammy heat dissipating as he opened his eyes. His pupils were slightly dilated, but otherwise he seemed restored. 'See? Much better.'

Ellery was unsure. Her head was still ringing, her stomach churning but she was afraid of what the stone did to her. On the other hand, she did want to feel better. Ugh. 'All right,' she said. 'But keep an eye on me, okay?'

Taking a deep breath she touched her tallus stone with the tip of her finger. The effect was instant, intense. She was above her pain, feeling as though a river was rushing through her whole body, clearing away the poison from the night before. She gave herself up to the sensation, floating away in fresh water...

Someone slapped her on the cheek and her eyes flew open. Deryck was leaning over her looking worried, his hand still on her cheek as he said her name over and over. He lifted his hand as though to hit her again and she grabbed at it, shooting him an injured look. Relief washed over his face.

'I'm so sorry,' he said, sitting back. 'It's just, I couldn't wake you.'

'Wait, what?' She rubbed her cheek, the sting already fading as the sensations from her stone flowed through her. 'What do you mean? I only closed my eyes for a second.'

Deryck shook his head. 'You were out for ten minutes. I was shaking you, calling your name. I'm sorry I hit you, but there was nothing else I could do.'

Ellery was aghast. 'It's getting worse,' she whispered. Her hangover was gone, but she was terrified. 'This is why I don't want to use it. It takes me. I don't know why it does it to me, but I don't like it.'

'I don't like it either. Maybe you need to talk to Father about it?' Ellery shot him a look and he snorted. 'Yeah, you're right,' he went on. 'Um, I don't know. I don't think you should use it though, not till we figure out what's going on.'

Ellery nodded, saying nothing. All being well, she would have a fake stone soon – it would be easy enough to pretend, to close her eyes and sigh whenever she touched it. Deryck smiled and put his arm around her, hugging her to him.

'Come on,' he said in response to her surprised look. 'Let's go back inside and get some proper breakfast. You feeling hungry now?'

Ellery thought about it carefully, not sure she was fully recovered. But she actually was hungry. She smiled at her brother.

'Yes, let's go.'

BERAN MADE HIS WAY TO THE KING'S TOWER, WORRY WITHIN him. He started up the familiar stairs, remembering a time when Artos was King and he was young - a newly minted steward, conscious of the honour. Artos had been nothing but kindness to him; despite all the pain and loss he'd suffered he had remained noble. But now he was missing. Beran had arrived early that morning to find the apartments deserted – no Artos, and no Alma. He'd left immediately to find Thorion.

He knocked twice on the heavy oak door. It opened almost immediately, but instead of Edric it was the King himself, resplendent in his council robes, gold around his brow.

'My Lord.' Beran went to bow, but Thorion stopped him, a hand on his arm.

'Peace, Beran. How are things? I trust Artos made it back– What is it?' Thorion's smile faded, his eyes sliding towards grey.

'My Lord, he has not returned. And I am worried. Forgive me, I had forgotten about the meeting. Perhaps I should go–'

'Go to the Gate. And let the guards know. Do it now.' The King's handsome face was stern and Beran nodded.

'My Lord. Thank you.'

'And let me know when you return,' Thorion called after him, his voice echoing down the stairs.

Beran nodded, picking up the pace. He paused in the Foyer. There were already a few Elders there, both Dark and Light, waiting to enter the Hall. He needed to be discreet. Tamping down the urgency in him, he went to one of the guards by the door. Taking him to one side, he spoke quietly. 'I am going to the Stone Gate, on the King's orders.'

The guard's eyes widened and he tilted his head slightly. Beran held his breath. He needed no scenes. After a moment, the guard nodded.

'I will let the Captain know, sir. Will you need assistance? I can call for someone.'

Beran shook his head. 'There's no time. I must go now. If someone could meet us–' He stopped, realising he had given something away. 'Please, be ready.'

The guard inclined his head. 'Of course.'

Beran turned, trying not to run as he left the Foyer through the double doors. Once outside he headed for the stables, running into the yard and calling for a groom.

'A horse, and quickly. The King's orders.'

The groom nodded and bowed, running off. Beran chewed on his lip, crawling anxiety all through him. But he didn't have to wait long. The groom returned leading Artos' own mount, a grey stallion called Mercury, saddled and bridled.

'Thank you.' Beran mounted, turning the horse and clattering from the yard, letting the animal have its head as they raced across the fields towards the Stone Gate. Panic was blooming in his stomach and Mercury seemed to sense it too, picking up the pace, fresh morning air streaming around them.

After a while Mercury started to slow, his breath blowing hard. In the distance Beran saw the estate of Lord Denoris, long windows catching the light. The Gate came into view, fingers of stone stark against the green slopes. There was something on the ground near the Gate, and Beran's heart dropped. As they drew closer the shape resolved itself into a body, lying on its side, one arm flung out. A glint of silver grey hair was visible, and Beran knew.

'Oh no.' He dismounted, running over to Artos, fearing the

worst. He knelt down beside him, horror at the amount of blood. Artos was breathing, short shallow breaths, but his eyes were closed. Beran laid a hand on his shoulder.

'My Lord!'

Artos opened his eyes, but only slightly, slits of ice-blue. He rolled back slightly, and Beran could see the movement caused him pain.

'My Lord,' he said again. 'I am here. Let me help you.'

Artos nodded. There were tears on his face, squeezing out from under his eyelids as Beran carefully placed an arm under his back, manoeuvring him into a sitting position. Artos gasped.

'Can you stand? Mercury is here – he'll carry us back.'

Artos nodded, holding up one hand. Beran waited. Artos placed his hand flat against the grass and closed his eyes. His breathing faltered, then deepened, and Beran, awestruck, saw faint colour come back into his pale cheeks. After a few moments Artos opened his eyes.

'Take me to Thorion,' he said. 'The Dark is moving, and we must stop them.'

Beran took in a breath. 'But, you're hurt—'

'It will hold long enough to get us back to the Palace. Come, there is no time to waste.'

With Beran's help Artos got to his feet, but he groaned with the effort and Beran could see fresh blood blooming on his side. It took more effort to get him onto the horse's back, Beran managing to get up behind, holding Artos as he slumped against him. He turned Mercury and they started back across the fields. The pace was agonisingly slow compared to his mad dash to the Gate, but he couldn't risk going any faster.

Finally they reached the stable yard. A groom rushed over to help Beran, whose arms were aching with the strain of holding a semi-conscious Artos. A blanket was brought and laid down on the cobbles, several more grooms coming to help. Gently they laid Artos down on the blanket – he was pale and starting to shiver, the dark patch on his side growing ominously larger. Beran knelt next to him.

'We need the Healer, and fast!'

'But, my Lord, there is a Council Meeting – Marlin is there–'

'Danae is here – she is working with Lord Cedran's horse–'

'But she is not–'

'Get her, please!'

One of the grooms nodded and ran off, disappearing into one of the stalls lining the yard. A muffled conversation was heard and eventually he re-emerged, followed by a woman in shirt and breeches wiping her hands on a cloth, her long black braid like silk. Her eyes widened when she saw Artos lying on the blanket. She came to kneel at his side, one hand checking the pulse at his throat.

'What has happened?'

Beran shook his head. 'I don't know. I found him, er, out in the fields.'

She felt along Artos' side, her long fingered hands gently probing. 'He has been stabbed.'

'What!?'

'I must heal him, and quickly. There is no time to lose.'

She ripped open the bloodstained fabric, revealing a dark slash in Artos' side, still faintly welling blood. Beran swallowed, horror in him. What had happened? Danae laid her hands over the wound and closed her eyes, lashes dark against her caramel skin. She took a deep breath in through her nose, blowing it out through her mouth. A faint flush came to her cheeks, sweat beading her brow. She held her position for a minute or so. All at once she gasped, pulling her hands back. The wound had almost closed, an angry red line dotted with blood. She looked at Beran.

'I've done what I can for now. I'm sorry- I've been up all night tending animals and my energy is not what it should be–' She was pale and Beran put a hand on her shoulder to steady her as she swayed.

'Will he be all right?'

'I've managed to stabilise him for now, but he's lost a lot of blood. He needs more healing—' She broke off, lashes fluttering, putting a hand out to support herself.

'Is she all right?' Artos had opened his eyes.

'Artos! Er, my Lord, I mean.' Beran flushed. Artos smiled.

'It is fine, Beran. We are old friends, are we not? And, Danae, is it not?'

The Healer, her head hanging forward, nodded. 'My Lord,' she murmured.

'Where is Marlin?'

Beran answered. 'At the Council Meeting.'

'The Council Meeting!' Artos tried to sit up and Danae protested, her hand on him.

'My Lord, you are going nowhere except to your chambers. You need rest and healing.'

'But Alma—'

Beran's stomach dropped. So he hadn't found her. Still, Danae was of the Dark and the less she knew the better. 'My Lord, it is fine,' he said, half smiling as he inclined his head, though he widened his eyes slightly.

Artos stared at him. 'Of course,' he said. 'To my chambers, then.'

DENORIS STOOD IN THE FOYER. HIS CLOAK BRUSHED AGAINST his bare arms as he watched Gwenene approach, sleek in icy velvet, blue eyes gleaming with suppressed excitement. He could feel it as well, coursing through him – it was all he could do not to pull Gwenene into the shadows and have his way with her. She smiled at him as though she knew, moving close to run a hand over his armoured chest and he growled, low in his throat. Maybe there was time, before the meeting started, to step into the gardens together. But a voice called his name and he turned to see Nevros and Ghislaine, the former in red Council robes, the latter in her customary blue armour, coming towards them. What now? Denoris raised an eyebrow, Gwenene moving close to his side.

'Well met, Denoris, Gwenene.' Nevros smiled, gold dust glittering on his high cheekbones. Ghislaine nodded a greeting, her expression circumspect. She was one to watch, thought Denoris, still waters if ever he saw. He smiled, though he didn't let it reach his eyes.

'Ghislaine, Nevros. A fine day, is it not?'

Nevros tilted his head. 'Indeed. And you are well?'

'As always,' replied Denoris.

'And your plans—'

'Are best not discussed here, Nevros,' said Denoris, his smile becoming tight.

'Rest assured, Nevros,' Gwenene said in her husky voice, 'that things are progressing as they should, are they not, Denoris?' She smiled up at him and he bent a tender look on her, excitement coursing through him once more at the thought of Etras and what he was doing at that moment. Just an hour or two more and the girl would be his, finally.

'And you have not forgotten us?' Ghislaine moved closer, dark red hair rippling around her form.

'Of course not,' said Denoris. 'How could I ever forget one such as you, my Lady?'

'You know that's not what I mean,' replied Ghislaine, eyes like dark blue glass, sharp and glittering.

'And you know that I cannot say much more,' said Denoris, narrowing his eyes slightly. 'But I will tell you both this. There will be a development, today. During the meeting. You will know when it happens.'

'Indeed?' Nevros raised his eyebrows. His sensual mouth tugged into a half smile, robes rustling as he turned to Ghislaine. 'Well, that is good to hear,' he went on. 'After all, if we can resolve this without resorting to any further... unpleasantness, it will be good for us all.'

'Oh, it may be unpleasant for some people. But not for us, rest assured.' Denoris looked up as the door opened to admit more Elders, this time of the Light. He nodded a greeting to them, feeling generous. It would not be long before he held the power here.

~

THE MEETING BEGAN, THORION PACING THE CIRCLE AS WAS custom. 'Lord Artos will not be joining us today, and sends his apologies,' he said, as he moved around. Denoris tensed. Was he imagining things, or had the King's gaze flicked to him? He narrowed his eyes slightly, keeping his impatience under control, reaching to the stone at his neck. When he held power he would do away with all this, he thought to himself, all this civility. And Thorion would–

He realised Thorion had paused in front of him, his expression vaguely amused. Denoris bristled, drawing himself up to full height, meeting Thorion eye to eye.

'I am pleased to see you here with us, Lord Denoris, especially after your opinions expressed at the previous meeting,' said the King, inclining his head.

'Where else would I be?' Denoris smiled, his hands held wide. Thorion did not smile.

'The Library, perhaps?' The King raised one dark eyebrow. 'Or out in the hills, visiting friends?' Denoris could see his blue eyes turning to grey.

'You are well informed, my Lord,' he said, the tension in him almost unbearable. *Where* in darkness was Etras? 'Though perhaps you do not know all.'

Thorion lost his amused expression. The rest of the Circle were silent, their faces ranging from reserved to avid. Denoris knew they were all waiting to hear the King's response. But Thorion wouldn't give him the satisfaction.

'Perhaps,' was all he said, pausing a moment longer before moving to Gwenene, who bowed her head to him. Denoris was seething, but held his tongue. Just a little longer, he thought, and then the balance of power would change in his favour. His gaze slid to the great doors, but they remained closed, for now.

CHAPTER 22
UNDER STONE

'Right, let's get on with this.'

Merewyn bounced to her feet, looking fully restored. Alma got up a little more slowly. Feeling cold, she paused to untie her hoodie from her waist and shrugged it on, before following Merewyn across the green grass to where the old curtain wall still stood, the thick construction withstanding all the years. The arched doorway was still there, though the timber door was long gone. Merewyn began examining the stones, trying to find the one that Iorweth had pressed. Alma just stood there, staring out to sea as reaction washed over her. She hugged herself against the cool breeze and watched the water change colour. A gentle hand touched her arm and she jumped.

'Alma, hey,' Merewyn's hazel eyes, though still bright, were full of concern. 'You all right?'

Alma frowned. Was she all right? Her mind was reeling under the weight of everything she'd just learned. She shook her head. She needed to pull herself together.

'Sorry,' she said. 'It's just, there's a lot to take in, right?'

'Yes, but, Alma, we need to act, and we need to do it now. The Castle will close soon.' There was an urgency to her tone and

Alma's frown deepened. Reluctantly, she started examining the stones, not really sure what she was looking for. Then she saw it.

'There.' She pointed. Merewyn took in a breath. The light was changing, the sun starting to slide into the west and a beam had shone at just the right angle to illuminate a five-pointed star etched into the stone, so faint and rubbed it could barely be seen. Merewyn went to press on the stone, but Alma stopped her, one hand on her arm.

'Are-are you sure?' she whispered, starting to tremble. 'I mean, this could just be some graffiti, right?'

Merewyn paused. Around them the breeze blew off the ocean, whistling through the ancient stones, ruffling the long grass and brambles growing along the seaward side of the mound. 'This is the right place, I know it,' she said, her voice quiet. 'It's too much of a coincidence for it not to be, you know this. C'mon, we need to do this, right?'

Alma swallowed. 'Um, okay,' she said, still whispering. 'Okay, let's try.' Merewyn pressed on the stone – set slightly in from the others in the wall, it wasn't something that could be opened accidentally, and she had to exert a fair bit of pressure to get it to move. Finally, she got it. There was a faint grinding noise and a dark opening appeared in the thickness of the wall, the air blowing out of it musty and cold. Merewyn stepped through. 'Come on,' she said, again in that urgent tone.

Alma stared at her. *Here goes nothing*, she thought. She stepped through the gap to find herself on a small landing, damp stone walls rising to a curving roof. She could see, by what little light came through the still open door, a flight of stairs leading down into the darkness.

'We're goin' to have to close the door. We can't leave it like that, they'll be checkin' it once the Castle has closed for the night.'

'But how?' said Alma, turning around in the tight space as she looked for some way to close the door. She noticed another five-pointed star carved into the wall, over which an ancient iron bracket, probably for a torch, still hung. She pressed it without thinking and the door shut suddenly, leaving them in complete and utter darkness. She heard Merewyn gasp and froze, not wanting to unbalance the other girl and send her falling down the stairs.

'Well, good work, Alma.' Merewyn sounded amused, despite their situation.

'Sorry.' She reached into her pocket and pulled out her phone, running her fingers over it, waiting for the screen to light up. It did, and she heaved a sigh of relief. Merewyn had obviously had the same idea, her face lit strangely by the faint electronic glow. Scrolling through the icons, Alma found the one for her torch. She pressed it and a strong beam of light appeared, illuminating the stairs.

'Well now, that's a handy thing,' said Merewyn.

Alma took a deep breath, her heart beating fast at the strange unreality of their situation. They were actually doing this. 'Right, so, let's go.'

She handed her phone to Merewyn who held it out before her, illuminating the worn stone steps. The walls were running with damp, more iron brackets spaced at intervals. As they started down the stairs Alma touched one gently, rust staining her fingers. Wiping her hand on her jeans she descended further, gradually becoming aware of a deep booming noise, strangely muffled, and a faint vibration coming through her feet.

'What's that noise?'

'It's the sea,' replied Merewyn. 'We must be heading below the water line.' Alma put her hand out to steady herself on the wall and could feel a soft pulse coming through the stone. She closed her eyes and concentrated, sensing the waves as they crashed against the base of the Castle mound, feeling the power they held. She realised that, if she wanted to, she could tap into it.

'Hey, Alma. Pssst!' Alma opened her eyes. Merewyn was

standing at the bottom the stairs, looking up at her with a puzzled expression.

'Sorry, sorry,' she said, as she came carefully down the last few stairs. 'It still takes me by surprise, sometimes. Whoa...'

The staircase ended in a small domed chamber, the floor laid with worn flagstones. Several small wooden crates were dotted around, one with an old wine bottle and dusty glass on top of it next to a small pile of paper. Dust was everywhere, light as air, coming up in little puffs as they walked. Merewyn picked up the glass and blew on it, releasing another cloud of dust. Alma wandered along the edge of the room, her hand brushing the smooth stone walls. There was an open doorway at the opposite side from the stairs, a darker rectangle in the gloom. Putting her bag down on the floor, Alma realised she felt drawn to the opening, and wondered what lay beyond. Perhaps the Gate to Ambeth was in there. Then she realised.

The doorway *was* the Gate.

Energy pulsed through her feet and air twisted in the open space, sparking in the darkness as she reached out her hand. Her stomach lurched as she realised how close she'd come to going through.

'Merewyn.' The other girl turned and Alma heard her sharp intake of breath.

'It's the Gate?' she said, sounding incredulous. 'I just thought it was a doorway. Well I never...'

Alma nodded, swallowing. 'But, all the Gates are... known, aren't they?'

Merewyn shook her head. 'Alma, you know how long I've been livin' here, don't you?' Alma nodded. 'Well, I never knew of a Gate here, and I don't know that anyone else would remember either. I wonder if Davies knew it was down here? I mean, Iorweth must have chosen this location because of the Gate, right?'

'Davies had been studying the Castle for years. Maybe he just... found the way down here one day?'

Merewyn shook her head. 'I don't know. And he was with Gwenene... I wonder.' She turned away, hand on her chin, the other arm folded at her waist. Alma was mesmerised by the Gate and the energy she could feel, twisting and fluctuating. If she concentrated she could almost feel where the two realms touched... She jumped, startled by the sound of a crate scraping against the floor, the old wood creaking in protest as Merewyn sat down.

'Well, well.' Alma turned to see her holding a piece of paper, waving it so shadows flickered around the chamber. 'These are Davies' notes. So he did find his way down here.'

'What?' Alma went over and picked up another of the sheets, flapping it around to get the dust off, trying not to sneeze. Squinting in the light from her phone she held the page close, struggling to read the familiar scrawled handwriting.

My love took me to the Library the other day and showed me the greatest treasure of her kind, a book of what she called 'skye lore'. It was a beautiful thing, a thing of power. I want it, and I want her, and I worry she will tire of me soon if I do not match the power of her other lover. For I know she is with the tall blond one as well, I see the way he looks at me. I will take his book, and with it his power, and then she will be all mine.'

'Huh, good luck with that,' muttered Alma, shaking her head. 'I mean, was he nuts or something? To try and match Denoris? Huh.' She realised Merewyn was staring at her. 'What?'

'Did that say 'skylore'?'

Alma looked at the note again. 'Yeah, actually, it did.' Realisation dawned. 'So that's how Denoris knew, how he knew about me! I always wondered about how Ellery knew to target me.' The paper crumpled in her hands as she stared at Merewyn. 'He's reading the skylore!'

'But the Dark gave up on that years ago, it was thought,' said Merewyn, aghast. 'We have to tell Thorion. He needs to know about this! Not to mention the Gate.' Her pixie face creased with worry and Alma chewed on her lip, realising what the other girl was about to say.

'Well, can you just send him a message, or something?' she asked, her voice shaky. 'I mean, we could do that, right?' Wanting to change the subject she picked up another sheet, brushing the dust off and reading aloud.

They will not find the Grail here. They have forgotten even their own lore, and so I have brought it through the hidden Gate, keeping it safe in our old Castle. I knew as soon as I saw the picture in the book, the star charts taken from Iorweth's stronghold. It was my own Castle, could be nowhere else! I was right, I was right! And soon I shall bring my love here to see it, and she shall walk with me again for all to see.

Merewyn's mouth dropped open. 'Is that... is he talkin' about the Cup?'

The paper fell from Alma's slack fingers, drifting and turning to the ground. Crap. She remembered the cool tangle of energy she'd sensed, looking at the Castle from her bedroom window under a starlit sky. 'So it is here.' Her stomach flipped, half exulted, half terrified at the thought that she'd done it again, another line of the Prophecy fulfilled.

'You knew there was somethin' here, didn't you?'

Alma shook her head. 'I sensed something, I guess. I just thought it was the Gate...' She looked around, wondering where Davies might have hidden it.

'It must feel good, knowin' you were right.' Merewyn's voice was quiet.

'Caleb was right,' she replied, her heart clenching at the thought of him that long ago day in the Library, his excitement at finding the diary pages. *Wherever you are*, she thought, *I hope you know that you were right. And that I miss you so.* A cool breeze, soft and gentle, blew around her and she felt a kiss, soft lips on her brow. She looked up in wonder as the strange wind swirled through cobwebs on the wall nearby, revealing another star traced on the wall, dust almost hiding the fine carving. Unbelieving, emotion harsh in her throat, Alma went to the wall and brushed the dust away. She paused briefly, closing her eyes. *Thank you,* she thought, then pressed hard on the carving. There was a grating noise and a small section of the wall sank back and slid away to reveal a stone alcove. A glow lit the chamber.

'Oh my.' Merewyn came to stand next to Alma, squeezing her hand. Alma could hardly breathe, tears coming to her eyes. For in the alcove was a cup of great beauty, silvery metal shining smooth, ruby gems dotting its gentle curves, the rim and stem decorated with delicate curling leaves and vines.

'Can you feel it?' Merewyn's voice caught on the words. 'It's so very beautiful, more than I even remember.'

The Cup glowed with its own light and Alma *could* feel it. A gentle warm energy passed through her, so different from when she had found the Sword, all blood and pain. Gently, reverently, she reached up and lifted the Cup from its niche. At the touch of her hand the glow increased, illuminating the little room like a burst of sunshine, soft and golden. Holding it carefully she looked into the gold-leaf lined bowl. Merewyn reached out to touch the Cup. Her eyes closed for a moment and she let out a long breath. She smiled at Alma, beatific.

'We found it,' she whispered. 'I can't believe it.'

'I know,' said Alma, also whispering. 'So, what do we do now?'

'Why, we take it back to Ambeth.'

CHAPTER 23
DARKNESS FALLS

'What, now?' squeaked Alma, fear rising in her. Her stomach flipped, despite the calming energy from the Cup. 'Can't we just, I don't know, take this home and, well...' She looked at the Cup, the silvery curve of gleaming metal and knew there was no way she could take it home, not with the Dark on the move. She looked pleadingly at Merewyn. 'Could you take it? Please?'

Merewyn shook her head. 'I am not the one of the Prophecy,' she said. 'You're the one who is destined to bring it back to Ambeth.' Alma stepped back, shaking her head. Her foot knocked the crate and the wine bottle fell over with a clatter, making her jump. Merewyn frowned, folding her arms. 'Alma, I didn't want to say anythin', but... someone is comin'.'

Alma froze. 'Someone – who?'

'I don't know, but they came through the Stone Gate about an hour ago. If they are trackin' us, if it's who I think it is, we need to move fast.'

'Who do you think it is?' whispered Alma, feeling the blood drain from her face. She clutched the Cup to her chest, breathing in the glow of it, taking strength from it. 'You mean, the Dark?' Her voice trailed off in a squeak, icy fear deep within as Merewyn nodded. 'You aren't making this up t-to make me go through there?' She jerked her head towards where the Gate waited.

Merewyn looked shocked. 'I would never!' she said, sounding hurt.

Alma immediately felt terrible. 'No, I'm sorry, I know you wouldn't. I'm just... so scared, you know?'

Merewyn's mouth twisted. 'I know you are,' she said. 'I also know that you have this in you, that you can do it. You just need to find it as well.'

Alma bit her lip. She could feel the twisting pull of the ancient Gate, the thunder of the sea against the walls of the chamber. They were deep beneath the Castle, the room carved out of the bedrock itself and she realised that it was the second part of the prophecy, 'in stone'. She'd found the Sword in the mists and had always thought that getting the Cup would involve a cave, or maybe even some diving, but once she'd left Ambeth she hadn't worried about it any longer, not thinking she would ever be back there again. She'd never really believed in the Prophecy anyway, felt her role in finding the Sword had been chance more than anything else. But Caleb had always believed in her. Holding the Cup close she closed her eyes, tears falling at the thought of him, so serious, telling her she could do it. She looked within, trying to find the spark, the pulse, the thing she needed to help her to make the right choice.

And it all came crashing over her.

The lost summer in Ambeth, Deryck and Caleb, Artos, gentle Adara and proud Thorion. But instead of turning away from it for the first time she accepted it, accepted them all, even the pain, because behind it all, behind each and every one, she realised, was love. And with that realisation came the spark, leading her back to the person she was supposed to be. She savoured the warmth of it within her, realising it was never really lost; it had only gone dim for a while. She opened her eyes.

'I'm ready.'

Merewyn kissed her on the cheek. 'I know,' she said. 'Shall we?' Alma nodded. 'Remember what I told you, though, about crossin'.'

She walked to the Gate and stepped through, leaving Alma alone in the chamber. But instead of being afraid Alma put the Cup into her backpack, zipping it closed, still holding onto the spark, the feeling of acceptance. Reaching within for the power she knew she possessed she passed through the Gate in one easy motion, emerging the other side with hardly any dizziness at all.

Which was good, as she appeared to be in a box.

'What the hell is this?' she said, coming up hard behind Merewyn in pitch-blackness. Reaching out to either side she hit solid stone, but as her eyes adjusted she could see small slivers of light piercing the blackness in front of them. She realised suddenly that it was gaps between timbers, and that Merewyn appeared to be fumbling with something.

'Blast this latch!' she muttered. Alma could hear it rattling.

'Is it locked?' She started to panic. Still, the Gate was behind them; they could go back through if they needed to.

'No, just stiff. I think it hasn't been opened in a while,' hissed Merewyn. 'Ouch! There, got it, though it's snagged my finger nicely.' She pushed on the panel in front of them. It opened slowly, as though something were stopping it from swinging out all the way and Alma could see, as the gap grew wider, that they were behind a heavy embroidered curtain. Merewyn, sucking on her injured finger, used her other hand to push back the fabric. Over her shoulder Alma could see a small dining room, luckily deserted. Merewyn stepped into the room, Alma following, the tapestry swinging back to cover the door once more. A large wooden table, its surface well-polished, sat in the centre of the room with six heavy-looking wooden chairs around it, all of them carved with vines and flowers. A fire burned in the fireplace, while the small arched windows let in bright daylight.

'Well, this is definitely Ambeth,' said Merewyn, hands on hips as she surveyed the room.

'But where?' Alma was starting to shake. Now she was in Ambeth she felt sick to her stomach, knowing if the wrong person were to find them it would all be over. Taking deep breaths she closed her eyes, trying to control her trembling, which was spreading to her legs.

'Alma.' Merewyn touched her lightly on the shoulder. 'Alma!' Her voice became more urgent and Alma opened her eyes to see Merewyn's face close to hers. "We're in one of the rooms off the Great Hall. We cannot linger here.'

'I know,' Alma said through gritted teeth. 'I just can't seem to move, that's all.'

The sound of voices came through the closed door. Moving quietly Merewyn laid her ear to it, listening for a moment. Her eyes widened and she beckoned to Alma, sliding her hood up over her head.

'Come on!' she hissed.

Alma finally managed to get moving, swallowing hard as she crept across the stone floor towards Merewyn.

'What? What is it?' she said, pulling her own hood up.

Unexpectedly, Merewyn smiled. 'It's a Council Meetin'.'

CLAD ONLY IN SHIRT AND BREECHES, ETRAS STUMBLED THROUGH the small gate to find himself on the street, the soft laughter of his hosts ringing in his ears. He grinned, raising a hand to wave, swaying as the streetlights blurred. He had drunk an awful lot, really. Some more of that cider, then something in tiny glasses that went down smooth then kicked like a mule. There had been dancing, he knew that, the girls swaying and twisting in such a way he could not believe, clapping and roaring his approval. There had been kisses, soft kisses from the three of them as he caressed their smooth skin, felt their warmth and sweetness. Then more drinks, lying on his back as they poured them into his mouth, laughing as he drank it down, more kisses. They had unlaced his armour, peeling it from him as he protested, leaving it in scattered pieces on the floor and touching him until he gave in, unable to resist. Finally he'd remembered he was supposed to be doing something and had pushed them away, not ungently, thanking them for their hospitality, promising he would return once he had done what he needed, his body thrumming with desire. Ah, this human world and its delights!

'Straight down the hill,' called one of them, the one with the braid – Bronwen, he thought her name was. 'You can't miss it.'

'And then come back,' called the one with dark curling hair, laughing her head off. He grinned – he had particularly liked her. Waving once more he turned in the direction that seemed best, surprised at how difficult it was to keep in a straight line. He took the next street, then the next, keeping the Castle in view. The road dipped and turned and he found himself at a crossroads, one road snaking under a high stone bridge, the other heading back up the hill. Unsure where to go he scrambled up the slope, stones scraping his hands, brambles catching at his clothes. Angrily he brushed them off, emerging to stand unsteadily on top of the bridge. There was the Castle, lit up on its mound, stars coming out above. He reached for a sense of the girl, but there was nothing. Frowning, he rubbed both hands against his blurry eyes, his head spinning. He tried to reach out once more, the ground moving beneath his feet. He really shouldn't have drunk so much. There was an unearthly screeching and he looked around in alarm to see a bright light bearing down on him, huge in the darkness. Before he could move something hit him and he was gone, his body flung into the air and dissolving like mist.

THE DRIVER FINALLY MANAGED TO STOP THE TRAIN, SWINGING down from the engine and running back up the tracks, hand to his mouth. He'd just been standing there, right on the tracks! There was nothing he could have done. Anxiously he walked the length of the train on both sides, looking down the embankment. The engineer came to join him, both of them increasingly mystified as they walked further along, crossing the bridge and going down into the road below. But there was no sign of the mysterious figure. Finally they came back to the engine, both of them silent. The engineer shook his head.

'Maybe it was a trick of the light...'

'But I swear, I saw someone there...'

'How 'bout I take over for a while, you make yourself a cuppa. You've been driving for hours.'

The driver looked at him, a long look, then nodded.

With a hiss and rattle, the train started up again, driving into the night.

CHAPTER 24
REVELATIONS

Ellery knocked on the plain wooden door, looking around to make sure no one was watching. She didn't think she'd been followed, but wouldn't put it past her father to be spying on her.

The door opened. An older woman stood there, salt and pepper hair, her face lined with laughter and a life lived. 'Yes?' she said, though not unkindly. Ellery drew herself up tall.

'I am looking for Mari the jeweller,' she said. 'My foster mother gave me this address.'

'That's me,' said the woman. 'And your foster mother...?'

'Is the Lady Hillary, of the Dark.' Mari's eyes widened, and Ellery saw her throat move.

'Won't you come in?' She moved back and Ellery stepped into the cottage, relieved when the door closed behind her. She followed Mari through to a room at the back of the property, a large window overlooking the garden and woods beyond. A row of cupboards ran along one wall while a wooden workbench, well worn, sat in the centre of the room with a stool next to it. Curls of precious metals glittered on its scarred surface, and a small piece of velvet was home to several sparkling gems.

'Won't be a moment,' said Mari, smiling at her. 'Please take a seat.' She indicated a chair, then disappeared from the room. Ellery gingerly sat down, the skirts of her brown riding habit spreading around her. What was she doing? This plan was madness, really. Now that she was here she wasn't sure at all.

'Now, my dear, what can I do for you?' Mari had returned, bearing a tray with a pottery jug and two mugs, which she set on a small table.

This was it. Ellery took a deep breath and reached into her pocket for the small velvet pouch. Undoing the ties she tipped her necklace into her gloved palm, holding it out to the other woman.

'I would like a copy of this, if you please,' she said. 'I understand you're able to reproduce these stones?' She raised her eyebrows. Mari, on seeing the necklace, had sat back, a furrow appearing between her brows. 'You must not touch the stone.' Mari nodded, her brown eyes fixed on Ellery. 'And, please understand, I need this to be accurate to the last detail. It is,' she paused, 'important that it be so.'

Taking a small scrap of leather from her workbench, Mari reached out for the necklace and Ellery gave it to her. She held it carefully in her hand as she studied the fine work of the mount and chain. Finally she looked at Ellery. 'I can do this,' she said. 'An exact copy, just as you've asked.' A frown started on her pleasant face. 'A thing of power, this. Do you not wish to wear it?'

'It's none of your business as to why I want a copy!' Ellery went cold. 'I'll pay you well to keep this a secret.' Mari looked shrewdly at Ellery before nodding.

'You can trust me, my Lady.' Ellery at once felt awful, noting the change in tone. Mari tilted her head to one side as though considering something. Ellery shifted in her chair, feeling under scrutiny. She glared at Mari, her guilt changing to anger. How dare she! She was a Princess of the Dark and–

'You're very like your mother,' Mari said, the words tumbling out of her mouth as though she had been holding them back. Ellery recoiled, her anger gone.

'What do you mean? How do you know my mother?' She couldn't believe it, twisting her gloves in her hands. 'Is my mother... here?'

Mari put down the necklace. 'Here? Well, of course she's here.'

Ellery was thunderstruck. 'She's in the village? Why has no one told me?' Hope surged through her and she leaned forward, reaching for the other woman. 'Can I see her? Will you take me to her?'

~

'AND I STILL CONTEND, THORION, THAT IT'S TIME FOR THE Dark to work alone. Have you had a chance to further consider my point of view?'

Thorion suppressed a sigh. This again! Denoris had his arms folded, his handsome face set. Beside him Gwenene was all icy defiance, though her blue eyes kept flicking to the double doors. Thorion glanced at Adara – her lovely face was calm, but he could see her hands twisting together, while next to her Meredan looked ready to explode, one leg stepped forward with his fists clenched at his side. Something was up. There was an undercurrent in the room, murmurs from the other Elders in the circle, particularly Ghislaine and Nevros, who seemed unusually impatient.

'Well?' Denoris' arrogant tone rang through the Hall and Thorion, at the end of his patience, was about to respond when he heard a creaking sound. He turned to see two dusty hooded figures emerging from a door near to the two thrones.

'What is this!' cried Thorion. He glared at Denoris – was this one of his stunts? But he could see the other man was just as surprised as he was, for all that he fought to hide it with an answering snarling glare. The rest of the Circle were agog, all looking at the two figures, the hoods over their heads hiding their identities. Fury surged through Thorion. He went towards the intruders, his robes billowing out behind him.

'Who dares to enter my Hall, during a private Council!'

They were both female, that was obvious, one of them carrying a bag, her arms wrapped around herself as though for protection. The other, the smaller one, stepped forward, raising one slender hand. Thorion stopped, shocked at her boldness. Before he could speak she fell to one knee and pulled back her hood to reveal spiky blonde hair, bowing her head.

'Forgive us, Lord Thorion. We did not mean to interrupt. But we bring you something of great worth.'

A gasp went up from the watching crowd and all eyes turned to the other figure, whose identity was still hidden. Thorion, though, had guessed who it was and his heart lifted. Merewyn had done it. His anger gone, he raised her to her feet, kissing her gently on one cheek.

'Well met, Merewyn.' He turned to the other figure, starting to smile. 'But who is this you bring with you?'

He could see her pale hand trembling as she pulled back her hood to reveal herself, shaking out her red hair. A second gasp, louder than before, went up.

'Alma.' Relief poured through him to see her again, though she was thinner, paler than she had been and his heart broke again at what she'd been through. He gently placed his hands on her arms, holding her blue gaze with his own. 'It is so very good to see you again, dear heart,' he said. 'Do not fear, nothing can harm you here.'

At his words, spoken softly but still audible, a hiss went up. Thorion ignored it, focusing on Alma, wanting her to calm down. He could see she was fighting fear, and it was a few moments before she managed to speak.

'I have something for you,' she began, the words catching in her throat. Thorion released her so she could slide her pack from her shoulder, struggling with the zipper before managing to get it open. As she reached inside he saw calm come over her, and felt an answering pulse in his own mind. Surely not...

She smiled at him and pulled the Cup from her bag.

Thorion gaped, disbelief giving way to joy bubbling in his chest. She had done it for them. Despite all she had lost, all they had lost, she had triumphed.

Pandemonium ensued. Cries of pleasure came from many but were dwarfed by the shriek of rage from Gwenene.

'It is mine!' screamed the Elder, making as if to run at Alma, her hands curved into claws. Thorion moved to stand in front of Alma, his hand going to his knife.

Denoris, though his own face was stony with rage, grabbed Gwenene's arm with a grip like iron, holding her back.

'This is not the way!' Thorion heard him say. 'You cannot be seen to do this! You know of what I speak!'

'But it's all wrong!' Gwenene shrieked, struggling and thrashing in his arms for a moment longer before acquiescing, her long dark hair falling forward as she hung her head. Denoris, surprisingly gentle, turned her around, his arm still around her as they left the Circle, heading for the double doors. Several other Elders of the Dark followed, their rage and disappointment plain to see, leaving the remaining Council members standing as though stunned. As the doors closed behind the Dark Thorion eased his protective stance, Adara's golden eyes meeting his as he sheathed his knife. He half smiled at her before turning to Alma who was clutching the Cup to her chest, her face white as paper.

'Now, my dear, where were we?' he said, trying to diffuse the tension in the room. He winked at her, but she only stared at him, her hands still tight around the Cup. 'It is all right,' he went on, moving closer. 'They are gone.' She took in a shuddering breath and slowly untwisted her fingers, holding the Cup out. He took it from her, leaning in to kiss her cheek before turning to face the remaining Council. He raised the Cup to his lips, kissing it before lifting it high above his head where, lit for a moment by light from the great stained-glass windows, it seemed to glow like a jewel. Moving forward, he placed it in the alcove next to the

Sword. Immediately the golden glow increased and a sigh went up from those watching.

There was a thud. Alma lay on the floor, her eyes closed and one arm outstretched, her red hair tumbling about her pale face. Merewyn turned, her face stretching with shock, but Adara was the first to reach her, dropping to her knees in a rustle of silk, her hands gentle on Alma's brow. 'It has all been too much for her.' She turned a worried face to Thorion, who had rushed to her side. 'Help me lift her.'

Merewyn was on Alma's other side, her hand on her arm. 'Will she be all right? I shouldn't have pushed her—'

'She'll be fine,' Adara slid her arm under Alma's shoulders. 'Peace, Merewyn – we just need to get her upstairs and safe.'

Thorion signalled to the guards at the door. They both came over, saluting smartly. 'Help the Lady Adara take Alma to her room, if you please. Do not leave her unguarded, even for a moment.' The guards bowed and the King turned to the remaining Elders. 'Marlin, would you be so kind as to accompany them? I'm sure your healing talents will come in handy. I will be along shortly.' He was polite, as he felt he should be, but the implications of what had just happened were rolling over him. And where was Artos? He blew out a breath, wondering whether Beran had been able to find him.

Marlin helped Adara to lift Alma. Her eyes were still closed, her head lolling back and Thorion felt a dart of alarm at how pale she was. Marlin scooped her into his arms. 'She'll be all right,' he said.

'Take care of her,' Thorion replied. Adara linked arms with a shaken Merewyn and the group left the Hall, the guards following behind.

Thorion surveyed the remaining members of the Council. They still looked stunned. Some of the Dark, including Lord Cedran, had remained after Gwenene's outburst, an interesting development that Thorion filed in his mind for future reflection.

Now he needed to manage things. There was no point continuing the meeting, not after what had just happened. But there was no reason to abandon protocol completely.

'My fellow Elders,' he said. 'This was unexpected.' An understatement. He paused for a moment then began to laugh, joy from the Cup bubbling through him. The sound echoed around the room, bouncing off the rafters. The Elders looked at each other, starting to smile, caught up in the King's hilarity. Eventually Thorion brought himself under control, knowing he needed to end the meeting. He paced the circle once more.

'My Lords, you are free to go. May Light shine on you all.' With the ritual words the meeting was ended, though no one turned to go.

'My Lord.' Seren Stargazer came up to him, lilac robes dragging on the mosaic floor, eyes shining like her namesake. 'We must celebrate.'

'And we will, dear Seren. Let the word go out, three days hence, shall we celebrate the return of the Cup.' His voice rang out and there were nods and smiles.

'I will make the arrangements.' She smiled at him, her voice thrumming with excitement. 'But first, I think I need to look upon the Cup once more.' She moved past him and, as though her words were a signal, so did the remaining Elders, crossing the Hall to stand at the alcove, their voices humming through the room, an undercurrent of joy. Thorion watched them for a moment before making his way from the Hall. The Cup could wait for now. He needed to know that Alma was all right.

CHAPTER 25
MOTHERS AND DAUGHTERS

Mari had an uneasy feeling growing in her stomach. She bitterly regretted ever mentioning the girl's mother – curse her loose tongue, it always got her into trouble! She had wondered, they'd all wondered why the young woman in front of her had never been to visit her mother's grave. The villagers had taken it upon themselves to tend it year after year, wanting to mark the memory of the distraught young woman whose life had ended so sadly. Did she really not know? This one's father was powerful and not someone to cross, so she needed to tread very carefully indeed. Settling herself on her stool, she asked gently, 'Do you not know of her story, child?'

Ellery stiffened, sitting up straight. She looked very like her father, her green eyes blazing and Mari quailed inwardly. She opened her mouth to apologise, but before she could do so Ellery slumped down, going from Dark princess to young woman again, one with sorrow and stress printed plain on her pale face. She swallowed hard and Mari felt for her. 'No.' Her voice was a rasp, a whisper. 'No, I know nothing of her, other than the fact she is human.'

'That she was, and beautiful, as beautiful as any of the Lords and Ladies in yonder Hall,' said Mari, trying to stay positive.

'Was? Do you mean, she's no longer... alive?' Ellery's face crumpled. Mari, unable to look at her, picked up her pencil and started to work, roughing out a sketch of the silver mount, her work-worn hands falling easily into the rhythm, calming her mind and helping her to think.

'Please, will you tell me?' Mari looked up to see a pleading Ellery and her heart clenched with pity. All trace of the girl's resemblance to her father was gone, other than the vivid eyes, and she looked so like her mother that Mari blinked.

'This is not easy to tell,' replied Mari.

'Please.'

It was only a whisper, but it broke Mari. She set her pencil down and sighed. 'If you're sure,' she said. Ellery nodded, and Mari got to her feet and went over to the small table. She needed a moment to gather her thoughts and wished, with an inward chuckle, that there was something stronger than water in the jug. Filling the mugs she brought one over to Ellery who took it, eyes wide with trepidation. Mari held on to the other and sat down again, facing Ellery

'You were born in this village, just a few doors from here,' Mari started, choosing her words with care. Ellery opened her mouth as if to speak and then closed it. Mari took another sip, her mouth tightening for a moment before she went on. 'I remember your mother being brought here—'

'Wait, brought here? Wasn't she already living in the village?'

'Ah, no,' Mari paused. How best to tell this? 'She was in the woods, near the Oak Gate. It was Frank who found her, while he was out collecting wood. She was in some distress, I believe there may have been some sort of disagreement with your, erm, father.'

She paused again, wanting to measure the effect of her words. Despite her hands being steady as they curved around the mug, Mari's heart was beating fast. This was dangerous ground. Ellery chewed on her thumbnail, her distress apparent. Then she burst out, 'He left her in the woods!? While she was—'

'Pregnant, yes, and heavily so. Your mother was already in labour when she came back here, so we did the best we could for her, made her comfortable and tried to help her. But she was so distressed...'

Mari trailed off, not wanting to say any more. After all, it was the girl's father she was talking about. Who also happened to be one of the most frightening people in Ambeth. Ellery had her face in her hands and Mari, worried now, put down her mug and went to her, laying a gentle hand on her shoulder.

'I'm sorry, my dear. Perhaps I shouldn't have said anything, I did not realise. Your father—'

Ellery took her hands away from her face and looked at Mari with despairing eyes. 'I have no illusions about the type of person my father is.' Her voice was barely a whisper. 'But this! To know that he left her there...' A single tear slid down her cheek, more hanging on her dark lashes that she blinked away. She grabbed Mari's hand, shocking her. 'I never knew about her, what had happened to her. No-one would tell me and I always wondered... Tell me, did she love me?'

Mari was taken aback. What could she say? She placed her other hand over Ellery's, deciding. She'd come this far, no point not telling the rest of it. And this poor girl needed to know, hang the consequences. 'She didn't live for long after you were born. But it was long enough to hold you, to name you and to name your father. She cuddled you for as long as she could, told you she loved you, that she didn't want to leave you – I'm so sorry.' Mari broke off as Ellery sagged forward, the girl's long dark hair hiding her face as her shoulders shook. She stayed that way for a moment before straightening up and fixing Mari with a long look. Mari bore her scrutiny, once again reminding herself who this girl's father was, knowing that her life rested on a knife edge. Wiping away her tears, Ellery finally spoke.

'Thank you,' she said. Inwardly Mari sagged in relief.

'You're welcome.' She smiled. 'And I can have your necklace ready in a week's time, should you still wish–'

Ellery nodded. 'I do.'

Standing, she was about to take her leave, when Mari stopped her. She laid her hand lightly on Ellery's arm – Ellery looked at it curiously but said nothing. What the hell, thought Mari, in for a penny, in for a pound. 'Your mother lies in the graveyard here,' she said. 'Her name was Grace.'

The devastation on Ellery's face went straight to Mari's heart. It was obvious that this young woman, for all her privilege, was alone. She patted her arm, her sorrow genuine. 'And, if you ever need someone to talk to, I'm here for you.'

Tears welled in Ellery's eyes as she nodded. 'Thank you, again.'

'MY LORD!'

Thorion, about to go up the stairs, paused. He turned to see Beran crossing the Foyer, his clothing dishevelled and hair wild, quite unlike his usual dapper self. There were darker patches on his tunic, an ominous sign. He started to bow, but Thorion stopped him, going to him and placing a hand on his arm.

'What is it?'

'My Lord Artos.' Beran's face crumpled.

Thorion felt a dart of horror, despite his recent joy. 'Tell me.' He drew Beran to one side, into the shadow of the pillars.

'He is injured, stabbed. He has been taken to his chambers. We need Marlin, my Lord.'

'Marlin is with Alma.'

Beran's face lit up. 'She's here? Oh, that will be a relief. Artos has been so worried, that Etras–'

'Etras?' Thorion squeezed Beran's arm involuntarily and the other man winced. 'I am sorry.' Thorion let go, his mind whirling.

Etras, of all people. Rage surged through him at the thought of the Dark Elder, the memory of Laurel lying broken and blood-stained on the floor. 'Take me to him.'

'At once.'

Thorion followed Beran up the stairs, his joy at the return of the Cup tempered by his worry for Alma and now Artos. Stabbed? By *Etras*? He ground his teeth, hands clenching. He should have killed the Elder himself, all those years ago, rather than sending him into exile. His gorge rose at the memory and he swallowed, pushing his guilt and sorrow down, Laurel dancing in his mind, blonde and beautiful like their son. He rubbed a hand over his face, all at once weary. They had reached the door to Artos' chambers and Beran was looking at him, expectant. Thorion pulled himself together.

'My Lord, if you please.' Beran opened the door, holding it. Thorion entered, pushing the door to the inner rooms open, not wanting to wait. Artos was lying on the sofa, a dark-haired young woman kneeling next to him. He recognised her – Danae of the Dark. She was paler than usual, her energy obviously depleted. On seeing him she got to her feet, swaying as she attempted to bow. Thorion raised his hand. 'It is fine. How is he?'

'Just a scratch, Thorion.' Artos tried to sit up, but Thorion could see how it hurt him to do so.

Danae frowned. 'I told you not to do that!' Thorion hid a smile at her scolding tone. 'My Lord.' She turned to Thorion. 'I have done what I can to stabilise the wound, but my energy was already depleted when I was called. The wound is deep, and should have killed him. Truly, I do not know how he survived.'

Thorion raised an eyebrow and Artos waved his hand. 'Long story,' he said, his voice a pale thread of its usual hearty tones.

'I'm sure.' Beran, who had disappeared through another door, returned with a tray holding four cups, a steaming teapot next to them. Placing the tray down he poured the tea, bringing a mug to Danae who took it.

'Thank you.' She took a sip, her eyes closing briefly. She was still very pale and Thorion was worried for her.

'Danae, you have done more than enough. Truly, dear one, you must rest, or you will become ill yourself. The meeting is over and I will call Marlin shortly. In the meantime, Beran and I will look after him.'

'Thank you.' She took another sip, putting the mug down. 'This is lovely tea, but I do need to rest. I'll take my leave then.' She turned to Artos. 'Remember, no getting up and running about.'

Artos nodded. 'I'll try and remember.' His tone was dry and there was a familiar twinkle in his eye. He reached and caught Danae by the hand. 'And thank you, my dear, for everything.'

She smiled, her face lighting up. 'You are most welcome, my Lord. I wish you a strong recovery.'

She left the room and Thorion came to sit in the chair near Artos. 'So?'

Artos shook his head slowly, shifting against the cushions. Danae had bandaged his side and his chest was bare. 'It was Etras. He came through the Gate and surprised me. Bastard.' His face twisted. 'I couldn't find her, Thorion, I'm such a fool! And now she's out there alone and he is chasing her and I cannot—'

'Peace, Artos. She is safe. There is no way Etras can get to her.' His voice stumbled slightly on the hated name, but joy at the news he was to deliver kept him going. Artos said nothing, just stared at him. 'She is here. Here and with the Cup in hand, coming into the Hall by what means I cannot imagine, but she has done it! Surprised us again.'

Artos' face crumpled and he huffed out a sob, rubbing his eyes. 'Truly?'

'I would not lie to you about such a thing. And, can you not feel it?'

Artos looked distant for a moment. He smiled, as though he heard music, far away. 'I can. Truly, this is a joy.' His eyes brightened. 'I must see her.' Before Thorion could stop him, he pushed himself to his feet. 'Ugh!' He collapsed back onto the sofa, his hand to his side, and Thorion could see fresh blood on the bandages. Artos grimaced, pushing himself upright again and Thorion, unable to bear it, reached out.

'No, my friend. What you need is rest and healing. She is safe, under guard, and you will see her, I promise. But not if you kill yourself before you get to her room. Please, let me send Marlin to you.' He paused. There was no way he was letting Artos know Marlin was with Alma – he wouldn't be able to stop him from going to her if he knew the healer was with her. 'I will get him, now.'

'I must see her. I need to talk to her.' But Artos' voice was fading, sweat beading on his brow and Thorion could see he knew he needed to wait, hard as it was.

'I will look after him, my Lord.' Beran stood next to the sofa, tea in hand.

Thorion nodded. 'I will tell Alma you will be in to see her soon.'

'But nothing more, Thorion! Nothing more.' Artos gasped and sat back, a hand to his side.

'You have my word.'

Standing, the King left the room, heading for the stairs, and Alma, once more.

THE DARK BROWN SKIRTS OF ELLERY'S RIDING HABIT SWISHED around her legs as she left Mari's cottage. She was near to breaking, but she couldn't, not here, not with the curious eyes she could feel on her as she walked along the rutted lane, her head held high. Past wooden gates set into low stone walls she walked, the extraordinary heartbreaking fact that her mother was here, had been here all along, ringing in her mind.

Set on a central green, the little chapel was of no particular religion but rather just a sacred space, somewhere the village inhabitants had created for ritual and respect – all were welcome. And it was to this place, if Mari was to be believed, that Ellery's mother had made her final journey. The pain inside her was almost unbearable and on more than one occasion she reached into her pocket for her tallus stone, only pulling her hand back at the last moment. She owed her mother more than that.

She stood for a moment at the lych gate, breathing deep, trying not to cry. Pushing the gate open with her hand she stepped into the circular green graveyard. It was dotted with markers, some made of stone, others of wood, all of them marking the lives of those who had chosen or been forced by circumstance to end their days in Ambeth. It was a peaceful place, for all that – the stone chapel flanked by dark green yew trees, fallen leaves from the nearby woods blowing across the short grass. Ellery frowned – where should she look? She couldn't wander here forever; her absence would be noted soon and there was no way she could tell her father where she'd been. Stepping off the gravel path she chose a direction at random, but couldn't stop her cry of surprise when a figure rose up in front of her, seemingly from the ground itself. Her hand to her heart, Ellery stepped back. The figure bowed.

'I'm sorry, my Lady, I was tending the graves. I did not mean to frighten you.'

Ellery, gasping, took a moment to answer. 'It's fine,' she said. A thought occurred to her. 'Do you know this place well?'

'That I do,' said the man, a stooped individual who looked to be in his fifties. 'Is there someone you're looking for?' He tilted his head to one side.

'I'm looking for my mother,' replied Ellery, and her voice shook. Summoning the last of her self-control, she managed to say, 'Her name was Grace.'

Understanding dawned on the man's face and his eyes grew wide. 'Follow me, if you please, my Lady. I'll take you to her.'

Stepping carefully around the graves, Ellery followed the man across to a small stone marker, set close to the curve of the wall and sheltered from the wind that blew cool across the grass.

'She is here, my Lady.' He bowed once more and took his leave, perhaps recognising he could offer no further comfort. Ellery stood for a moment, looking at the square stone with a single word, 'Grace' carved into it. Then her legs wouldn't hold her up any longer and she sank to her knees before her mother's grave. Her head dropped into her hands and she wept.

CHAPTER 26
HE HAD A KEY

'Be *quiet*, I tell you!'

Deryck, sprawled in a chair and half asleep, jerked awake and sat up, running a hand through his hair. He frowned, wondering what the hell was going on. It sounded like Gwenene in the hallway outside, shrieking at his father and he rolled his eyes, not wanting to get involved. But then a sound like a slap followed by a gasp brought him to his feet and he ran to the door, opening it. He stopped, shocked. His father and Gwenene were struggling in the hallway, Denoris holding her arms as she tried to scratch at him, a red mark on his face where the slap had landed. He shook her hard, so her head went back and forth. Deryck, aghast, grabbed his father's arm.

'What the hell is this? Father, stop!'

Denoris turned to snarl at him, shaking off his grasp, but it was Gwenene who answered, her eyes wild.

'That little bitch of yours,' she glared at Deryck, 'has brought back the Cup. And it should have been mine!' she moaned, her voice rising to a shriek. 'He promised it to me!'

'Gwenene, stop this nonsense,' roared Denoris, his hands squeezing her arms so hard Deryck could see the bruises starting on her pale skin. 'Enough, I tell you!' His shout rang around the hallway and Gwenene turned an anguished face to him, her dark hair tangled around her delicate features.

'I always thought he was joking,' she whispered, white and distraught. 'I never dreamed he actually took it, that he did it for me...' She trailed off, weeping, and Denoris made a sound of disgust, pushing her away. She sank down onto the bench, sagging forward with her head in her hands. Denoris shoved roughly past Deryck, heading for his study.

Deryck's heart was beating fast as he took in what they were saying. *Alma was here.* 'Where is she?'

At Deryck's words Denoris stopped dead. Deryck, seeing the fire in his eyes, took a step back. 'Your human,' hissed Denoris. 'Or, should I say, half-human,' he stuck his face close to Deryck,' is in her tower room, I should imagine. I don't fancy your chances of getting near her though.'

'Wait, what – half-human?' Deryck's stomach dropped like a stone and he followed his father into the study. Denoris let the door swing back in his face and Deryck, all at once furious, pushed it so hard it crashed against the wall. 'What is this? What do you know of Alma?'

'What does it matter?' snapped Denoris, who was looking in his desk drawer for something. Deryck walked up and slammed his fist down on the desk.

'It matters to me,' he snarled. 'It always has.'

'And there is your problem, my son.' Denoris pointed at Deryck, his whole body vibrating with rage. 'This is why once again our plans have come to naught. Your *obsession* with this girl!'

'*What. Is. Alma?*' shouted Deryck. 'What do you mean when you say 'half-human'?'

'She is Galen's daughter. That is who she is, that is why I cannot take her, that is why you were supposed to make this work!' Denoris' voice rose to a shout.

Deryck was utterly taken aback. He stumbled back and sat

down heavily in a nearby chair, rubbing his hand over his face, feeling cold all through. '*Galen's* daughter?' He shook his head, completely astounded. 'How long have you known this?'

'Since before she was born.' Denoris closed his desk drawer so violently the whole desk shook, carved dragon eyes glittering. 'I lost track of her for a while, so I didn't realise until I saw her again, standing in the Hall next to Thorion. The resemblance is there, it's unmistakeable. Ungh!' He wrestled with the lock on another drawer, still looking for whatever it was he could not find.

'You knew, all along...' Deryck's voice trailed off, his heart breaking all over again, the pain of losing her now worsened with his father's betrayal. No wonder he'd sent Deryck after her, not daring to capture her himself. Swallowing, he turned away, his hand going up almost automatically to his stone. Then he stopped. No, he wouldn't do it, not now, even though hurt bloomed inside him.

'Yes, I knew,' said Denoris. "It was the only reason I went along with your ridiculous plan in the first place. I – damnation, where is the thing!' he roared, finally opening the locked drawer.

Deryck said nothing, staring at his father. Denoris looked up and met his gaze. 'Oh, come on,' he said. 'Do you really think I would have let you dally with her that long if she were just some human?'

Gwenene, who had come to stand in the doorway, began to laugh and Deryck, finally, had had enough. He got up and left the room, pushing Gwenene roughly out of the way. Heading outside, he strode through the garden, and those who saw him moved quickly out of his way. Upon reaching the Great Hall he presented himself at the double doors, the two sentries bowing, though they exchanged concerned glances as they let him through. He didn't care – let them think what they wanted. Halfway across the foyer he stopped, putting both hands up to his face, running them through his hair. The anger that had brought him there was dissipating, replaced with nervous tension at the thought of seeing her again. He looked to where the stair started, twisting up to her tower. Taking a breath he moved towards it.

～

ALMA WOKE TO FIND HERSELF LYING IN A COMFORTABLE BED under a familiar ceiling painted with stars. A gentle hand was stroking her hair while another held her wrist, fingers pressing on her pulse. Unbidden, the memory came to her of the last time she had wakened in this room, of Deryck, beautiful against the white pillows, his green eyes warm as he held her close. She groaned, her free hand going to her head.

'How are you feeling?' Adara was sitting next to the bed and it was her soft hand on her brow. Marlin the Healer was holding her wrist, eyes closed as if concentrating. Merewyn stood further back against the wall, pixie face full of concern.

Alma struggled to sit up and then wished she hadn't, her head pounding like an army of hammers. She tried to speak, but her mouth was dry and only a croak came out.

'Here.' Marlin let go of her wrist. 'Drink this but slowly at first.' He smiled, his brown eyes twinkling in his angular chiselled face. Alma realised that, despite their concern for her, the two Elders were bubbling over with happiness. She could feel it inside her as well, the restored Cup working its magic. She remembered feeling that way after finding the Sword, riding with Caleb on a madcap dash through the woods, shrieking with laughter. Taking a sip of the drink she realised it was the strawberry and lime cordial she so loved, that Caleb had given her the first time she visited. Sorrow flared through her at his absence. This was going to be very hard.

'I'm... okay now, I guess, though I still feel a bit dizzy.' She wanted to reassure them, even though they were blinking in and out, changing from energy lines to people, then back again. Merewyn came to sit on the other side of the bed.

'How're you feelin'?'

Alma made a face. 'I've been better.'

'Well, you certainly gave us all a shock!'

'Sorry, I guess I just– I don't know.'

Merewyn grinned. 'I'm just glad you're all right.' She paused, her eyes twinkling. 'So, we did it.'

Alma leaned over and hugged her. 'I could never have done it without you,' she whispered. 'Thanks, for everything.'

'I'm just glad I could help.' Merewyn hugged her back and Alma clung to her for a moment, needing her comfort.

The door opened to admit Thorion, whose face lit up with obvious pleasure when he saw Alma. He went over to Marlin, who'd been preparing something in a bottle on the nearby table, and murmured something to him. Alma saw the other Elder's eyes widen, then he nodded, but she couldn't hear what they were saying. As the door closed she glimpsed two burly guardsmen standing outside her room. She turned to Adara, a question in her eyes.

'We thought it best, that you feel safe,' the Elder said, her gentle voice quiet.

'But... he had, he has a key.' Her heart contracted with pain at the memory of Deryck sitting on her bed in the twilight, dangling a golden key from his hand.

'He may have a key,' said Adara, 'but I have had the locks changed. So rest easy – none will enter here that you do not wish.'

Alma nodded, tears in her eyes. Energy lines were still flashing in and out, all over the room. She took a breath, feeling for the thread in her mind, wanting to get her power under control. She managed, sort of.

Thorion came to sit by her bed, pulling up a chair. He was smiling but, looking closer, Alma could see he wasn't quite as mellow as the others, jagged edges to the coiled pattern of light within him. 'Are you feeling better, Alma? We were all so worried about you.' He touched her arm and she jumped. She bent her head, hating feeling so weak. But her tears were so close to the surface, Caleb's absence a hole that no-one could fill. She knew she would need to cry about it properly at some point, but she didn't want to do it now, not in front of everyone. She could feel the silence in the room, the warmth and love coming from everyone around her as they waited. She knew she had to do something so she reached out to touch his hand.

'I'm sorry,' she said. She knew he meant well, they all did, but this was so hard. She tried to explain. 'It's just, it's difficult to be back here. I mean, I love it, I love seeing you all and being here in my room, but, well, you know...' Her mouth twisted. Thorion took her hand, rubbing it, and she could feel his strength, his soothing energy. She began to feel calmer.

'Alma.' His blue eyes were full of affection, dark hair falling around his flawless face and she gazed at him, amazed once more by his beauty. 'You have done it for us again, and I cannot thank you enough for restoring the Cup, especially after all you have been through.'

'We weren't sure, you see,' continued Adara in her soft voice,' whether you would want to come back to us. And we understood.'

"But we have been watching you, making sure you were protected,' said Thorion, and her heart clenched.

'I-I know.' She managed a wobbly smile. 'And I'm grateful. Although to be honest, if it weren't for Merewyn I don't know that I would have ever come back here.'

Merewyn grinned, looking pleased.

'It seems we owe you a great debt as well then, Merewyn,' said Thorion. 'Convincing Alma to do anything she does not want to is a feat in itself.' He winked at Alma and she made a face, while Adara laughed.

'How do you feel, Alma?' Marlin came over to lay a hand on her brow, nodding to himself and looking satisfied.

Alma thought about it. Sad? Definitely. Scared? Not so much, anymore. But there was one feeling she needed to address. 'I'm hungry, I guess.' A general chorus of laughter erupted at this and she looked around frowning. 'Hey! It's been a long time since lunch, all right?' But her injured tone only made them laugh more and finally she joined in, seeing the funny side.

'Well, it looks as though I am no longer needed,' said Marlin. He glanced at Thorion. 'I shall bid you all farewell, and arrange for food to be sent up. I've left a tonic as well,' he went on, indicating the bottle on the table.' If you feel faint again, a single capful should do the trick.' He smiled at her once more. 'Take care, Alma. And, we are forever grateful to you.' He bowed and Alma stared at him for a moment before she remembered her manners.

'Oh! Um, thanks,' she said. 'I do feel okay, really.'

'Good. But don't hesitate to call for me if you feel unwell.' He left, the guards closing the timber door behind him.

DENORIS MARCHED INTO THE STABLE COURTYARD. A GROOM saw him and scurried away before he could call out. Another one was not so lucky.

'My horse,' Denoris snapped.

'But, my Lord, your face...' Denoris glared at him and he stopped talking, bowing instead. 'At once, my Lord.' As he ran off Denoris put a hand to his cheek, feeling it come away wet. He wiped the blood on his armour, feeling as though he was about to explode with rage. He'd sent Gwenene away, tired of her hysterics, but she hadn't gone quietly, striking at him again. Normally he would have taken her, the aggression stoking his lust, but not today. Where the hell was Etras? He looked to the distant hills, straining his eyes to see if anyone was coming.

The groom arrived with his horse, fiddling with the saddle. Denoris shoved him away, checking the girth himself before mounting. He dug his heels hard into the horse's side and the animal bounded forward, hooves clattering on the cobbles as they headed towards the mountains and the Stone Gate. Something had gone wrong, for the girl was here and Etras was not. First she had managed to evade the Dark Hunt, and now Etras, one of the most powerful trackers in Ambeth. Powers from her father notwithstanding, he reflected, Alma had been remarkably lucky. Now he needed to act. And then her luck would change.

CHAPTER 27
GALEN'S DAUGHTER

'Merewyn, did you know there was a Gate under Iorweth's Castle?' At Adara's question Merewyn looked up from her sandwich. She swallowed a mouthful before waving her hand in Alma's direction.

'It wasn't me, it was Alma who figured it out.' She took another bite, obviously enjoying her meal. All eyes turned to Alma. Her mouth came open. She was about to answer when the door to her room opened again.

It was Artos, dressed in his usual ivory and brown, wavy silver hair tied back. Alma's stomach flipped with nervousness, but at the same time she was so glad to see him. However, something wasn't right. His energy was depleted, shining more faintly than the others and, when he blinked back into focus, she could see he was moving slowly, his face pale.

Adara must have felt something too for she came to her feet, her hand to her mouth. 'Artos!'

'It's fine, my dear, I'm fine.' He flapped his hand at her, though he grimaced as he did so. Narrowing her eyes, Alma could see a knot of darkness, red and black, to one side of his torso. She blinked, and he came back into focus. Adara was still protesting.

'You are not fine—'

'I am. I am now. Now that I know Alma is here and safe and, if I'm not mistaken, brought the Cup with her too.' He bent an affectionate glance on her and she blushed, not sure what to do or think. This was her grandfather. A thought too amazing and mind-blowing to manage. She knew there was no way she could talk to him about it, not here in front of everyone.

'Adara, dear one, I'm sure Artos will want to hear about how Alma got here.' Alma thought she saw a meaningful glance pass between Thorion and Adara. Well, she already knew about her father, so they didn't need to worry.

Artos came over to the bed. 'How are you, my dear?'

Thorion brought a chair for him and he sat down. Alma could see the movement hurt him. 'I'm all right,' she said. 'But,' she bit her lip,' are you?'

'I'm fine, my dear. No need to worry.'

'But I can see—'

'It's a story for another time, dear one. Now, tell me how it is you've managed to achieve the impossible again.' He winked at her and she grinned.

'And discovered a new Gate in the process,' Merewyn piped up, waving her sandwich around. She nodded her head meaning-fully in Artos' direction. Alma frowned at her.

'Oh, well, it wasn't like I *knew* there was a Gate there,' she said. 'It was more, one night I looked at the Castle and could see something was there, so we decided to go and have a look. Plus it all seemed to tie in with the notes, you know, that, um, Caleb and I made. In the Library,' she added, wondering why everyone looked so confounded. Artos burst out laughing.

'My dear!' She looked at him, startled. 'You said to me, did you not, Thorion, that she was full of surprises? Well, you have surprised us again, dear one.' His lined face was soft in the light from the fire. 'We are all so proud of you.'

Oh, this was too much. Reaching for her drink Alma took a long sip, wanting to hide her face for a moment.

'And the Gate led through to the Great Hall? This is a wonder, Thorion.' Adara looked fondly at the High King.

'Well, to an antechamber.' Thorion smiled at her, his eyes blue. Alma shot Merewyn a glance, raising her eyebrows. The other girl shrugged. 'To think it was there, all those years, just lying dormant. No wonder we could not sense it.'

'There are probably others, you know, that we have lost track of over the years,' said Artos.

Thorion nodded. 'Yes,' he said.' The thought had occurred to me. Perhaps it would be worth looking into, perhaps we need to do an inventory. He paused, shaking his head. 'And so this is how Llewellyn got in, taking the Cup from under our noses. Another mystery solved.'

'It's a sad story.' Adara's voice was soft. 'I remember him, you know, when he was here. I would often see him standing at the alcove, just staring at the Cup. I could feel the yearning in him, but thought it just for Gwenene.'

'And she served him badly in the end, poor man.' This was Merewyn, frowning. 'If only he'd met someone else when he first came here.'

Thorion nodded. 'It was a stroke of bad luck, indeed. But I wonder how it was he found the Gate in the first place?'

'Well, he knew that Castle like no-one else,' said Merewyn. 'Although I didn't know he'd found anythin', not till we got down there and I saw his notes. I mean, he was all over the place at that time, with Gwenene and all. I just wish I'd seen–'

'Peace, Merewyn. You did all that you could. I suppose we'll never know what it was led him under the stone mound, and to the Gate. It matters not, and now the Cup has been returned to us.' He smiled at Alma, who blushed. God! Thorion always had that effect on her.

Merewyn yawned, leaning back in her chair and stretching her arms over her head. A cool breeze came through the unshuttered window, causing the flames in the fireplace to dance. Adara got to her feet, drawing the shutters closed. Alma yawned as well, leaning back into her pillows.

'Alma, will you be all right if I go? I'm feelin' tired, all of a sudden.' Merewyn grinned, but Alma could see she was paler than usual, her hazel eyes drooping.

'I'm fine,' she said. 'You go.'

Merewyn came over and, sitting on the bed, gave her another hug. 'You did well today,' she whispered. 'And we'll go back tomorrow. Although, can we go back in the afternoon? I think I might need to sleep in.'

Alma nodded. 'Sounds good to me. And, er, I have some stuff to do.'

Merewyn's hazel eyes met Alma's and she nodded, once.

Adara touched Merewyn's arm. 'Your room has been made ready,' she said, 'and I've arranged guards there as well. Just as a precaution, you understand?'

Merewyn nodded. 'Thanks.' She got up from the bed and waved at everyone, then she was gone, the guards closing the door behind her. Artos got to his feet.

'I think I'll go too, my dears. I confess I need to rest a little,' he said. 'I just needed to see you. Merewyn was right. You did do well today.' He nodded at Alma, his eyes bright. 'But then, you always do.'

Alma smiled. She still couldn't believe he was her grandfather, yet it also felt like the most natural thing in the world. 'Would it be all right,' she asked, her voice faltering. 'If I came to see you tomorrow, before I left?'

Artos' face lit up. 'Of course, my dear. My door is always open to you.' He reached out, his hand gentle as he smoothed her hair. 'Rest now, and I'll see you tomorrow.'

Once he'd gone Alma turned to Adara and Thorion, who were both pretending they hadn't been watching her.

'It's all right,' she said, laughing at their surprised expressions. 'I know about my father. About Galen.'

Adara looked at Thorion, her golden eyes wide. Thorion took in a breath. 'Alma, you understand, we could not tell you.'

'I know. I know why you couldn't. I-I get it, that you wanted me to choose.' She nodded at Thorion. 'It all makes sense. A lot of things make sense now.'

Adara bit her lip. 'How did you find out?' She reached to take Alma's hand and Alma could see the glow of energy in her, golden and swirling, beautiful. She blinked, taken aback so it took her a moment to answer.

'I found some letters,' she said. 'At my grandmother's. Then my mother told me. She told me everything.' Her eyes teared up as she thought of Eleanor and her sorrow. 'It's so sad.' Adara squeezed her hand, her golden eyes also tearing up. Remembering Adara was an empath and not wanting to upset her, Alma tried to control herself, looking up at her starry ceiling, so like the night sky over the ocean near her grandmother's house. Her eyes widened. That reminded her.

'Er, Thorion, Adara?' She shifted against her pillows, letting go of Adara's hand. She could still see her energy glow, and also Thorion's and, this was interesting, they were twining together, connected somehow. She shook her head to dispel the image and they both changed from light to people again, people who were looking at her with worried expressions. 'Sorry,' she said. 'It's this Channelling thing, sometimes it catches me unaware and I see things and get distracted.'

Thorion looked astounded. 'Then it is true, you are a Channeller?'

'Well, yes, I am, or at least Merewyn says so, but that's not what I wanted to tell you. When we were under the Castle, we found some of Davies' notes, some more of them and they mentioned that Denoris had a book of skylore, that he was using it to read the skies.'

Thorion's jaw dropped and Alma almost laughed at his expression. It wasn't funny, not really, but she had never seen the High King so thrown off guard. Next to him Adara was equally shocked. Her hand, Alma noticed, had now linked with Thorion's. This was very interesting. Could they not see it?

'The Book of Avernath?' Thorion's voice sounded strained, quite unlike his normal deep tones. Alma shrugged.

'Well, I don't know, the book wasn't there or anything, but in his notes he mentioned that he was going to steal it, to compete with Denoris for Gwenene.' She made a face. 'As if. What chance did he have? But that's how Denoris knew about me coming through the Gate the first time, I'm sure. It's the only way. And of course he couldn't just take me, knowing who my father was.'

Adara and Thorion both looked so amazed by Alma's revelations that she giggled. Totally the wrong reaction, she knew that, but she just couldn't help it. She shrugged again. 'See? I told you things were starting to make sense. But, what's that book you mentioned?'

Thorion took a moment to answer, his mouth working as though he didn't know what to say. Adara seemed equally speechless. 'You are very special, Alma, but then I have always thought that. Your father was a good friend of mine.' He reached out to touch her hand. 'There is much we need to discuss, dear one, but for now I will try to answer your question about the book. In the old days, before I was born, Light and Dark used to read the skies together, each side contributing to the lore. There were two books that were consulted, and the Shield Stone, which has always stayed with the High King or Queen. But then the Dark fell away, stopped using the knowledge, or so it was thought.'

'And now?'

'Now we have only the one book, Serennos, and the Shield Stone to light our way. Avernath has been missing for centuries. And all this time it has been with the Dark! Well, this is news indeed, Alma. As you say, things are beginning to make sense.'

Rummaging in a pocket at his waist, he produced something that he held out to Alma. It was a flat circular stone shimmering with crystals, lines radiating out from a centre point. Alma, intrigued, reached out and touched it gently with the tip of her finger. There was a ping! and light flashed out for a second, a pulse that echoed the shape of the stone. Adara gasped, and Thorion raised his eyebrows before putting the stone away.

'What was that?' asked Alma. Her finger was tingling, but it was a pleasant sensation, like feathers swirling just below her skin.

'That, dear one, is the Shield Stone of Ambeth, which we use to read the skylore,' said Thorion, smiling, dark hair in waves around his high cheekbones. 'And it looks as though Merewyn was right about the Channelling, too.' He sat back for a moment, his hand coming to his mouth, his blue eyes sliding to grey. Adara put her hand on his arm, firelight shining on the silk of her gown. Alma leaned back on her pillows, starting to feel weary. She yawned, then yawned again, her hand over her mouth, her eyes starting to close.

'Come, my dear,' she heard Adara. 'We should go, and leave Alma in peace.'

'Of course,' she heard Thorion reply in his deep voice, then the rustle of his robes. Her eyes snapped wide open and she reached for Adara, grabbing her hand.

'Oh no, please, can you stay, just a bit longer?' She didn't want to be left alone, didn't think she could handle the memories. Plus she still wasn't sure Deryck couldn't just walk in. She hung onto Adara, not wanting her to go.

'Of course. We won't leave you,' she said, surprise and sympathy mingling on her lovely face. 'We can sit for a while and talk if you like.' She glanced at Thorion.

He nodded, sitting down again. 'You are safe here, dear heart.' He touched Alma's hair. 'Your room is under guard and will remain so. Do not worry.'

Relaxing, Alma let go of Adara's hand and sank back against

her pillows. The fire crackled in the grate, throwing shadows to dance on the glimmering ceiling and she could hear, faintly, the distant sound of the sea. She slid down further under the covers, enjoying the smooth cotton sheets under her hands, the soft weight of feathers from her quilt. Blowing out a long breath, she closed her eyes, listening to Thorion and Adara as they talked of this and that, Thorion's deep rumble blending with Adara's light voice.

'I guess I just need to find the Crown now,' she murmured, and the conversation stopped. Her eyelids were so heavy, but she managed to open them enough to see that Thorion was next to her. She felt his hand warm on her cheek for a fleeting moment.

'Help will come to you, Alma, you will not be alone.'

Then she slept.

DERYCK RODE HARD ALONG THE CURVING BAY, PUSHING THETIS faster and faster as though trying to outpace his anguish. The guards at Alma's door had turned him away and so, crestfallen, he'd gone to the stables, unable to bear the thought of her so close. Tears burned hot then cooled on his cheeks in the frosty air as he rode, his breath sobbing in and out. Gradually he slowed Thetis, coming to a stop. Reining her in, he dismounted, standing with his head clutched in his hands. He sank down to a cross-legged position and sagged forward, gentle Thetis nuzzling him as though she didn't like seeing him in such pain. Deryck leaned his cheek against her, reaching one hand up to stroke her. Never had he felt so low. It was bad enough that he'd failed, that he'd come back through the Gate empty handed, that she wouldn't come back to him. But knowing she was here in Ambeth, sleeping in the bed they'd once shared, was torture. Anything his father did paled in comparison to how that made him feel. And for her to be Galen's daughter! His hand went to his wrist, to the leather bracelet she'd given him – he'd never taken it off, and now turned it around and around his wrist as he sat there looking out to sea. The light changed around him as the sun began to set and all at once he realised he was sitting close to where he and Alma had spent their first blissful day together, a lifetime ago it seemed. He remembered her soft in his arms, her joy at the beauty of the sunset, showing it to him through new eyes, as though he had never seen or appreciated the wonder of it before.

This was not to be borne.

With a cry of anguish he lay back, finally giving in to the urge to touch his necklace. But the stone couldn't help him, not for long, the energy surge dissipating as soon as he released it. Frustrated, he grabbed at it, pulling and breaking the silver chain as he crushed the stone within his fist, so hard he could feel the edges cutting into his skin. He cried out again as darkness pulsed through him like electricity, burning away his sorrow and pain. Shuddering and gasping he gave himself up to the darkness, letting it consume him.

CHAPTER 28
MEMORY AND LOVE

Alma woke slowly, that lovely feeling where there is no alarm clock, no shock to the system, but instead just warmth and comfort, a feeling of coming back to life. The click of her door closing had woken her and she rolled over, opening her eyes as she realised where she was. She braced herself, waiting for the pain, but it was only mild, nothing in the room to harm her except her memories. The fire was freshly laid and burning in the fireplace, breakfast waiting on the small table. Light came through the slits in her shutters, bright with morning sun and Alma wondered what time it was. She pushed herself up against the pillows, reaching for the soft robe lying across the foot of her bed and pulling it around her shoulders. Reluctantly she slid her legs out from under the covers, shivering despite the fire and soft carpet underfoot. Padding over to the window she opened one of the shutters, letting in bright sunlight and frosty air. Picking up the tray she hurried back to the warmth of her bed and settled herself against the pillows, pulling the covers up to her chest and pouring herself a cup of tea, toes wriggling as she enjoyed the luxury of breakfast in bed.

Lifting the lid from the covered dish she noticed a note

tucked under the plate and froze. He wouldn't have, surely? Did he even know she was here? Heart pounding, she carefully slipped the note out from under the plate. A single sheet of heavy cream paper, rough edged and folded in two. She blew out a breath, unsure what to do. Briefly, she thought about ripping it up. Turning it in her hands, she noticed a wax seal on the other side. It was marked with the symbol for Light. Oh, thank God, she thought. Taking a long sip of sweet tea, she broke the seal and unfolded the paper to find a few lines of text written in black ink.

Alma,

I hope you slept well and are feeling rested this day. When you are ready, would you care to meet me at my chambers? The guards will escort you. We have much to discuss, dear heart, and what better time to start than today.

Thorion

The King's writing was strong and spare, a curl on the 'T' the only flourish to his name. Alma smiled, folding his letter and tucking it back under the plate. She picked up some warm bread, spreading it with honey and taking a bite. She would go to Thorion, then to her grandfather.

DERYCK'S HEAD WAS POUNDING. HE'D NEVER HAD A HEADACHE like it. He groaned, reaching out from under the covers for the water he knew was at the side of his bed. He managed to sit up and take a sip, his stomach turning against the smell of breakfast left on the small table near the window. He felt hungover – why, he wasn't sure, as he'd drunk nothing the night before.

He'd wanted to, at first, riding Thetis back to the stable in darkness, leaving her with a sleepy groom, stars blazing above him as he made his way home. His father was gone, his sister closeted in her room. He'd knocked on the door, but she'd ignored him, and he'd found he didn't care about any of it anymore. Getting into bed he'd drifted into sleep, everything muted around him, all the sharp edges smoothed out.

Alma was here.

The thought that had sent him to sleep was with him again as he woke. The pain in his heart at the thought of her was gone – in fact, he could think about her as much as he wanted. Reaching for his stone he sighed out a breath as it cleared his headache. That was better. He couldn't imagine why he'd wanted to stop using the stone, couldn't even remember, really. His hand was sore and he opened it to see the shape of his tallus seared red onto his palm, small blisters at intervals as though it had burnt him. Huh. That was interesting, but then it slipped away and he didn't care anymore. What had he been thinking about? Oh yes, Alma. He closed his eyes, remembering her red hair, her blue eyes, the way she'd felt against him. He smiled, enjoying the fantasy, longing for her. One day she would be his again. It was all that was left, now.

THORION WENT OVER TO THE SMALL TABLE AND PICKED UP A goblet, filling it with cordial from the jug. Strawberry and lime. He knew it was Alma's favourite. Caleb had always asked for it when she was here. At the thought of his son there was a familiar tug of pain – he supposed there always would be. He took the drink over to Alma. She was curled up on his sofa, leaning against the soft velvet upholstery, looking much better than she had the day before, faint colour in her pale cheeks. She took the drink, smiling. 'Thank you.'

He sat down next to her. 'Are you well, dear heart?'

Her smile slid away and she looked down. 'I'm better, I suppose,' she said. 'But... it's still hard to be here, after everything, you know?'

'I do know.' He paused, not wanting to upset her. Her talaith bracelet caught the light and he reached out to touch the stone so it sparked, golden flickers of light dancing above the blue. 'You are still wearing your bracelet? I would have thought you did not need it any more. Not that you ever did, really.'

'Uh, well, I guess I don't need it.' Alma turned her wrist, looking at the stone, then at Thorion. 'But, it reminds me of my father, so...'

Thorion nodded. 'He had it made for Eleanor – for your mother, I mean.' Alma's eyes widened. 'They are love tokens, you see. Oh, they have power, of course. But they are so fragile that they are symbolic as much as anything. When a human wears one, they are considered pledged to the Light.' He stopped, thinking of Caleb's mother, his eyes going to the flowers she had painted, bright as the day he had given them to her, now frozen in time. He had given her a talaith as well, but Etras had destroyed it. He swallowed.

'What do you mean, fragile?' Alma's fingers went to her stone and it sparked again, making her jump. She laughed, but it was shaky.

'Well, as you know, one touch from a pure-blooded member of the Dark will destroy the power of the stone, making it nothing more than a bauble. But Galen knew what it meant when he gave your mother her talaith. It was a symbol of both his protection and his love for her.'

Alma's head was bowed. 'She still loves him.' Thorion felt a dart of pain. How could Eleanor have kept her heritage from her? Still, he understood, and could not find it in his heart to fault Alma's mother for the difficult choices she'd had to make. 'I get it, you know,' she went on. Her lips twisted. 'Deryck has a stone too. He told me it was sort of like a talaith, but Dark.'

Thorion took in a breath. 'Yes. Though the tallus stones of the Dark are much stronger. They are not symbols of love but of power, Dark energy fused into solid form. Very dangerous, and difficult to control.'

Alma blinked. She was trembling, her hands twisting in her

lap. 'Will it hurt him?' She whispered the words and Thorion's heart broke for her.

'I do not know. It is not a good thing, for one so young to possess.'

'Oh.' She huffed out a sob. 'I'm sorry, I don't even know why I care.' The words were fierce, her breath panting and Thorion felt terrible.

'My dear, I am so sorry we did not protect you more, that you were hurt—'

'No.' Alma cut him off. 'I'm sorry, Thorion, I don't mean to be rude.' She blew out a breath. 'I chose him.' She held his gaze. 'I chose him.' Her voice broke and she reached for her drink, taking a sip as she visibly fought for composure. Thorion put his hand on hers.

'Alma, I know that he loved you, we all knew that.' Of course they'd known. But no one could have guessed what the end result would have been. 'And in a way, he had no choice, at the end. He was caught between his own nature, and his father. I don't think he meant to—' He stopped talking, feeling his eyes slide to full grey.

'But it doesn't change what he did,' said Alma, her voice low.

Thorion blinked, tears prickling his eyes. 'No. Nothing will ever change that.' He stood up. 'I have something for you,' he said, going over to a small cabinet. Opening one of the doors he took out an item wrapped in silk. Bringing it over he sat down next to Alma, handing the small parcel to her. She looked at him, puzzled, before carefully unwrapping the soft fabric.

'Oh!' Her hand came to her mouth. 'Oh, Thorion.' Her voice caught.

'He told me. About the gift you'd given him. I think it meant a great deal.'

Alma said nothing, looking down at the tin in her lap. It was square and covered with stars. When she opened the lid the faint smell of fruit and spices wafted out, ghosts of the mince pies she'd made for him. She looked up, her eyes bright with tears. 'Don't... don't you want it?'

Thorion shook his head. 'I think he would have liked you to have it.'

Alma reached a trembling hand into the tin, lifting out a small sheaf of notes scribbled with Caleb's familiar writing. Underneath them was a small ivory shell, delicately whorled, and he saw her pause before picking it up. She huffed out a sob. 'He gave this to me. At the beach. I thought I'd left it there.' Her face crumpled and she wiped her eyes, closing her other hand around the small shell. Thorion put his arm around her shoulders, pulling her close.

'I miss him so much,' she said, her head on his shoulder. 'I think I always will. It's just not the same, being here without him.'

'So do I, Alma, more than I can ever express.'

He pressed his lips to her brow, fighting the waves of sorrow. She looked at him. Her eyes widened, and her lips parted. Thorion's heart lurched. 'Oh, Thorion,' she whispered. 'I never knew. Caleb never knew. Oh, I'm so sorry.' Thorion bowed his head, feeling as though he was about to break. All the weight of all the years of secrets and sorrow came to rest on him as Alma went on. 'He thought the world of you.'

'And I thought the world of him, too,' said Thorion. 'I wish—' His voice broke and finally Thorion, High King over Light and Dark, let go of the rigid control that had driven him for so many years. He sagged forward, sorrow overwhelming him. Alma's arms came around him and he laid his head on her shoulder, weeping. For Caleb, yes, but also for his long dead Laurel, finally acknowledging the loss he had carried for so long. Alma was also crying and they clung together, the mingled sounds of their grief filling the room.

'I'm so sorry,' sobbed Alma, 'I'm so sorry, Thorion, it's all my fault.' Thorion raised his head.

'No, Alma,' he said, his throat raw. 'These events were set in motion so long ago. I could have acknowledged him, but I did not.' He touched her cheek, smoothed her red hair, so like her father's. So much sorrow, so much loss there had been, over the years. He hugged her close again, wanting to comfort her as she had him.

There was a knock at the door and he turned to see a worried looking Adara enter the room. Alma gently disengaged herself.

'Adara,' she said, wiping her face. 'I think Thorion needs you.' She kissed him on the cheek, then stood up. 'Thank you,' she said, 'for everything.' As she went to the door, Thorion called out to her.

'Alma! You are not leaving, are you?'

She smiled, tucking her hair behind one ear as she did so, again so like her father. 'Not yet. I think I'll go to my room and freshen up, then there's a grandfather I believe I need to see. So I'll see you both later, before I go,' she went on. 'That is, if you're around.' She left the room, the door swinging shut behind her.

Adara sat down next to him and he turned to her, still stunned at what had just happened. It was as though something, some vital part of him, had broken away. Yet it had left him feeling free, rather than bereft. Adara still looked worried, her golden eyes dark with concern. 'Are you–'

But before she could finish he reached for her, bending his head to hers, the barrier that was broken finally allowing him to acknowledge how he felt about her. He kissed her, gentle at first, but then increasingly intense, his arms tightening around her as she responded to him, sweeter than anything he could have imagined. Eventually the kiss ended, leaving them both breathless, Thorion unwilling to let her go. He smoothed the curls back from her face, a gentle flush of pink staining her cheeks as she looked at him in wonder. He smiled at her, knowing his eyes had gone to blue, deep as the ocean, as his love for her.

'Alma was right, my dear,' he said. 'I do need you.'

She smiled, and his heart thrilled to see it. 'And I need you, my dearest Thorion.'

'Then let us waste no more time apart, my beloved,' said Thorion. He stood, holding out one hand to her. She rose gracefully to meet him, sliding her hand into his as they moved towards his bedchamber, closing the door behind them.

~

ALMA WALKED ALONG THE CORRIDOR, A GUARD FOLLOWING close behind. She was still reeling from the revelation that Thorion was Caleb's father. Her heart ached for Caleb, that he had never known. The guard spoke, breaking into her thoughts and she stopped, moving closer to him, glad of his presence. It was taking all she had to walk around, to overcome her fear of seeing Deryck again.

'This is the place, my Lady.'

They were at a large timber door, studded with nails, set deep into the thick stone walls. Taking a deep breath, she smoothed the fabric of her skirt with shaking hands, trying to keep her composure. Once she had herself under control she reached out to the large wrought iron knocker and banged it, once. Then she waited. After a moment the door swung open. A tall bearded man stood there, smiling.

'My Lady.' He bowed. 'I am Beran. Won't you come in? I believe Lord Artos is expecting you.'

'Um, thank you,' she said. Beran stepped to one side, holding out his arm and she nodded at the guard before following Beran in. They crossed a small antechamber, heading through a second wooden door into a stone chamber with wood panelled walls, much like her own tower bedroom. This one was laid out as a sitting room, with comfortable chairs and small tables of carved wood, a full bookshelf against one wall, the volumes obviously well read. A fire burned in the stone fireplace and, sitting in front of it, was Artos. He turned as Alma entered, his face lighting up when he saw her.

'Lord Artos,' Beran began, 'The Lady Alma is—'

Before he could finish, Artos was on his feet, coming over to take Alma's hands and lead her forward into the room.

'It's a pleasure to see you!' he said. 'Tell me, are you fully recovered? Come, come in, sit with me a while. Beran, will you bring tea for us both?'

'Of course, my Lord.' Beran bowed and left the room.

'Um, I'm much better, thank you. Are you feeling well?' Now that she was here, facing her grandfather, Alma found herself unaccountably shy and unsure what to say. Looking around, she noticed a small frame on a nearby table – set within were two miniature paintings, both of red-haired young men, so similar in looks as to be almost twins. Artos followed her gaze, then came back to look at her and all at once, seeing his ice blue eyes bent on her with such tenderness, it was easy.

'Lord Artos, I know about my father, about who he is.' There. The words came out as a rush and their effect was immediate. The old Lord's face softened and his eyes brightened.

'Oh, my dear,' he said. 'I am so very glad.' He gently gathered Alma into a hug and she found herself crying for the second time that day.

CHAPTER 29
NO BIRDS TO CATCH

Ambeth - Three days later

'You cannot escape it, my dear.' Lord Artos smiled, his eyes bright in the sunshine. 'Your finding the Sword and Cup has only proven the Prophecy reads true.'

Huh. Unable to help it, Alma made a face. Artos laughed, squeezing her arm where it linked with his. They passed under an archway, twisting brown vines clinging to the carved stone, emerging in another garden bounded by high hedges. Artos was almost recovered, or so he'd told Alma. She'd been checking his energy, though – he wasn't going to get away with hiding something like that again. She was still in shock at how close Etras had come to her, to ruining everything. He still hadn't returned, as far as anyone knew, but she didn't care. He wasn't someone she ever wanted to meet. For now she was happy to walk in the gardens, feeling safe with her grandfather. Even though she still didn't know how much she wanted to be involved with Ambeth, she knew she wanted to spend time with him.

'But, I didn't even really do anything,' she said, scuffing

along the gravel path. She kicked at a stone, irritated. 'Especially with the Sword. I was just in the right place at the right time. And the Cup – well, if Merewyn hadn't been there to help...'

'You're too hard on yourself,' said Artos. 'Only you could have made the connections that led us to the Sword and Cup. And you won't be alone in your search for the Crown, either.'

'Hmm.' Alma nodded, her breath puffing clouds into the air. They were both muffled against the cold, Artos in a heavy cloak and Alma in jeans and warm jacket, bright woolly hat covering most of her hair. 'Thorion said something about that, that help would come to me.'

'Then you must trust to him, my dear. He would not lie to you.'

They strolled a little further, Alma thinking how different the gardens looked without their summer glory of green and flower. Still, they were beautiful, she thought, admiring the delicate tracery of bare branches against the sky. Here and there evergreens shone dark, berries bright against the frosted leaves. Her grandfather spoke again, breaking into her musing.

'Are you sure you won't attend tonight, dear heart? I promise I won't let anything happen that you do not wish.'

Alma squeezed his arm, leaning in close, enjoying how easy it was with him, how comfortable it all felt. After her revelation about Galen, she and Artos had talked for several hours before she went back through the Gate, promising to return. But going to the Ball was a step too far. She shook her head.

'It's not just seeing Deryck,' she said. 'It's also that last time, at the last Ball, well, Caleb was there and I just, I can't do it. I'm sorry.' She felt guilty, not wanting to upset him. But she just couldn't face another Ambeth Ball, not yet. There was disappointment in her grandfather's eyes, but also understanding.

'Then will you let me speak for you?' Alma tilted her head. 'Had you come tonight,' he went on, 'I would have acknowledged you as my granddaughter in the eyes of the Court. However, I can still do so in your absence.'

'Um, well, okay. I mean, that sounds nice, I'm just not sure what it means.' She laughed and Artos put his arm around her, hugging her close. She could feel the joy in him, see it in his face when he looked at her.

'What it means, Alma, is another layer of protection for you. As my acknowledged kin, you'll have a status here above that you already hold. And any, shall we say, interested parties, will need to go through me should they wish to approach you.'

Alma frowned. 'What, like, if they want to speak to me? I don't get it.'

Artos stopped, turning to face her, his hands on her arms. 'My dear one,' he said.' I have waited so long to know you, and the day I saw you walk into the Hall, the very image of your father, to be named as part of the Prophecy and put in the direct path of the Dark, well, it was the proudest and most terrifying day for me, all at once.'

Alma swallowed, taking in the lines in his face, the marks of sorrow and loss, but also joy. She felt the pain of it in her own chest, saw the coiled Light within him, the power as it linked to her, the bond of family and love. She blinked and the pattern went away, becoming Artos again, smiling at her.

'You've achieved more than I could ever have imagined, but there are those who still seek to control you. By acknowledging you it takes away much of their power.' He touched her cheek, gently. 'And I am so proud of you, so happy that you're in my life once more that I wish to tell the world – what better way than this?'

Alma's eyes filled with tears and her lip wobbled, her heart spilling over. 'Oh, I get it,' she said. 'No, I understand. I'm sorry I can't be there.'

'It's fine,' he said, folding her into a hug. 'Whatever you want is fine. Just promise me you'll come back soon?'

She hugged him back. 'Of course,' she said. 'I promise.'

He kissed her on the forehead. 'Now, if you come with me,' he said, 'I can show you a shortcut to the Gate, so you know where to come next time.'

He linked his arm with hers again and it reminded her of Caleb, and how they used to walk together. Smiling, she fell into step with him, wiping her tears with her other hand, happy and sad and joyful as she walked with her grandfather, letting him lead the way.

Darkness had fallen by the time Denoris, magnificently attired in navy brocade, crossed the gardens, heading for the torch-lit Palace, gleaming golden among the trees. The Ball was already well underway when he arrived, and he held his shoulders back as he entered the Foyer, nodding to acquaintances as though all was well, as though his plans had not once again been thwarted. He knew Gwenene's outburst would be news. He also knew the cuts on his face would excite more comment, but he was beyond caring.

Deryck and Ellery trailed behind him, also dressed in their best as he'd requested. Deryck looked fine enough in green velvet, his blond hair brushed back. Ellery, however, was pale, despite her gown of russet embroidered silk. Frowning, he caught her eye. She flinched then smiled, but he could see something behind her eyes, a defiance that reminded him of her mother. He marked it to be dealt with later. Looking at the milling crowd he nodded slightly. Fine. He could do this.

A cold voice spoke a greeting and he turned to see Nevros and Ghislaine emerging from between the great stone pillars, the former in red, as was his custom, Ghislaine in deep green velvet, though her lack of armour did nothing to dispel her air of menace. She was obviously not impressed.

'Not quite the development we were expecting, the girl returning with the Cup. Surely this was not what you meant?' Her dark blue eyes were cold as a night sky. Nevros moved to his other side, glittering and crimson like spilt blood. Denoris tried not to sigh. This was all he needed.

'All is not lost, Ghislaine,' he said, keeping his voice low. 'Although I appreciate your concerns.'

'Do you?' Nevros folded his arms, dark eyes hard as he leaned in close. 'For I tell you, unless you have the Crown hidden somewhere I do not see how the Dark can gain any advantage from this latest turn of events.'

Denoris paused, momentarily taken aback. Surely he did not... He pulled himself together, fixing Nevros with a hard stare. 'Oh, there is still advantage to be gained. Though I would keep your thoughts to yourself, especially here.' He looked pointedly at the crowd.

'Please,' scoffed Ghislaine. 'As if they are concerned with your petty schemes! No, they are here to celebrate the girl who, once again, has come through with the goods.'

'If you think my schemes petty, why then were you so interested in being involved?' He grabbed her arm, squeezing.

Ghislaine seemed unfazed, night blue eyes snapping with anger, her hands clenched into fists. She leaned in so close he could smell her musky perfume. 'Because I thought you might have something to offer, something to change things, that the Dark be second class citizens no longer!'

Denoris half smiled, stirred by her defiance. Maybe Deryck was onto something; redheads did seem to possess a certain fiery temperament.

'Peace, Ghislaine.' Nevros put his hand on her arm and she snapped her head around, red hair flying.

'Peace?' She laughed without humour, her voice rising. 'No, there will be no peace for me, for any of us, until the Balance is righted once more. The Dark have every right to rule here!'

'Calm yourself.' Denoris squeezed her arm harder. He was hurting her, he could see that, anger and lust mingling inside him as he put his head close to hers. 'This is not the place, nor the time. It is not over, not yet. Bear with me and you shall yet see results.'

'Huh!' She snarled at him and Denoris recoiled back, releasing her.

Nevros pulled her away, eyes dark above his glittering cheek-bones. 'I apologise, though you must be able to understand our distress.'

'I promised you nothing,' Denoris folded his arms, his temper close to lost. 'Nor do I still. Yet—'

'Denoris.' It was Gwenene, paler than usual and dressed in black and silver, her gown spangled with stars. She wrapped her hands around his arm, caressing the muscles under the silk and he felt his temper turn to something warmer at her touch. 'Are you well?' She bent her blue gaze on Nevros and Ghislaine. 'And two of our fellow Elders. How nice to see you both.' She smiled coldly before turning her attention back to Denoris.

'I am well, my Lady,' he said. 'And you?'

'I am fine.' She smiled, but it was more like baring her teeth. Denoris hadn't seen her since their argument in the hallway. He realised he'd missed her. Strange. He smiled, not hiding his feelings. She took in a breath, colour coming to her pale cheeks.

'You are looking well,' he murmured, sliding his arm around her waist.

'As are you,' she said, dark lashes covering her eyes. Her hands came up to his shoulders and she moved closer. Nevros had led Ghislaine away – glancing briefly to one side Denoris could see them having what looked like a heated conversation. Deryck and Ellery were also nearby, the latter looking worried. He didn't care. Tightening his arm around Gwenene, he waited for her to look at him. She did, finally, and he bent his head to hers, kissing her hard. She kissed him back, purring against his mouth.

'So I am forgiven?' she said, once she could talk.

Denoris raised an eyebrow. 'Hmm, well, I don't know about that. I might need to punish you further.'

'Is that so?' She laughed, red mouth curving around the sound and Denoris felt a thrill through him. Maybe he should just take her home now. But he knew he couldn't, not yet. He needed to be seen here. She put her hand to his cheek, fingers tracing the scratches she had left there.

'I am sorry I marked you,' she murmured.

He smiled. 'Why? Now all who see me know I am yours. They will heal, in time.'

Gwenene's eyes widened and became bright as though she fought back tears. She pushed a strand of hair out of his eyes, her fingers lingering on his skin.

'Any word of Etras?' she asked, and he did not mistake the catch in her voice. He shook his head.

'Nothing. I rode out to the Gate these past two days, but he has not returned.'

'Ah.' She looked down, her mouth twisting and he put a hand under her chin, lifting it so he could see her face.

'So here we are, at another Ball.'

Her mouth quirked up into a half smile. 'No birds to catch this time, sadly.'

'No,' he said, pleased to see he had distracted her. 'Though there are still opportunities to hunt, my bloodthirsty one. I have not given up, not yet.'

'Nor have I,' she said, blue eyes glittering. 'We will get her, one way or another.'

CHAPTER 30
JOY RESTORED

Ellery nudged Deryck, leaning into him with her elbow, not wanting to watch her father and Gwenene any longer. She wanted to find Tomas but knew they had to wait for Denoris, that he would expect them to stand with him during the speeches. Deryck, staring into space, didn't seem to notice. She pushed him again, harder.

'Hey,' she said. 'Are you all right?'

'What?' He turned, his eyes focusing as though only just noticing she was there. 'Er, yeah, I'm fine.'

Ellery frowned. 'Really?'

'Yes.' He shrugged. 'Why wouldn't I be?'

Ellery took in a breath. 'Well, um, because you seem kind of... different?'

'I'm fine. 1 promise you.'

At that moment Lissa went past with her group of friends. She smiled at Deryck, looking hopeful, but his expression didn't change and her face fell. He reached up to his throat, touching his tallus and his eyes closed. Ellery took in a breath. This was the first chance she'd had to talk to him since Alma had returned with the Cup and she knew something was wrong. He'd spent most of his time in his room, ignoring her knocking at the door, though she'd heard him go out, late at night. She'd wanted to tell him about her mother, about what she'd found out, but knew she couldn't without revealing her errand. Still, she missed their closeness of late. She tried again. 'Deryck, please talk to me.'

'I am talking to you,' he said, looking mystified. He took her arm. 'Come on, let's get a drink.'

ARTOS HELD A GLASS IN ONE HAND, THE OTHER SMOOTHING HIS brocade tunic as he took in the scene. The Great Hall shone with light and colour, the ornate lanterns burning overhead, the assembled Court in all their glory moving around the room. Conversation ebbed and flowed, music lifting the mood and the alcove glowing brighter with the Cup restored once more. He took a sip, enjoying the fine vintage, the company and the feeling of joy emanating from the Cup. That his own Alma should have returned it! He could not be happier, had not been this happy for so many years. There was a gasp in the crowd and he caught sight of Thorion coming through the double doors, Adara on his arm, both of them attired in their finest robes. The King paused, raising Adara's hand to his lips to kiss, smiling at her. She smiled back, glowing pink and gold, beautiful in silk and lace. More eyes turned to them, murmurs running around the room and smiles from many to see them finally together.

'What is this?' Artos came through the crowd, arms held wide as though to embrace them both, his joy almost overwhelming. He kissed Adara on the cheek and clapped Thorion on the back. 'Finally! Have you two figured it out? I've been waiting so long I thought it would never happen!'

Adara smiled up at Thorion. 'Yes, though it took Alma to make him finally see the light,' she laughed, her arm around Thorion's waist as she leaned against him.

'And since then, we have not wanted to be apart,' added Thorion, his eyes shining blue as he gazed at her.

'Is that so?' smiled Artos. 'I wondered that we had not seen you both for a day or so – now I know why.' He winked and Adara, blushing, hid her face in Thorion's shoulder.

'Can you blame us?' Thorion laughed as he wrapped his arms around Adara. 'After all these years, I could not be happier.'

'Neither could I,' smiled Artos. 'For you both, and for my Alma, who is finally part of my life.'

'So you've spoken to her?' Adara's golden eyes lit up. 'Oh, Artos, I'm so happy for you. Is she here?'

At this Artos' mood fell slightly. 'She is not,' he said. 'She couldn't face it, face him.' He glanced across to where Denoris stood with Gwenene and his children, Ellery pale and serious, Deryck expressionless. Adara followed his gaze and understanding dawned on her face.

'Oh, my dear...' she said, but he smiled at her.

'It's fine. I saw her this morning, and we plan to meet again. And tonight I'll acknowledge her publicly as my own kin, if you'll allow it.'

'There is no need to ask permission, my friend,' said Thorion. 'I will address the assembly now and then, if you wish, you may speak after me.'

Artos nodded, falling in behind Thorion and Adara as they moved through the crowd towards the dais where the musicians played. As the High King drew near they stood, laying down their instruments to bow deeply before stepping aside. Thorion acknowledged them with a nod and a smile before stepping up onto the dais, waiting for the crowd to quiet down. Realising the music had stopped, the Court turned to face him, conversation dying to a faint murmur and then silence.

'Welcome, everyone,' Thorion said, smiling round the room, his arms held wide to the crowd. 'Once more it is a day of joy for Ambeth, that the Sacred Cup has been returned to us.' There were cheers at this, and applause, the mood buoyant as he went on. 'I will not keep you long, wishing you only Light and Celebration. Alma, who returned the Cup to us, could not be here tonight, but there is one here who will speak for her.' Turning, he beckoned to Artos, stepping aside as he took the stage. Murmurs went around the room once more, people glancing at each other in confusion, though there were several, Meredan and Cedran among them, who smiled, no doubt having some idea of what was to come.

'My Lords.' Artos' voice rang around the vaulted room, light sparking from the great hanging lanterns as he addressed the crowd, choosing his words carefully. 'Many years ago I lost my son Galen, a day of such black sorrow it still pains me to think on it.' He paused for a moment, feeling the familiar pang of loss, the crowd grown silent at his words. Then he moved past the pain, feeling for joy, the joy he wished to share with them all. 'But all was not lost. Galen had a daughter, kept safe in the human realm these many years.' Surprise rippled through the room and he smiled, nodding in acknowledgement. 'And it is therefore a pleasure to be here on such a joyous occasion, and to acknowledge the role my granddaughter, Alma, has played in bringing our sacred objects home.' The noise grew louder and he raised his hand, waiting until the crowd had ceased talking to continue, wanting the next words to be heard clearly. 'As she cannot be here tonight I will stand in her stead, both to acknowledge her as my kin and heir to my ancient line, and to congratulate her on her achievements. Light be with her, and with you all.'

With that he bowed his head, then stepped down to applause. He could see the looks around the room, amazement at his revelation and he hid a smile. That should put the cat amongst the pigeons, he thought, glimpsing Denoris through the crowd. The Elder's face was tight with rage – next to him Deryck was pale and impassive, reaching to his throat while Ellery looked stricken, her green eyes wide. Was that a tallus stone? Artos squinted, trying to see, but the crowd moved once more and his line of sight was lost. The musicians moved back onto the dais and struck up a lively tune. Couples began to dance and across the room he could see Thorion and Adara, engrossed in each other as they moved around the floor. Smiling, he took another drink from a passing waiter and entered the throng, feet light and heart filled with joy.

~

'WE ARE LEAVING.' HER FATHER WAS OBVIOUSLY FURIOUS, HIS green eyes blazing. Ellery held back a sigh, trying not to curl her lip. Ugh, she was so tired of his rages. And of his lies. It all made sense now, the reason her father hadn't just taken Alma, and had sent Deryck to do his dirty work! Her heart filled with sorrow for her brother and all he had been through. He hadn't seemed surprised by Artos' revelation, though – perhaps that explained why he'd been hiding in his room since Alma returned with the Cup. She wondered when, and how, he'd found out.

She folded her arms, not ready to leave yet, wanting at least to dance with Tomas. But her father, after muttering something to Gwenene, took her by the arm and started pulling her along, Deryck on the other side of her so she could do nothing except try and keep up as they exited the Hall, moving quickly through the Foyer and out into the gardens. At the turning to the apartments her father let go of her arm. 'Go home, Ellery,' he said, his tone dismissive. She bridled, sick of him pushing her around.

'Why can't I go back to the Ball?' she said, her brows drawing together.

'What?' Denoris, who had walked away, turned around and came back towards her, shoulders forward and fists clenched, his cloak flowing behind him. 'What did you say?'

Ellery took a step back, her eyes widening as her father bore down on her. She tried to dodge, but he grabbed her by the arm, holding her so she groaned with pain, his fingers digging into her flesh. Deryck opened his mouth as if to protest, but instead he reached for his stone and his face went blank again. She started to cry, as much from the pain as from seeing him that way. Her father pushed his face close to hers.

'I told you to go home. Do not make me ask you again.' He squeezed her arm even more, fingers grinding into the muscles and she cried out. He pushed her away so she stumbled, managing not to fall, her hand coming up to her arm. Her father met her gaze for a moment and his expression changed from anger to something else that made Ellery go cold. He turned and walked away, beckoning Deryck to join him. He did so, with a backwards glance at his sister. Then they were both gone, disappearing into the dark gardens, leaving Ellery alone and crying on the path. Her arm felt like it was on fire, throbbing so she could hardly move it. She turned away, sobbing her heartbreak as she made her slow painful way home.

LEFT ALONE IN THE GREAT HALL, GWENENE TRIED TO KEEP A brave face on things, though her disappointment was profound. After all they had done, all they had schemed, their plans were coming to naught and all because of Galen's daughter! She nodded and smiled to a passing member of the Dark, knowing she needed to keep up appearances, that Denoris making a swift exit was bound to be noted. 'Wait for me in my rooms,' he had muttered as he left, a searing glance from his green eyes leaving her in no doubt of what he intended. She sighed. Anger, pain, the wind changing – it didn't take much to stir Denoris into passion, though it was mostly directed at her these days. Not that she minded – when this was all over she meant to force him to set Aeres aside, so the two of them could rule together as they'd planned. She stopped a passing waiter, favouring him with a dazzling smile as she picked up a drink from his tray. She took a long gulp of the cool wine, savouring the sour sweet honey taste, the sting as it went down her throat. Then she moved into the throng, searching for those she knew would be most useful. It was all she could do, for now.

CHAPTER 31
MASTER PLAN

Deryck followed his father through shadow and darkness, deep into the gardens. As the path twisted and turned, he realised where they were going. The Garden of Shadows. He took in a breath, remembering the last time he'd walked this path, and where it had taken him. A shard of pain cut through his stupor and he reached for his stone, the movement so automatic now he barely noticed he was doing it. He hoped his father wasn't going to send him after Alma again.

Upon reaching the curving stone wall Denoris unlocked the wooden door and they stepped inside. The lamps were already lit, flickering shadows echoing the fast-moving clouds above, smudges on the face of the moon.

Deryck wondered what was going to happen. His father still hadn't said a word, not since he'd sent Ellery on her way. Deryck felt a flicker of sadness. He knew his father had hurt her, had seen the stricken expression on her face. Strange that she was the one who loved their father more. Though he wasn't sure about that now.

Denoris was kneeling at the dark pool, the liquid turning and sparking as he accessed his power. A shimmer appeared in the air and Deryck bit his lip. He could hear, faintly, the sounds of the distant Ball, the night air cool on his face. All at once he was fully present in the moment, his skin prickling as though it knew what was to come. He closed his eyes.

'Deryck!' His father's voice was strained and he opened his eyes to see him curved over the pool, the muscles in his arms standing out against the brocade. 'Go through, now! I will follow. Do it!'

Fine. Deryck, pushing his misgivings away, reached for his stone as he stepped forward and through the Gate. He braced himself, just in case Alma was going to be there again, blue eyes hostile. But he emerged into a stone chamber with a vaulted ceiling. It was empty, no windows, lit only by soft concealed lighting in the walls, casting golden patterns of light on the mellow red bricks. A flight of stairs at one end of the room led upward, more golden light coming down from above, the air pleasantly warm. A moment later his father joined him, sweating and gasping as he closed the Gate behind them. He went to lean against the wall, reaching for his tallus stone as he caught his breath. Colour came back to his face and he stood straight, restored. Deryck went over to him.

'Where are we?'

'We are in the human realm,' his father replied. Unexpectedly, he smiled. 'Come on, follow me.'

~

THORION LIFTED HIS HEAD, HIS EXPRESSION DISTANT AS though listening to something only he could hear, his blue eyes darkening like storm clouds.

'What is it?' Adara touched his face, concerned.

'It is the Dark. They are opening a Gate.'

Adara frowned, pushing herself up against the dark red velvet of the cushions in the booth. 'Denoris.'

He nodded, dark hair falling forward to tickle her skin, his body warm against hers. 'Yes. And that means only one thing, beloved.'

'That the game is still in play.'

'Alma is protected. They cannot get to her, not without me knowing, and now that Artos has acknowledged her...'

'So what are they doing?' Her voice was soft, but she knew Thorion could still hear her, even over the music and merriment around them. Unexpectedly, he smiled, one hand coming to caress the curve of her cheek.

'It doesn't matter. Not right now, anyway. We have the Cup and the Sword and Alma is safe. There is only so much they can do.'

'But Thorion—'

He cut her off with a kiss. 'It doesn't matter,' he said again, lifting his head, his eyes back to sea blue. 'And I can think of many things I would rather do at this moment than worry about the Dark.' He grinned and she smiled back, enjoying the feel of him against her, wanting to be alone with him once more.

'Why don't you tell me?'

He pulled her hard against him and she laughed, gasping as he kissed her neck, lips moving along her jaw to whisper in her ear. 'I'd rather show you.'

DERYCK FOLLOWED HIS FATHER UP THE STAIRS INTO A LARGE airy hallway, sunlight streaming through panes of stained-glass around a panelled front door. There were more doorways either side of the hallway and another flight of stairs leading up, light glinting from small crystal chandeliers. Denoris went through one of the doorways and Deryck, still following, found himself in a spacious room with fine furnishings, delicate mouldings on the ceiling. Two large windows at the front let in more light, illuminating the soft colours of the rug, the dark green silk on the walls.

'What is this place?' Deryck was surprised enough he was shaken out of his fugue state. He went to the window and slid it open, leaning to look out, breathing in the strange scents, the cool air.

'This is my home, Deryck.' Denoris went to a large desk against one wall, opening a drawer to take out a set of keys.

'So why have I never been here before?' Deryck frowned, wondering what was going on, but Denoris just smiled. Deryck was shaken, both by the suddenness of the crossing and all the smiling. This was not the father he was used to. Denoris went on, his tone almost jovial.

'Because of the ban on crossing, Deryck. And you have been here before, but you were only a babe in arms, so you won't remember.'

'I have? But why—'

'I come here when I need to. That's all you need to know. And this place has been mine for nearly two hundred years, so I make sure it's looked after. The ban cannot hold forever.' Denoris looked briefly annoyed.

Deryck raised his eyebrows. 'So this is the human world?' Alma's world. At least, that's how he'd thought of it. But now, of course, he knew that wasn't entirely true. 'Huh.' He made a face. 'So, what do we do now?' He looked out of the window again, intrigued by the sounds from outside. People talking, heels clicking, a strange hum of honking horns and growling noise. 'Are we going out there?'

'Yes, so you'd better get changed.' Denoris slid a key from the cluster in his hand and tossed it to Deryck, the brass gleaming in the light before he deftly caught it. 'Second door on the left at the top of the stairs. You'll find all you need in the cupboard there.'

Deryck looked at the key, then at his father. He grinned, leaving the room to take the white painted stairs with their curving timber banister two at a time. He found the door he needed and slid the key in, opening it to find a well-appointed bedroom. The furnishings were masculine, dark timber in clean lines, and Deryck looked around approvingly, a faint thread of excitement in him. He didn't need his stone. He went to the square-paned window and looked out, surprised to see a great river, boats and people everywhere, bridges arching across its expanse in both directions as it snaked through a vast city. Across the river were large buildings, some like nothing he had ever seen, strange expanses of glass and metal, while others were made of stone cut into classical shapes, more like the palaces he knew. He tried to take it all in, fascinated by the endless traffic. Craning his head to look along the river he could see what looked like a large metal wheel arcing into the sky, and near to it a tower, four sided, with what looked like a clock face just below the pointed top. He thought he heard it chiming faintly. Looking the other way a large domed building caught his eye.

'Deryck, are you ready?'

He heard his father's footsteps as Denoris came upstairs, entering the room next door. There was a thud of cupboard doors opening and closing. Reluctantly he pulled himself away from the window and the panorama outside. Going to the wardrobe he opened the doors to find several pairs of dark trousers on hangers, along with shirts in different colours and folded jumpers on the shelves, shoes lined up below. He looked at the clothing, his brow furrowed. What was he supposed to wear? Alma would know. She always wore jeans. He remembered her calling them that and the way she spoke, laughing as she explained them to him. He wished she was there to help. If only she would come back to him. The thought was without pain, but it still tugged at him and he found he needed the stone after all, reaching for it and taking a deep breath as he sought to focus. His feelings under control, he pulled out a pair of jeans, dark denim, and found a shirt in soft cotton on a shelf below. Quickly he got dressed, pulling a jacket from its hanger and throwing it on the bed as he sat down to put on a pair of leather boots. He figured they were his father's, surprised that they fit. He shrugged on the jacket and left the room, running down the stairs to find his father, similarly dressed, waiting in the hallway, looking impatient.

'Come on.'

Denoris opened the large front door. They went down a small flight of stone stairs to join a stream of people, heads turning to look at them so Deryck felt self-conscious for a moment, hunching into the upturned collar of his jacket. But Denoris didn't seem bothered, striding out in his usual style, Deryck hurrying to keep up. At a gap in the buildings Denoris stopped.

'This way.' He handed Deryck a small blue rectangular card. It was hard and felt strangely slippery under his fingers, the word 'Oyster' written on it. Deryck turned it over in his hands, looking quizzically at his father. 'Hang onto it. You'll need it.'

Deryck tucked it into his pocket as they started walking again, Denoris taking one street then another before leading Deryck down a flight of stairs into a tiled underground space, large pictures on the walls bright screams of colour. They came to a row of black gates. Deryck watched his father put the blue card against a panel on the front of one of the gates. It opened like magic and Deryck tried to follow his father through, coming up short as the panels closed again. 'Use the card!' Denoris scowled at him. 'And hurry up!'

Deryck pressed his card to the same panel and the gate opened. Amazing. Alma's world was truly a place of wonders. He went through, turning to watch as it closed behind him again.

'Come on!'

He followed his father down yet more stairs, emerging on a platform in a rounded tunnel, warm air blowing from the darkness at either end. He looked around, trying to take it all in, glad of his tallus stone, of its calming influence. A girl with long red hair came onto the platform and his eyes widened, but then with a crash and hiss a large metal vehicle emerged from the tunnel, coming to a stop. Deryck took a step back, restrained only by his father's hand on his arm.

'Come on. We need to get on.'

'On *that*?' Deryck was gladder than ever that he'd given himself over to the stone. There was no way he would have been able to handle this otherwise. He touched his tallus again, sighing as everything muted. He stepped onto the strange vehicle, through doors that slid open and closed, though no-one was touching them. Another wonder.

'Hold on.' His father nodded to one of the long yellow poles running between floor and ceiling and Deryck grabbed onto it just in time, the vehicle jerking and lurching into motion, picking up speed as they entered the tunnel. He took a deep breath, hanging onto his pole, then realised he was being stared at. He flushed, hanging his head. Three young women, all sitting together, were looking at them, wide-eyed and whispering. As he looked around, Deryck realised that nearly every woman in the carriage was staring at them. His father ignored them all, shoulders back. He caught Deryck's eye and snarled a smile at him.

'Not long to go.' He nodded at the diagram painted above the windows. Deryck frowned as he took in the tangle of coloured lines and names he didn't understand. Well, he'd better trust his father for now, he guessed. The vehicle jerked to a stop and several passengers got on and off, more stares. It started up once more, rattling and swaying through the darkness as Deryck hung onto his pole, half lost in a daydream of red hair and blue eyes, barely noticing when they drew to a stop once more. He felt his father tapping his arm. 'This one. Let's go.'

He followed his father once more, the young women calling out a farewell as they left the train, their giggles echoing. There were more flights of stairs, one of them moving, another wonder, then more black gates and all at once they were out, standing in what seemed to be a forest of tall buildings stretching to the sky.

But there was no time to stop and look around, no matter how much he wanted to. His father was on the move again, taking a side street that opened out into a large square bordered by a mix of buildings, ancient brickwork set against strange light-coloured stone and glass, curved in unusual shapes. Denoris walked briskly across the vast paved square towards a building with a pale façade, the large arched windows with stone decoration reminding Deryck of the Great Hall.

The doors to the building were strange, four panels that moved around in a circular fashion. Deryck paused for a moment, confused, before figuring out he needed to push one of the panels to make it work. He emerged into a wide carpeted foyer with stairs going up and down, just in time to see his father taking the flight of stairs heading down, booted heels clicking against the white and grey marble. Deryck followed him, jogging slightly to catch up. Finally, his father stopped, in front of two sets of grey metal doors. He pressed a circular button set into the wall and it began to glow. Deryck stood next to him, content to let the strangeness of the day wash over him. He thought again of Alma, and how he would love to explore her world with her. There was a ding! and two of the doors slid open to reveal a small metal room.

'Get in,' said Denoris, jerking his head.

'What?' At his father's glare Deryck obeyed, startled to feel the room move under his weight as first he and then his father stepped inside. Denoris stabbed another button set into the wall and the doors closed, the room dropping so Deryck reached for the wall, fear darting through him. But it was over quickly, the doors opening with another ding! to release them into a darkened hallway, white writing and an arrow on the wall.

Giving up any idea of being told where they were, Deryck followed his father along the corridor into a large underground room. The floor was carpeted except for several sandy areas separated by a small step, curving ancient stones set into the earth as though they had been there before the building was constructed around them. Timber cases with glass covers were set at intervals around the room. With a gesture Denoris cleared the space, his banishing spell causing the few other people there to leave without protest, the atmosphere changing to one of menace. Unaffected, Deryck wandered over to one of the cases, intrigued to see they contained some sort of artefacts, his hand wandering over the glass.

'Deryck!'

He looked up in surprise to see his father waiting at one end of the room, against a black wall covered with green figures and shapes. As he hurried over he saw Denoris move his hands, twisting them as he murmured something. All at once a darker space appeared, an opening in the wall.

'Come on,' Denoris beckoned him. He shrugged. Fine. If that's what his father wanted, that's what he would do. He hitched at his jeans, unused to the heavy fabric around his legs, though they were surprisingly comfortable. Alma always wore them, he thought, the idea of her somehow comforting as he stepped through the opening into a dark and dusty space. His breath caught in his throat and he stepped back, stumbling a little on the stony ground, shocked once again out of his stuporous state. He felt his father's hand on his shoulder.

'So what do you think, my son, of our master plan?'

What did he think? All he could do for a moment was stare. 'Is that...?'

Denoris smiled his wolfish smile as he surveyed his creation. 'Yes, Deryck. It is. It is the Crown.'

CHAPTER 32
SET IN MOTION

Deryck's mouth dropped open. So this was it. His father's great plan. But what the hell was it? A spidery contraption of delicate metal rods and wires, twisted together and anchored into the ground, was lit by two torches that burned with a strange blue flame. Beyond the contraption low tiers of stone seats circled back into the gloom, and Deryck realised they were standing in an ancient arena, hidden beneath the modern city. The Crown was part of the machine, suspended high above a hollow in the ground. Moving closer, Deryck could see the hollow was a whirling pool of dark liquid, similar to the one in the Garden of Shadows, though much larger.

Emotion washed over him, tears hot in his eyes. He thought of Alma, of her quest to find the Sword, the Cup and the Crown, and how much she'd worried about it, never sure she was doing the right thing. And all along the Crown had been here, darkness knew why. He wondered whether his father had lost his mind. 'What...what is this?' He turned to his father, who was watching him with a smile on his face.

'It is my design. Do you like it?'

'Well, it's... um, amazing.' He didn't know what else to say, moving around the network of rods, reaching to touch a whorl of silver wire.

'Careful!" His father's voice rang out and he pulled his hand back. 'All the elements are delicately balanced. And the pool is pure energy, a vortex that would tear you apart should you fall into it. So stay back.'

'But, what does it do?' Deryck turned to his father. 'I mean, what are we here for?'

'This, Deryck, is the key to our future. To the Dark having power once more in Ambeth, holding the throne there. Watch, if you will.'

Denoris went towards the machine, careful not to touch it as he positioned himself in the hollow space beneath the Crown. Feet apart and legs braced, he took hold of two thick metal rods driven into the ground. Deryck, fascinated despite himself, moved closer.

His father's eyes closed and his head snapped back as the machine moved into life, the metal pieces turning in a strange, hypnotic dance. All at once what looked like strings of light appeared above them, coming from all corners of the room and converging above the Crown. Forming one single beam they flowed through the circle and into his father, who bared his teeth, starting to shake. From the whirling pool came a burst of Dark energy, like a flash of black lightning, passing through Denoris and fusing with the light. It moved back up along the strands, turning the brightness to dark thundery onyx, moving back out to the edges of the room and beyond. The ancient arena was humming with energy, and Deryck could feel the hairs on his arms rise. Half fascinated, half horrified, he watched his father strain against the metal rods, his body rigid. Denoris held on a few moments longer before letting go of the poles with a groan. Immediately the light conversion stopped, the strings drifting away like mist. Denoris staggered away from the machine and dropped to the ground, unable to stand. Deryck rushed over to him.

'Father, are you all right?' He knelt down next to Denoris, who was lying half on his side, eyes closed as he breathed hard, his golden hair dark with sweat. Finally, he opened his eyes.

'I'll be fine in a moment,' he gasped, reaching for his tallus stone. Deryck helped him, gently untangling the chain from his father's shirt, careful not to touch the stone.

'Here.' He guided his father's hand to the tallus and Denoris nodded his thanks, taking in a deep breath as he grasped the stone, colour returning to his face. He managed to sit up, then got to his feet, waving away Deryck's offer of assistance. He went to sit on the ancient stone steps, beckoning Deryck to sit next to him. Shaken, Deryck obeyed. The denim of his jeans was hard against his legs, different than breeches – he rubbed his hands across the fabric, as though trying to connect with something real.

'What the hell was that? What did you do?'

'That was energy,' said Denoris. 'Light energy – all the good deeds and thoughts and ideas of this world, all that flows to the Light and gives them power.'

'But what were you doing with it?'

'I was stealing it. Changing it to Dark. Sending it back out into the human world, to take over their thoughts and minds, steering them away from the Balance. The Crown brings it in and I send it out again.'

Deryck's stomach lurched. He looked again at the machine. 'So you mean...?'

'Yes. The Darkness goes back into the world, perpetuating more dark deeds, dark thoughts and ideas. And then that energy comes back to us, increasing our power, while the Light stumble and fail.'

'But... why here? Why did you...?' Deryck fell silent, unable to take it all in.

Denoris nodded. 'This is a place of power, Deryck, similar to our own Garden of Shadows. But the energy here is darker even than that. You see the size of the pool?' Deryck nodded. 'It is a vortex, a portal to the point where two lines of darkness cross in the land. Such places are uncommon, and very powerful – even the humans knew it for what it was. This was a place of sacrifice for millennia before this great city grew over it, a place where humans came to die. Later, men and animals were killed for sport here, and then, when the arena was lost, the courts above us decided the deaths of many, even though they no longer knew this place was here.'

Deryck frowned. 'More powerful than the Garden of Shadows?'

'And the perfect place for me to build this machine, where it can most impact humans. This city is a microcosm of the world, all cultures, all types of humans finding their way here. And so here is where it will begin.'

'But, the machine... You can't do much, not for long – it looked like it was killing you–'

Denoris nodded, looking serious. 'True. I do not have the gift, nor do you, to channel the power properly, but there are those who do. All I need is to find one who sympathises with us.'

'The gift?'

'Yes.' Denoris laid a hand on Deryck's shoulder. 'You are an Opener, my son– oh, do not shake your head, I see the start of it in you. Are you not surprised, that you would take after me? So, like me, you cannot run this machine for long. But I have someone in mind who can.'

'Who?' Deryck stared at the silver wires, the jewelled crown sparkling in the flickering light.

Denoris huffed out a laugh. 'Oh, don't worry about that for the moment. All I wanted was for you to see this, to understand what it is we're working toward. This is the plan, Deryck, this was the plan all along. I already have the Crown, don't you see? The Sword and the Cup, they would have helped us, of course.' His expression darkened. 'But the Crown is still enough. And once I send enough darkness into the world, there will be no saving the Balance, and the Dark will finally rise to power.'

Deryck's mouth twisted. He wasn't sure about any of this anymore. But at the same time there was a pull; he could feel its allure, the whirling vortex seeming to speak to a deep part of him. Maybe this was the answer, after all. But he couldn't escape a sense of disquiet, faint yet insistent. He reached for his tallus stone.

His father spoke again. 'We need to talk. About Alma.'

Deryck looked away. 'I don't want to talk about her.'

'Please.' He felt his father's hand on his arm and flinched. But he couldn't talk about her, not to his father. Denoris spoke again. 'I...I wish to apologise.'

'*What?*' Deryck's jaw dropped. His father had definitely lost his mind. Maybe using the machine had been too hard on him. He turned back to him. 'I don't understand.'

'I should not have been so hard on you about her, should have understood how you felt.'

'But, you made me go and try and capture her, again – what–'

"I was hoping that you wouldn't have to, that she would come back to you of her own accord. It has not been easy for me, watching you in such pain these past weeks. That's why I gave you your stone, you know.'

Deryck, frowning, shook his head. He had no idea where this was coming from, nor how to respond.

'Tell me, when you saw her again, did she say she no longer loved you?'

Deryck thought back to the awkward confrontation in the playground, his mood darkening further as he went over it in his mind.

'No, not exactly. She said she would always care for me–'

'Aha!' Denoris smiled. 'But this is good news!'

'It is?'

'Yes, yes. She's a woman, Deryck, and you know what they can be like. Always thinking one thing and saying another. She still cares for you, so let us try together and get her back for you.'

Astounded, Deryck stared at his father. 'You-you would do that for me?'

'Of course. I have been thinking on the matter. She is Galen's daughter after all, an appropriate match for a Prince of the Dark. Perhaps Artos can help to persuade her. I know she has started to visit with him.'

'She has?'

'She has. And I will speak with him, I promise you that. If I am to succeed here, it's important to me that you and your sister are... taken care of.'

'It is?'

'Yes. Despite what you may think, I do care about what happens to you both.'

Deryck didn't know what to say. This day was stranger than he'd ever imagined it could be. Even with the calming influence of the stone, he was still finding it tough to take in. He yawned, all at once exhausted.

Denoris stood up, brushing dust from the dark denim of his jeans. 'Come on,' he said. 'Let's go. I can see this has been a lot for you to take in. We can rest a while before going home. I must say, I could use some sleep myself.'

Deryck nodded. A rest did sound like a good idea, the thought of the large bed in the room overlooking the river tempting. Besides, he needed some time alone to think. He stood up. 'Okay.'

When they reached the Gate opening, Denoris stopped. 'Remember how I told you that you're an Opener? Well, let us put it to the test.'

'*What?*'

Denoris grinned. 'I'll go through, then close this gate. You can open it yourself, then come through- oh, do not worry, I'll not leave you here!' He clapped Deryck on the shoulder. 'It's simple enough, just a straightforward Gate through a wall, not between worlds. You should be able to do this without any trouble.'

'Uh, I don't–'

'You need to focus,' Denoris went on, ignoring him. 'Focus on the idea of the opening, of the existence of the opening. Feel it in your mind, shape it, sense it, taste it. Make it as real as you can. Use your stone if you have to. Then, once you have it held steady, project it out to the wall, speaking the words of power.'

'But, what are the words–'

'Got it?' Denoris clapped him on the arm again. 'See you soon,' he said, and stepped through the Gate.

'Wait!' Deryck tried to follow, but the wall solidified as he stepped forward. The Gate was closed. He stared at the wall, unable to believe that his father had left him there, effectively trapped. He was alone. He turned, looking around for a rock or something he could smash his way out with. 'Father!' He shouted the word, fear making his voice rough. Panic thrummed within him, his stomach lurching, and he reached for his stone again. It helped, a little, but he was still stuck.

What the hell was he supposed to do now? He stared at the blank wall, feeling the darkness crowding him like wings. He didn't want to look at the machine, or the pool. He just wanted to get the hell out of there. His breathing was shallow, and he could feel himself sweating under his shirt. How could his father do this to him? The betrayal stung and he latched on to it, using his anger to sharpen his focus. What had his father said? Use his stone, and speak the words of power. Well, he had no idea what they might be, but he did have the stone. He reached for his tallus, letting cold energy wash through him. He closed his eyes, visualising a hole in the wall, a doorway he could walk through. He pictured the room on the other side, imagined himself there, walking among the display cases. He could almost see his father waiting with his arms folded, looking impatient. For a moment he faltered. Was he truly seeing? Was this what his father had meant?

He found the thread again, feeling the rhythm of his breath as he focused, deeper, harder. He was sweating now, his muscles tense and strained, his whole body shaking. He knew no words of power, but all at once it was as though he could feel the opening in front of him. He opened his eyes and saw a twisting in the air in front of him.

'Uh, open?' He sounded unsure, he realised. The twisting paused, hanging in the air as if waiting. He tried again. 'Open, I command you!' The twisting spun faster and spread, a darker space appearing in the wall. He stepped through to the other side.

WAITING IN THE UNDERGROUND ROOM, DENORIS WAS GROWING impatient. Where in darkness was the boy? He wandered around, trailing a hand across the display cases. Human rubbish, he thought, scornful. Why they hung on to the detritus of their past he didn't know – it all seemed worthless nonsense.

All at once he felt the pull of energy and turned to the end wall. A darker space opened and through it came his son. He staggered over to a nearby bench and sat down heavily, reaching for his tallus, visibly sweating. He had done it, and on his first try, too. Good. That meant the gift held true.

'Well done.' He went over to him. 'You did it, as I knew you could. Let's go.'

'Give me a second.' Deryck was still pale. He held onto his tallus, breathing heavily.

'Come now, it's not so bad. The first time is always the hardest. You need to practice, hone your talent.'

He saw Deryck's throat move, colour returning to his face. 'Fine. I guess.'

Denoris held back a retort. He needed the boy onside, and he knew the key to doing so. 'Come on.' He held out his hand and Deryck took it. He pulled his son to his feet and the two of them left the room, Deryck still walking slowly. Denoris kept pace with him.

'So you would be agreeable to it? A match with the girl?'

Deryck's mouth tightened, his green eyes glancing sideways. He paused before answering. 'Yes.'

'Then we'll make it happen. Come now, do not despair. We have great things ahead of us.'

Deryck nodded. 'I guess.' His mouth twisted. 'So what will happen, to that Dark energy you sent out?'

'It's probably causing trouble as we speak.' Denoris laughed. When they reached the lifts the doors opened and two women came out, their faces stretching in wonder as they took in father and son. He smiled at them, appraising as they passed him and the women smiled back, one turning her head to wink as they walked away. She said something to her friend, and both women laughed.

As they stood in the lift, Denoris could sense the excitement, the change in mood in his son and he smiled to himself. Yes, let Alma come back to Deryck. He would welcome her with open arms, then introduce her to the machine. For a little bird had told him that she was a Channeller.

CHAPTER 33
BACK TO REALITY

September

ALMA HURRIED UP THE STEPS INTO SCHOOL, HER BAG SLUNG over her shoulder. She was running late already and it was only her first day. The foyer was pulsing with noise, a cacophony of chatter and shouting and footsteps bouncing off the large glass windows and she paused, trying to figure out where she needed to go.

She'd got home late the night before, spending most of the evening, which amounted to a day and a night in Ambeth, with her grandfather. Though she still couldn't bring herself to sleep alone in her tower room, the guestroom in his chambers was comfortable, Beran taking good care of her whenever she came to stay.

But now it was back to reality. A new school year beckoned, and she knew she had to consider her future in this world, as well as in Ambeth. Besides, she still hadn't completely decided whether she was going to look for the Crown or not, despite her grandfather's gentle encouragement. The wounds of Caleb's death and her relationship with Deryck still ran deep.

As she moved through the crowd of students, her gaze was drawn to a boy standing near the wall, hands in pockets, talking to several other students. He was tall, with dark hair that flopped over his eyes. Her Channelling took over and he blinked into energy, light and dark coiling through him, incredibly powerful. She gasped as she felt a pulse through her feet and he blinked back into being a boy again. A boy who was looking at her, blue eyes quizzical.

He grinned and she blushed, heat in her cheeks, wondering why she felt so drawn to him, as though his energy was somehow linking with hers. Something about him seemed very familiar. Maybe it was just another weird side effect of her Channelling. Her new powers still surprised her at times, the gift not quite under control.

Someone bumped into her and she stumbled, the connection breaking. Looking up at the clock, she realised the time. Shit. She really was going to be late. Hitching her bag higher on her shoulder she pushed through the crowd.

AFTERWORD

Here ends Volume Four of The Ambeth Chronicles
Volume Five, *Light And Dark,* will be available from April 2021.

If you enjoyed *Under Stone*, please consider leaving a star rating or
review on Amazon, come see me on Goodreads, or visit me at my
website, www.helenglynnjones.co.uk

Thank you for reading.

Want more?

Join my mailing list for release news, sneak peeks, competitions and more...
eepurl.com/c9lzRD

ACKNOWLEDGMENTS

Thank you to Esther Newton for her editing insights, to Rich Jones at Turning Rebellion for another gorgeous Ambeth cover, and to my wonderful beta readers, Louise, Lucy and Angelika, for challenging me and giving me wonderful feedback. Thank you to bloggers far and wide for your generosity, to my family and friends for your support, and to my beloved Marcus and Isabelle, for being on this journey with me.

ALSO BY HELEN JONES

No Quarter

Volume Two of The Ambeth Chronicles

Alma has returned the lost Sword to Ambeth and is finally with Deryck, Prince of the Dark. But what's really going on? Deryck is struggling with his father, who wants to control Alma, while Alma is struggling with her best friend Caleb, who doesn't trust Deryck one inch. Plus it's getting harder and harder to keep up with her life in the human world. Falling in love shouldn't be this difficult. But things are about to get much worse...

*Praise for **No Quarter***

'The characters are complex, believable with their flaws and virtues. The story is nicely woven and has a wonderful flow; it was easy to get hooked.'

'I'm dying to get my hands on Hills and Valleys; I need to know what's going to happen!'

No Quarter

Available from Amazon as an e-book or paperback

ALSO BY HELEN JONES

Hills And Valleys

Volume Three of The Ambeth Chronicles

'Sometimes things call to us until we can no longer ignore them. And Ambeth is calling you, Alma.'

After the events of the Harvest Fair, Alma is finished with Ambeth - they can find the missing Cup and Crown without her. But Ambeth is not finished with her. First the mystery of her dead father comes back to haunt her, then the Dark reach out, hoping to trap her once more. And then there's the strange power she seems to have...

*Praise for **Hills And Valleys***

'Hills and Valleys is intense and without doubt the best in the series so far.'

'I have loved all the books in this series. Didn't want this one to end.'

Hills And Valleys

Available on Amazon as an e-book or paperback

ALSO BY HELEN JONES

A Thousand Rooms

You don't wake up expecting to die.

Katie is thirty-two, single, and works in advertising. She's also dead. A lost soul hitching rides with the dying, trying to find her way to... wherever she's supposed to be. And whoever she's supposed to be with.

Heaven, it seems, has a thousand rooms. What will it take to find hers?

Praise for A Thousand Rooms

'what I loved, loved, loved about this book was the incredibly touching and heartfelt expressions of human emotions, particularly grief and sorrow and, ultimately, of pure love.'

'One of those rare books I simply couldn't put down.'

'Highly recommended for those who like strong female characters, coming-of-age narratives, and true love -- just keep the tissues nearby!'

A Thousand Rooms

Available on Amazon as an e-book or paperback

ABOUT THE AUTHOR

Helen Glynn Jones is a prize-winning author of six novels.

Born in the UK, she has since lived in both Australia and Canada. A few years ago she returned to her native England where, when she's not writing stories, she likes to hunt for vintage treasures, explore stone circles and watch the sky change colour. She now lives in Hertfordshire with her husband, daughter, and wonderfully chaotic cockapoo.

Come and visit me
www.helenglynnjones.co.uk

www.ingramcontent.com/pod-product-compliance
Lightning Source LLC
Chambersburg PA
CBHW071851220626
47052CB00002B/76